PRAISE FOR *THE WILD LAUGHTER*

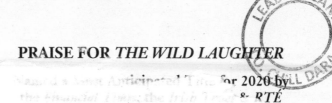

Named a Most Anticipated Title for 2020 by the Financial Times, the Irish Times & RTÉ

'I loved this book. So funny and bleak. I loved the madness, the tone, the ending, the realisation, *The Third Policeman* charge of the whole thing.'

Roddy Doyle, Booker prize-winning author of *Paddy Clarke Ha Ha Ha*

'A memorable, insightful portrait of a complex family in an equally complex economic and emotional situation. Caoilinn Hughes gets the balance just right: the pathos is real but never heavy-handed; the humour is black but never mean-spirited. *The Wild Laughter* succeeds on all levels.' **Patrick deWitt, author of** *The Sisters Brothers*

'*The Wild Laughter* is painfully smart, comically brilliant and boldly subversive. Hughes makes her subject matter entirely her own while providing a lacerating look at the world we live in.'
Olivia Sudjic,

'What a profound, much needed, u...
is dark and beautiful, and touches the...
our political systems have brought u... ...t seen in
that clearest way—intimately, microsco..., ..hrough family. The
myriad ways they can love, hurt and betray one another... So
well done.' **Fatima Bhutto, author of** *The Runaways*

'*The Wild Laughter* is a raucously intelligent, tough and tender black comedy written in jaggedly beautiful prose and confirms Caoilinn Hughes as a restlessly inventive, exciting new voice in Irish literature.'

Colin Barrett, author of *Young Skins,*
winner of the *Guardian* **First Book Award**

PRAISE FOR *ORCHID & THE WASP*

Named a 'Best Book of the Year' by *Cosmopolitan,
Sunday Independent, Hot Press, Irish Independent, RTÉ
& Sunday Business Post*

Winner of the Collyer Bristow Prize 2019
Shortlisted for the Hearst Big Book Awards 2019
Shortlisted for the Butler Literary Award 2018
Longlisted for the Authors' Club Best First Novel Award 2018
Longlisted for the International DUBLIN Literary Award 2020

'A remarkable, propulsive debut ... No precis can adequately convey the novel's startling, impressionistic prose, nor its corrosive humour. Jewels of observation glitter amid the earthy gags. Exuberant ... it zings with energy, ambition and daring.'

Times Literary Supplement

'Caoilinn Hughes is the real thing—an urgent, funny, painstaking and heartfelt writer. *Orchid & the Wasp* is a startling debut full of the moral complexity, grief and strange bewilderments of humanity. As the world spins ever more quickly in response to the demands of grifters, parasites and liars, this book offers a troubling, beautiful and wise response.'

**A. L. Kennedy, Costa Prize-winning author
of *Day* and *Serious Sweet***

'*Orchid & the Wasp* is an ambitious, richly inventive and highly entertaining account of the way we live now. Caoilinn Hughes writes with authority and insight, and her novel is as up-to-date as tomorrow's financial-page headlines.'

John Banville, Man Booker Prize-winning author of *The Sea*

'Caoilinn Hughes's highly ambitious fiction debut contains multitudes … Kick-ass, whip-smart and with "a tongue like a catapult", Gael belongs to a venerable tradition of feisty heroines … Some serious intellectual themes are explored: the crisis of late capitalism; the redemptive power of art and love; free expression in sexual matters; and much else besides. But maybe most strikingly, Gael Foess makes a telling contribution to the unlikeable female narrator debate … Readers are going to love her.' *Sunday Times*

'*Orchid & the Wasp* … is making waves because it is fiercely bright and moves like a bullet train.'

Sebastian Barry, bestselling author of *Days Without End*, for the *Irish Times*

'A gem of a novel about the way we live now.' *Elle*

'You won't forget Gael Foess.' **NPR.org**

'A winning debut novel … Hughes, a poet, touches the prose with a comic wand … *Orchid & the Wasp* delivers a fantasy of competence, the kind that is in dialogue, if not always complete agreement, with morality.' *The New Yorker*

'A razor-sharp wit and an astonishing psychological and emotional perceptiveness combine to yield uncommonly rich portraiture in this bracing book by a deadly talented writer, in prose so refined one slows to savour each beautifully unfolding sentence. Unsentimental, yet sneakily moving and given to surprising bouts of joy, *Orchid & the Wasp* becomes a referendum on the resiliency of selflessness in a contemporary world steeped in the logic of ambitious self-advancement.'

Matthew Thomas, *New York Times*-bestselling author of *We Are Not Ourselves*

THE WILD LAUGHTER

CAOILINN HUGHES

A Oneworld Book

First published in Great Britain, North America,
Ireland and Australia by Oneworld Publications, 2020

ISBN 978-1-78607-780-6 (hardback)
ISBN 978-1-78607-781-3 (export paperback)
ISBN 978-1-78607-782-0 (eBook)

Every reasonable effort has been made to trace the copyright holders
of material reproduced in this book, but if any have been inadvertently
overlooked the publishers would be glad to hear from them.

Printed and bound in Great Britain by Clays Ltd, Elcograf S.p.A.

This book is a work of fiction. Names, characters, businesses, organisations,
places and events are either the product of the author's imagination or are
used fictitiously. Any resemblance to actual persons, living or dead, events or
locales is entirely coincidental.

Oneworld Publications
10 Bloomsbury Street, London, WC1B 3SR, United Kingdom
3754 Pleasant Ave, Suite 100, Minneapolis, MN 55409, USA

for Seán, for Ailbhe

1.

The night the Chief died, I lost my father and the country lost a battle it wouldn't confess to be fighting. For the no-collared, labouring class. For the decent, dependable patriarch. For right of entry from the field into the garden.

Jurors were appointed to gauge the casualty. They didn't wear black. Don't they know black is flattering? The truth isn't. They kept safe and silent. I didn't. When is a confession an absolution and when is it a sentencing, I'd like to find out. I suppose there's only one outcome for souls like us—heavy-going souls the like of mine and the long-lost Chief's—and not a good one.

But I'll lay it on the line, if only to remind the People of who they are: a far cry from neutral judicial equipment. Determining the depth of rot that's blackening the surface can't always be left to deities or legislators—sometimes what's needed is to tie a string around the tooth and shut the door lively.

2.

He was a bright young thing. My brother, Cormac. His mind was a luxury. The face was rationed, it must be said, but there's not a body with everything. Part t-rex, part pelican. Picture that menace of features! Close-eyed, limb-chinned, skin thick as the red carpet he imagined laid down beneath his wellies. Tall as the door he expected to be let in. When he was twelve, he looked twenty. The mind was ahead too, as I said. The odd girl went in for such a harrow of a fella (the odd girl and not the even) on account of his brains and chesty conduct. Not that he was liberal with his cleverness. But there was the atmosphere of it, knowing at any moment something you'd say would be turned inside out like a child's eyelid to traumatise you, to show you the violence behind it that you never meant, or maybe you did.

I might have voiced some innocent idea. Some vague concern about a spray the Chief was sampling, and Cormac would go, 'Yeah yeah yeah. Atrazine. It's no fucken DDT, but it's been proved to be an endocrine disruptor. Environmental protection agency done a tonne of research on amphibians, showering them in the new compounds, and the creatures wound up with extra pee holes. A surplus set of balls, or quarter fanny, two-fifths bollocks— scrambled their sex organs, so it did. Foul stuff, in high doses.' And then I'd nod and mutter a bit, dizzying with the image of the two pee holes, as if a snake bit itself in its artichoke-green scales, and I'd be caught up in the symbolism to do with a snake snacking on its own tail, nodding along because Cormac didn't abet attention-wandering, and I'd get a clobber on the head if I asked was a snake an amphibian. He'd have clocked my yea-saying, and he'd go: 'So you're anti-pesticides, would you say?' On the main, I might answer, I am. There's natural ways to rid a field of pests—letting birds eat the ladybugs and all that—isn't there? Some of them chemicals do more harm than good. I might not be a fan of dogs, but teeny frogs are adorable. Then he'd look down his bucked nose at me, like a horse that couldn't be fucked to lep the last fence for the sugar cube reward. 'And I suppose you think seven billion people can be fed on a batch of organic carrots? Ya privileged, gentrified, self-serving colonial twit,' he'd say, 'letting billions starve, so long as they're out of sight, all to spare a few extra cunts on a toad.'

As I say, I didn't resent him his mind. Early on, its potential was fearsome, but he cached it away too long, until it curdled. He could have his intellect. I had the looks. The Chief's mud-coloured locks, yellowing now like a stack of cut grass drying out for haymaking, hey! Square skull, cultured nose, the kind of eyes that might be described as pea and mint soup, best served cold. I was shorter than my brother by a foot, but divvied up as good as David. I'd the emotions of every girl in the County Roscommon over a barrel. A fact he found hard to swallow, in spite of—or maybe because of—the pelican chin. Excepting gobshites, I liked people. And I was well liked—for no good reason, far as Cormac was concerned. I'd zilch to contribute in the way of knowledge or guile or points for the home side, and sure, how else can a person be of use? Sport lent him an absence note for the farm work that needed doing. For the care work. For the life sentence. His absence meant my containment. Stay put, Hart, he was telling me. Stay a mile wide of my circle.

There's only so many circles in a town the size of a souterrain. What I did and said reflected on him, so he wanted the sticks brushed from my hair, the charm wiped off my face. He wanted me capable of summing sums and changing tyres. To be mad on mechanics—Newtonian and Fordian both. To know a stock option hadn't to do with cattle. But I wasn't after his or his boyos' approval—that panel of experts. Where we're from, infants get swaddled in hessian sacks. I never bought into an alternative reality, no matter how low the interest rates limbo'd for the new millennium, no matter how you could go the whole way to Dublin on a test drive and, if you weren't satisfied, no one would lambaste you or demand a tenner for petrol. Cormac *did* clinch a deal with the new reality. Nothing daft: he didn't barter his youth, as many did, for a barge on the Shannon or a conservatory extension or an interior decorator or a rotary milking parlour or a personal stylist. No. He wanted a college education. A new way of life, less like subsistence—one that didn't stink of fear and survival. A challenge that called for grey matter and not gruntwork. He did fast maths on how the island was transfiguring—one of them scenarios like if a train is going at such-and-such a pace in the direction of a stone wall but it's absolute gas craic on the train, what are your options?

Land had been the Chief's idea of a fortune up to then. He was jubilant to get two extra acres in 2003 for twenty-two grand, on a five-year loan. High milk prices coupled with favourable weather conditions meant banks were lending freely for farmers to expand their livestock, upgrade machinery, to purchase double chop silage over single so the animals could eat shorter grass. Didn't they deserve it! Fatten them quicker. Growth, ladies and gentlelads. The Feelgood Factor.

Cormac wouldn't have advised our father to buy land. Not that year. Not in Roscommon. Not if all he planned to do with it was to work it himself and not let someone else's livelihood be exposed to fickle conditions and soil that would've needed gold in it to be amply mineral-rich. But then, he could respect the challenge that the Chief had lived up to when he'd been the same age, when his parents and small sister had burnt alive in a hay fire and he'd had to take over the farm. There followed a stretch of the Chief's life that was toilsome and lonesome. He had been left behind. Until he married Nóra in '82, when he was thirty-two and she thirty. By then, he had turned the arid earth over and over until it was fertile. So how could such a man's son see fit to question his choices?

3.

One muggy August Sunday the year following, after mass, we drove fifty miles to Offaly for the agricultural show. The four of us away together was a rare thing. (That said, our final trip together would be infamous, would be played out in the courts, reported on the telly. But back then, we were culchie innocence incarnate.) I was a yoyo-voiced fifteen, in my Junior Certificate year. It sank in then I mightn't do the Leaving Cert., but Cormac—nearing seventeen— would do it well enough for the pair of us. It was the last stretch of holidays before his last year in school, and he was jockeying up accordingly. We hadn't gone to Tullamore since it was cancelled in 2001 thanks to foot-and-mouth (the year Cormac collected my Easter eggs in a bin liner, saying 'twas all over the news that Nestlé chocolate had mad cow disease and your brain could get infected; it took the sight of his brown teeth later for me to cop on to my robbing), but by 2004 the Celtic Tiger was on the prowl even in the midlands, and the place was a big trough of milk for her to lap up.

Sixty thousand country people the colour of rain turned out in complicated hairdos and rosette-augmented breasts. They sashayed between alpaca-shearing competitions, pig agility exhibitions and Herefords with weird clean arses being spruced for the stock judging. A new fad among the women was to wear skirts atop trousers—the height of meanness, leaving no view to take in but drooping peach udders mocking us from every angle. Needlework, arts and crafts, fashion shows, food stands, cookery demos, bread-baking tournaments and flower-arrangement tents were in among hundreds of trade stands, advertising everything from insurance to religions to hypnotherapy tapes, soaps, sausages, jams, universities for the high and mighty and jammy. Cormac carried his six-pack from one trade stand to the next, conversing with fellas in pinstriped suits that weren't even Adidas. He opened beer bottles with his belt. Since we'd each been given twenty-five euros to spend, it was an economy I couldn't fathom, bottled beer when cans were half the price. But what did I know about economics? Only that it's a creed we're all baptised into against our will, and our heads can be pushed back underwater and held there if ever the fealty wavers.

'Agribusiness,' Cormac declared to the Chief later, who was stationed at the vast machinery exhibition at the heart of the fair, 'is not the same as agronomy.'

Another father might have clipped his ear. But the Chief clutched his wrists behind his back and squinted at his son's puffed chest, inviting a lesson on the difference between agri and agro, and it nearing forty years his occupation. There were youngsters in Monaco majoring in Luxury Studies, and yet the Chief hadn't taken a day of luxury in his life, to get some distance from his work, to see where efficacies could be won. Cormac was telling him: 'If the old combine harvester's on the bust for even a pair of hours on the wrong day, the tiny margins in tillage mean you're well and truly—you know yourself, Dad. *And* it's versatile, like.'

The Chief heeded Cormac that afternoon because it was fine to have sons who wanted your ear. Because of the report card that had come in the post, marking his eldest the first family member bound for university. Because of the Excel spreadsheet that had been a Father's Day gift in the early summer, by which Cormac had made the case for various technological investments—a new power harrow with trailing serrated discs, for example, whose loan could be paid off quick 'if Hart contracted himself out with the machine when it's not needed on our own farm. New streams of income.' My brother's sums had my submission worked into them.

'If we're flush enough to buy new machines,' I said, 'what about a holiday abroad?' A thing we'd never done in our lives. As I suggested this, a few tractors paraded past like blown-up toys, shiny red and green, the tyre nodules pleasingly Lego-edged. 'I want to go to Barcelona, with the skull balconies and lizard-skin roofs, and Athens, with the crumbly anfitheatres ...' I paused then, thinking up a joke to do with Excel columns versus Roman, but Cormac was off again, saying we were all so wet for *buildings* and *holidays* because any stunted eejit can understand them things, and the government could only fathom factories and stadiums besides—more of the same. There's more helicopters in Ireland than high-speed modems. Yeah yeah yeah, it was normal to covet our own places after a century's occupation, he said, but we'd need to get wise if all this luck wasn't to be idled away. He flung his arms out to the fair, like a ringmaster whose arena encompasses the far reaches of the imagination. But he wasn't imaginative. He was a ledger.

He gestured to the thriving gala, but me and the Chief looked past it to the real fortress behind the bouncy one—the gorgeous grey, gothic Charleville Castle, the land it looked over—and the truth was we both saw it as evidence of what he'd been describing. The national wealth and the luck. What it meant to prosper. Heritage worth restoring. 'Do they do bullfighting still in Madrid,' I said, 'with matadors and the pole through the pate?'

'A lance, it's called,' Cormac said, watching the Chief's gaze connecting the castle back to the big machine that had been in question—a sort of building, surely.

'Horns blowing for the start of the fight!' I said to myself, vaguely searching among the bulls for my slinky cousin Shane, who we'd given a lift to, and who'd made a needle of himself soon as we arrived at the haystack. (That he baled a fashion model, as he'd insist upon later, was a tall one. She was a twelve-year-old who came Highly Commended in the All-Ireland Farm Skills competition—in the First Aid category and not, as he'd try to imply, in Manual Handling. 'Ah ya havta throw some shnazz on it, lads.')

'Bugle,' Cormac muttered. He opened his last two beer bottles on his belt and offered one to the Chief, who declined. Cormac didn't press him, hoping it was because he'd be driving heavy machinery. A fine thing in a bright red fleece walked by, and we clocked her. I'd've held out the spare beer to her with a broody smile. Instead, Cormac took turns swigging from each bottle.

'The bulls'll be after her,' I said.

Cormac tutted. 'Bulls are colour-blind, you mong.'

That was no time to admit confusion. I pivoted. 'Why didn't Mam bring Big Red for the poultry competition?' Her prize-worthy rosecomb cock.

'Ah now,' the Chief said from his great height, with his arms crossed so I could barely see his face. 'Watching and appreciating's more her style. She's not competitive.'

'Why not?' I said.

'Just, it doesn't suit her,' the Chief said. He spotted his pal, our neighbour Gerry, across the way and waved. The Chief had nothing else to say about our mother behind her back. A peculiar sort of romance, but largesse and courtesy can amount to the same.

'She's more private,' Cormac said, as if to conclude the mention of her positively. He sympathised with her for what she couldn't speak of—the same ordeals, he supposed, that explained her estranged siblings. She had four, apparently, but we didn't know if they were alive or what. Cormac pitied that she'd never been given a challenge to live up to. The only challenge he knew she'd had was to keep on at it. Cormac must have deemed it too late for her, then, though I didn't.

'*I'll* show her chickens for her next year,' I said, 'if it's because she's embarrassed.'

'Then she'll have every right to be morto.' Cormac drained one of the bottles and put it in the back pocket of his jeans so he had a free hand to shake Gerry's.

Gerry wore his cap low to keep the sun off him but the skin around his eyes was stuffed against the band of it with his smile. He nodded at each of us and said our names, as if to prove he could recognise us out of context. Then he jabbed his thumb in the direction of the big green harvester the Chief had been studying. 'She's the one?' he asked.

The Chief shrugged gently. 'It's the bank has to say "I do".'

Gerry twitched his head diagonal. 'Well wear, Manus. It's lovely!' Then he stood side by side with the Chief and they looked at the machine.

I looked up too, at the sky that wasn't a thing we could modernise or beautify. It emptied out onto our fields when it wanted to, having no mind for our buildings and brand-new plans or for timing.

'Well, I'm getting a celebratory six-pack,' Cormac said, even including me in his mirthy eye contact. 'Any takers?'

'Oh,' Gerry said, 'in actual fact, I'm for the road this minute. I'm too long gone as it is. Thanks all the same, Cormac. I wonder will it be yourself operating this fine outfit?'

Cormac shook his head and let out a small burp. 'Excuse me,' he said. 'No, Gerry. I'm for college next year.'

'Oh?' Gerry said. Then he turned to me and pushed up the brim of his cap so all his moles were on display. It was a bit like the clouds clearing at night, showing a familiar constellation. Heralding nothing. Only constancy. The plough, the plough, the plough.

Cormac had left, and I don't know if he said anything more. But Gerry hadn't asked me the same question. He didn't want to offend me and he couldn't think of what to say. So there was a moment of silence, which was nice. Then the Chief said that he shouldn't speak for me, but that I'd only been saying I'd like to travel the world, 'and that *is* the other family tradition, so it is, Gerry. There's a whole band of Blacks down there in New Zealand.'

'So there is,' Gerry said. 'And I wonder ... how they pronounce Black ... do you think?' Gerry was too shy to say it—*Blick*—but he and the Chief laughed at the sound of it in their heads.

''Tis a bit zany, the accent alright,' the Chief said. He turned to me and put his heavy hand on my shoulder, like a loaded canvas saddlebag. Gerry said he thought I was more of a homebody. The Chief gave me time to answer, and when I couldn't, he hummed a little, to put the silence at ease. I was looking at the harvester. At that huge worldly thing my brother had been able to convince him of. How many huge nebulous things had he convinced me of, and for whose harvest?

But there was one time three years on—a hair's breadth of a moment in the tail end of our youths—when me and Cormac put our differences aside, pooled our minds and work ethics, and I'll tell you what, there was no splitting of hairs but splitting of atoms. That's where we were when it comes to what I'm confessing, and I'd rather it out of the way. None of this 'we'll wait and watch the tragedy to the last curtain', as Patrick Kavanagh would have it. This is the prodigal son *scéal* of our times, so out with it.

4.

Before the bubble burst, the conditions were set in by which the Chief would have to work his dying day, tilling his grave in the fields with the heatless sun hung low in the sky. Until then, we wouldn't know the goings-on of his mind, never mind the spoiling meat of him. To think of the foreign things he let eat him alive for he wouldn't leave his sons a worse debt than what he'd already accumulated. The foreign things we'll get back to. First, how did he get so sick as that, as if his lips had been stretched round a chimney flue? By association. Haven't we the Black Death and the well-fed crows and the Famine Roads going nowhere to teach us that in Ireland? Many a friend the Chief had despite his being largely silent. When he had something to say, he knew how to open the chamber of his throat and come out with something brief but mighty, so that everybody heeded him and the principles he lived by—hard-earned learnings. The stories he told were local in the sense of being local to the soul, not to the landlocked midlands culture. But primarily, he was a listener.

One day in the height of the country's delirium, he listened to a subsidy-suckling sheep husband by the name of Tony Morrigan, whose palms convened round a pint of Guinness of a Sunday morning. With a necktie he must've tugged up from his grand-father's grave, he'd come to our house midday midweek to show the lazy hours of a sheep-farming property owner (he'd hired shearers) with the advice of the centuries: 'There's azy money to be made off bricks and mortar. Spain's past its best now, so you've to know what you're at. I've four bought off-plans in Bulgaria. I'll keep one and dole out the rest to my pals with only ten percent atop the price I got them. Going up sure as escalators. More reliable even. Stairs! I'll be having me ease retiring before my own father, I'll tell you that for nothing. There's a ticket out of this slog, Manus, and here's me handing it to you on a platter.'

I won't make excuses for the Chief—he shouldn't have heeded such an infested-arseholed skiving prick, but they'd copied each other's algebra sums on the school bus, so why shouldn't they copy each other's assumption sums on the train to Dublin? The way you come to trust a thing you've known your lifelong is the way you come to trust the sea, until one day you're napping in your La-Z-Boy and a tsunami rolls in and wakes you with the lungful of salt water and the shame of dying without your feet on the floor. Like that, he wound up with an apartment in Malaga and the plan for one in Sunny Beach—the portent of it—on the east coast of Bulgaria by the time Morrigan had jellied him up like an aul sow in muck and introduced him to the creditor—citing the Chief's land for leverage, his cultivator, seeder, sprayer, the harvester he'd been prompt in his hire-purchase payments for. The three of them sipping lattes and our father who never had a latte in his life— who drank milky tea only. Our father who didn't have an atlas to look up where Bulgaria was besides—not for stupidity or naivety, but he was a working man with no time for atlases or affogatos or amortisations.

He looked for proof and he saw it in the Range Rover he was picked up in, in pals calling round on a Thursday afternoon, saying to leave the spade alone and join them for a jar in Monroe's, in the mansions going up along these boreens, the ribbon housing that made no sense for the development of townships. But no one voiced a word of provocation or changed the planning legislation or sought out unbiased advice or turned down the 10K loan when they'd only asked the bank teller for directions. They let it happen and our father saw that. He envied the people of Ireland their long driveways that Polish hands were weeding on the weekends. Their furniture imported from China and not fought over from the pickings of a dead relative. Underfloor heating warming their soles. Their kids driving themselves to school in Mini Coopers. It was true, he feared himself left behind. He'd been left behind before— as he saw it, his loved ones gone off to greener pastures. The scent of smoke had never left him. But mostly it was Tony Morrigan's visits and promises. He was buying from someone he knew—not some faceless developer. That was the way he got himself half a million in debt. Two sun-soaked chalets he'd never cross the thresholds of when he hadn't the roof above our heads paid off.

Us youths were staggered at his undertaking: the back for labour, the perseverance for farming, the mind for finance, the foresight for investment, hands big enough to hold everything in them at once. He was a veritable twenty-first-century Irishman as should be governing the country. Cormac took close measure of our situation. As to where he reckoned us headed, I only knew it was away from where we came. But as time went on and the forecast changed, the redness in the Chief's face never fully drained and we quieted down. He thumped our shoulders less often. Rarely. The food he shovelled down wasn't tasted. Like how you could settle the interest on a loan, and something would have been spent, but nothing would be paid. The working day ate away at the night hours till there was almost no break in his work but his back. Two silver coins in his pocket reminded him of what his great-grand-father set out with in the 1800s. The bottom line might have been writ on his brow: 'And I'm about to lose it all here.' We became a quiet house. Though I barely went to school, I was aiming for my Leaving Certificate, reluctant to sign on just yet—to be relied upon. Cormac had moved to Galway for college in '06 and only came back the odd weekend. He helped out when he was around so long as he could sleep in and take his pick of the jobs. But eventually, he avoided us. Home was some nugatory equation he couldn't solve, and so couldn't stand the sight of.

Nóra muted the radio whenever the Chief came in, for all that was on it was the R-word that should never have entered a countryman's vocabulary. He didn't tell us, but we knew well enough. Morrigan hadn't shown his wet-eyed weasel's face in months. The Chief was ruined—as were we all, by default—and the retirement that had been nearing slipped away like a pike till he lost sight of her entirely. That was when the brothers Black put differences aside and heads together to restore the pride of our father.

5.

Good Friday was only hours off, and our bellies already grumbled for the Sunday roast. Cormac was home from Galway for the long weekend and the atmosphere beefed up accordingly. We borrowed the antique Land Rover and told the Chief we were going twenty miles to visit cousin Shane. Cormac had to thrash out a business proposition with him that wasn't fit for the phone. The two of them being entrepreneurs, the story was credible, though the Chief recoiled at the suggestion of private enterprise and at the forty miles of petrol. (It being 2008, the sliding sensation was queasily felt, even if the country wasn't yet officially declared recessed.) Ketamine, syringes, head torches, scissors, knives, ice-filled cooler boxes loading down the boot, we stole into the night like two moths intent on lustre.

That night, *I* had a lesson for my brother: the 'quick brain death' manner of slaughter I described to him in the dark of the car parked a few fields down from Morrigan's ... until their sheepdog, out for a sniff, made the proposition catch in my gullet. Even with the protection of the car, my heart snatched at my throat like himself at the window. Airports, I realised that very instant, would be a problem if I ever wanted to escape this place. You've no choice but to let the sniffer dogs come right the fuck up to you, the way the darkness came right up to me then with a woozy haymaker's lurch.

Cormac didn't take it seriously. He thought I gave into it. The palpitations, sweat glands fizzing, stomach floating, leather-strapped chest. He thought I could control it if I put my mind to it, with the power of logic, as if it wasn't an infirmity that made my life a torture chamber, being reared in dog-ridden farmland. 'He won't touch you.'

'*You* go. You'll manage without me. Go on!' That was the way of my please, he knew well.

'Shut your face.' Cormac was there with me but I could sense him stood outside himself, watching our parochial ways, our inept, abortive solutions. 'Nothing to do with your hysterics,' he said, 'but we'll give the dog a dose of K to send him off, case he makes a racket.'

'That's a fair point,' I said, stifling the urge to whine. 'You'll do that so, will you?'

'Fuck you. I'll do everything.'

He had the job done by the time my heart was down to a canter. I heard the dog panting and whimpering, entering his cat-chasing dreams, and felt better directly. More so when Shane's Subaru rattled in. We leapt out into the field, igniting the head torches and readying the equipment like the neurosurgeons we could've been had we been born moneyed in Dublin—or maybe Cormac would've been that and me a gynaecologist, cutting out the browny petals as do the lotus flower a disservice. Oh for the road we're born on! It calluses more than our soles.

The spring lambs were comatose at our knees before long—fluffy slippers of things only two month old or around. We could barely see well enough for the job by the torches, so in spite of my 'gentle brain death' talk, we just slit the necks and hung them on the paddock posts. Shane panthered towards us from the road. He had the pelt for it—black, shorn, oily—and the lean, prowling body. His eyes wobbled through the dark field like a *púca*'s. 'He'll be giddy,' Cormac warned. This was the kind of thing Shane lived for—not that he was a farm lad. His father—our uncle-in-law Mitch's brother (Shane wasn't really our cousin, but close enough)—owned a hardware shop and planned to fob it off on one of them soon enough. But he took Shane hunting once and taught him how not to spoil a carcass in the gutting by sticking Shane's head into the hollowed-out innards of a wild goat and holding him in till he gagged. Shane would've flicked his father if the latter hadn't sworn the whole thing was ritualistic: his first kill, neat in the eye. His first good gutting. The head stuck in was traditional. The crock of shite that's swallowed in the name of man-making.

'Lads, look at the job on ye!' (Cormac was right about Shane being giddy. He might make the thing feel prankish, which I didn't like.) 'That's the stuff. Spuds! Slugger!' He clapped our backs. I was Spuds, for the obvious reason. Slugger meant someone who could hit a ball hard. Though it was a flattering nickname, Cormac would soon put an end to it. 'Ye've them docked and de-bollocked by the looks of it,' Shane said. 'That's half the job. Now we cut round the anus to free the tract, peel back their coats along the run of their necks to the rear trajectory, then draw the insides out.' He snapped on a pair of latex gloves as cocky as condoms. We let him have his moment. 'Skinnin' the animal proper afore spillin' the guts would be the ideal, but we've no time for that?'

'No,' Cormac snapped.

Shane threw him a look. 'Ye've buckets for the muck?'

'No buckets is the idea,' I said. 'To leave splattered guts for

Morrigan to slip on and learn what his like done to men like our father.' Seeing in Shane's gittish expression that he mightn't have grasped it, I added: 'It's metaphorical-like. For gutting the economy.'

'Hear fucken *hear*.' Shane slow-clapped. He liked me better than Cormac. I knew how to address him in his own talk. 'Listen, lads,' he said. 'The noggins on ye, with the day that's in it! These lambs are due to town in the morning to peddle for the Sunday roast.'

'The timing's no accident.' Cormac's words were clipped. 'Morrigan changes their breeding cycles for the swelled prices.'

'Is that right?' Shane opened the first lamb from chest to crotch and the guts flopped onto the grass, spattering the bin liner we loaned him.

'It takes some meddling to fuck with nature's cycles,' Cormac informed us. 'The cute whore. Want to know how he manages it?' He had an audience made of us all right. 'Tricks the ewes with hormones, so he does. He wanks the rams, upends the ewes on a cradle and forces the semen into them.' There was an ire in his voice that wasn't meant to entertain but to warn. He had the knowledge could do us the same. We were silent after that. Shane hadn't stopped working, though he'd heard Cormac well enough. He pulled out the long, shell-pink anal tract like a stiff squid, the full bladder, kidneys, gall bladder, all the innards of the first lamb. He lifted out the liver and held it on his palm like a red fortune fish.

'We want the livers.' I stepped in with a plastic container.

Shane grinned and stuck the arm in again. I watched the purple jelly pulse of it and didn't know how he could tell one organ from the next. That mess filled each of us. 'Now,' he commentated, seeing I was interested: 'Watch close. This is fucken needlework. I'm goin' through the gullet now, the windpipe ... separaten the diaphragm from the ribcage with a few ... wily ... scoops.'

I stepped closer, careful on the slimy grass, and heard the scraping flesh. Just then, the whole viscera dropped out onto the ground like a cut fishnet. Cormac bust into laughter behind, from a safe distance. Cold sweat tickled my forehead and I swallowed bile. 'You've a talent there,' I told Shane through a clenched jaw, the liver trembling in the container.

'Thanking you, Doharty.'

He knew the politics of the situation, and not to goad. Then he did me a favour I'll not forget. 'Slugger,' he said, 'root through them organs and see none are inflamed or infected. No boils or warts or pus on them. Dig out the heart too, will ya? I'll have the hearts myself if ye're not up to them. And if there's not a metaphor in that, I never fucked a dishtant cousin.'

I moved away from that scene and on to the next gentle lamb wilting in the darkness, our own father not enough unlike the sagging creature, all blood-let, bloodless. That's the way the world felt—as a post we were hung from, and no one willing to say who fixed the meat hook into the decade. Worse: the blood hadn't gone to some cause so we could've been grateful for the slow sacrifice. It hadn't been spread into the soil as it was on that night, to feed back into the rivers so the ones who'd done it could taste the contagion. No. The blood of the country had gone nowhere but gutters.

6.

Easter Sunday breakfast was hard-boiled eggs on brown bread with a sedimentary layer of butter. Nóra kept a palatial henhouse out back so we'd eggs to feed the bare-knuckled boxers of Longford. (We'd buy chocolate eggs when they were half price on Tuesday.) Eggs dropped from my armpits in the morning when I stretched, but I rarely sickened of them. Exposing the sunny yolks was a metaphysical occasion. After breakfast, we took the Land Rover to mass. Neither the Chief nor herself sniffed at the lavender air freshener. The notification—'Lambs to the Slaughter: Easter Embezzlement'—would be in the next *Roscommon Herald.* We'd see the look on his face then. But surely he already knew. We'd spied him going out to the shed for his toolkit to bleed the radiators, convinced no heat came from them at all. Would the mess we'd left be cause for our first true clobbering? Worse: would he be saddened? The Cranberries sang 'Linger' in the aromatised car.

That mass was the first we'd been dragged to since Christmas, but from that day until the fateful day I had to drive them weekly, with the Chief waning as slowly and irreversibly as an ice cap. The sermon started out promising. Cormac and I caught eyes. The Chief shifted in his seat. Nóra, for a brief moment, didn't look taxidermied. Had Father Shaughnessy been enlightened since Christmas? Had he Darwin checked out of the library? 'The world is a truly magnificent place, brothers and sisters,' he bellowed. 'The science of it is extraordinary and poetic in the highest degree. This world, *our* world, is made up of atoms and molecules. Galileo, Einstein, Newton … these were religious men, scientific men. These worshippers did what we must do now. We must see in this exquisite design, this infinitesimal complexity, the celestial architect and physicist behind it all: the Lord Jesus Christ our Saviour.'

The Chief's shoulders dropped. We didn't even skitter for the feeling there was of a man closing in on himself beside us, and not a particle of faith he could store away. The anxiety of being away from his work had returned already, after a scant hour's respite. His lumbering body put a bend in the pew, and dandruff flakes from his auburn-grey hair fell around him in his own weather system, slow to move on from winter and into spring.

We heard the rattle in his chest that had long replaced the rattle in his pockets. The collection came round and I saw the coin he slipped in. No notes or brown envelopes those days. The wicker basket, even, was coming apart: a discredit to its lavish past, when to weigh it down was to give weight to a hard-won collective. Perhaps the whole sect should have quit that Easter Sunday while it had some vestige of reputation, dignity, history about it. But our father got on his knees and convened his palms. I don't know what neurons fired in him, but I felt like standing up and wailing out to all the obedient parishioners in that hollow chantry to look at him: a hard-working man, brought to his knees.

And what? What then? Would I ask for their money, their diagnoses or their prayers? I don't know. I didn't stand to ask. Maybe this was the day the idea was planted into the minds of us Blacks: walk out of this world while you have the use of your legs.

7.

It rains 175 days of the year in Roscommon, with global warming set to triple that. Rain fizzed on the sill that April afternoon as I tucked my chair close to the table and Cormac forked peas from the bowl individually, flaunting his fine motor skills. Nóra was stood by the oven wringing her hands as we awaited the Chief, pulling off his boots in the garage.

Steaming carrots, peas, our own floury Kerr's Pinks, gravy and a basket of bread were on the table. In the middle was a mat for the roast to be set. I gave Cormac a freaked look to say: *Do you smell that?* By the dice eyes he threw back, he did. Then we heard the doors opening and closing beyond, in an effort to contain the cold, damp air. I had to blurt something out so the Chief wouldn't walk in on the quiet. 'How was the game anyways?' Cormac had had a hurling match. 'Is Brian back playing yet, with the glued forehead on him?'

Cormac sniffed, reluctant to be friendly. 'A learned wrinkle down the middle.' He indicated by fingering vertically between his brows. 'I christened him Wisecrack. Had the lads pissing themselves.'

'*An teanga!*' Nóra said. She was showing off for the Chief arriving in.

'*Céard é?*' He threw his wet cap on the counter and sat at the head of the table. His chest broke into a snare drum solo before she could respond. Cormac cracked his knuckles and inhaled as if he was going to say something over the coughing, deliver some insight. Then he busied himself tonguing pea jackets from his teeth. The Chief caught his breath and asked in a quiet voice that compelled Cormac to lean in: 'Did you score any points for the county?'

''Twas only a training match. We've all got college assignments. No proper matches till May.'

The Chief angled his gaze at me. 'A *no* if ever I heard one.'

I smirked quickly before Cormac caught sight. Then Nóra opened the oven door to *it*. We all turned to put an image to that mouth-flooding smell. The lamb had been roasted with garlic and mint and rosemary and was haloed in vapour. Not a word was uttered as she laid the weeping centrepiece on the table. The Chief stood up and took the carving knife in his fist. He stalled, seeming to inspect the meat for leanness, but he was taking measure of something else.

Nóra battled with this prolonged self-awareness, roping her hands. I came to know her awkwardness as a six-year-old boy, home from school after having won a Noddy book in a lucky dip, and only delighted. But when I got home to her, I began feeling strange and sick. The thing I'd been excited for wasn't the story itself, or it being the first book that was mine; it was the image I'd had of it being read to me with a mother's fluency and confidence, before a glowing fire. I'd held the glossy book out to her, hoping I wouldn't have to explain, but I did have to explain. And her stuck face revealed that she had no such experience of love or comfort to draw from, and she seemed embarrassed to be the stand-in adult in my fantasy. 'Ask your father,' she told me, knowing full well that the Chief never sat in front of the fire. I pictured him reading to me by an empty hearth, and cried.

On the Easter Sunday in question, she wore her collared, long-sleeved, raisin-coloured dress from mass with a bloodstained apron over it. She was uniquely equipped for some activity that neither she nor me nor the numen could name. For a minute, I thought she looked handsome, in the hoary way of a fossil—after all, she gave me the nose I have and the long eyelashes—but then, the way her eyes devoured her husband's face, she looked wicked again. The Chief winced with a pain we couldn't imagine and held his breath a while. At long last, he said 'Eaten bread is soon forgotten', and carved into the roast lamb in a tender way that couldn't have been further from the hacking of two nights earlier. That was the way he'd leave you shamed. I wanted to tell him all about it then. About the sheepdog and the fright I suffered, about the apprenticeship in butchery his sons undertook and the long hours spent contriving the only treatment our vernal minds could dream up for the injury. Though it wasn't a lottery win or a cancer cure, I wanted to know if it was something, anything at all—if it would do for the minute. But I already knew there was something nobler and far more difficult to be done, as soon as we were men.

8.

'You can't downsize a potato field … *agus sé sin an fhadhb,*' the Chief called from his tractor the following night when I went out with a sandwich. The Chief's parents—who, as I said, were burnt to slags in a hay barn when he was a youth—were Gaelgoirs. He kept on the bit of Irish to honour them. I made my way along the mud bank towards him. I wanted him inside in the sitting room with the paper flopped across his wide lap like a dead stingray and me sprawled sleepily on the couch, pretending to read *Philadelphia! Here I Come* (the Leaving Cert. play text, all about what Private wants to say but Public can't manage to get out because of the Indian cobra between his thighs and for fear of how the outside world would react, and couldn't we all relate to those obstacles?). I wanted to get straight to the point with the Chief, like the garrulous Private, and make frantic recommendations to do with the properties:

Wasn't there some poor illiterate creature who doesn't get out much or have the internet, who by some miracle doesn't know the home soil has gone to slurry, who'd happily lap up a villa in Malaga with a shared swimming pool and a dishwasher and a motorised awning and oversized tiles? Alternatively, wasn't there investing to be done, now that we were all in the pits and could only crawl upwards? Wasn't it time to let go of this outmoded life? If we could *sell* something—I'd live without a kidney, I had my looks—or arrange a countywide poker championship for Cormac to work the odds of with the Brobdingnagian brain on him ... for us to win ourselves back, slowly but surely? What I ended up saying, holding out the sandwich, was:

'There's lamb in that.'

He laboured out of the tractor. It was dragging a disc-type hiller behind for bringing earth up to the potato vines. Though the engine was turned off and its hoovering noise had fallen silent, the pattern of it carried on: the angled discs scooping in soil like a child's hands gathering sand to make a castle. The vines bowing down to let the tractor pass over them and then springing up behind—seeming renewed, devoted.

'Doing lines?'

We both squinted back down the length of the row that had been turned a deeper shade of earth, illumed by a flash of moonlight, leading straight back to our lit house an acre off.

'A manner of lines,' he said. 'I'll be doing it by hand before long. Spraying pesticide one squirt at a time.' He took the sandwich from me.

'Out of a Mr Muscle bottle?'

He winked and put a quarter of the sandwich in his mouth at once. Opportunities come in all ways and sizes: this time, in the form of a stuffed gob? No, it was too soon. But then my mind was so filled with the large things I wanted to say, I was stuck for small ones. The Chief chewed away and swallowed dryly. Never one to force talk. He was happy enough in his calm refuelling.

'We're back to school Tuesday. Tomorrow's off,' I said. He made a noise of acknowledgement. 'Cormac's doing college stuff.'

He looked at me sideways, then spoke with a full mouth: 'Have you enough to be doing?' I cringed suddenly at my school talk, so late in the day. I'd scraped together three of the six Leaving Cert. subjects last year: Irish, Geography and pass Maths. Managing the others this year was doubtful. 'You could help me widen the pond below,' the Chief said, almost optimistic, 'drain out the wet year that's in it.'

'Ya, I'll do that. I want to *do* something though, I don't know.' Some variety of physical mastery would've been the thing to want, but I tried not to lie to him. 'I like *making* things. Woodworking maybe, if I wasn't so tired from—' I looked from field to sky to lay the blame elsewhere for my wreckery. Huge iron clouds blockaded the moon. '*Gandhi* wouldn't've had the fortitude for stargazing in these parts.' I heard the promising outbreath of a laugh. 'Home-brewing's inevitable, one of these days,' I said. 'But maybe I should take that fiddle down from the attic. Learn to play a woeful recession tune.'

He grimaced. 'Woeful 'twould be. Don't be demanding fiddle lessons, is all I'll say.' I saw his hand go to his pocket in the gloom. 'Always on about the travel, you might take a look at your own country before scarpering off to Germany or Cambodia or wherever it is you're thinking? Walking's as good a pastime as any, to know yourself. There's history in these flatlands to fill a sizeable mind. No elbowing tourists along the stone wall.'

I looked across to let him read my expression.

'Oh. I do forget about the dogs.' He took in the last of the sandwich. He didn't press me on it. I handed him a flask of grey tea in exchange for the kitchen towels. Then I gauged him loosened enough, so I took a deep breath and spoke quickly:

'We could declare bankruptcy. It was Cormac came up with it, so it'll be well thought out. The thing is, neither of us wants the farm, Dad. It's a good life but Cormac's too arrogant for it. He said he will in his shite work for government subsidies ... And ... you can go anywhere with a face like mine! I might meet a girl who won't want this. I'm thinking Australia sounds the job. And the thing is ... if you go bankrupt you could retire then, that was the point of the houses and the whole mess anyways?'

He had the mouthful long-swallowed and was looking into the restless landscape, sporadically moonlamped, as if the night was giving sign to a dangerous reef up ahead. He was six foot two and had another year of standing to his full height, then a five-year crash and collapse. I felt a gossoon stood by him.

'You lads and yer grand plans,' he said, not to me but to the hours of work ahead. I was glad not to have his gaze on me then. There was no way of knowing how wrong I'd been, but I was relieved not to have the idea strangled in my skull any longer. 'You can tell your brother your ideas are for lining the pockets of men like Morrigan. And making them more self-righteous, while you're at it.'

I tried to understand him but it was a tone I hadn't heard. I guessed right that he wasn't talking bankruptcy: 'It was to get back at him,' I said.

The Chief lifted his stubbled jowl, the cap shadowing his face. 'On the insurance claim them lambs went, and Morrigan unable to sell them for the price he was asking, the fierce market that's in it. He was waiting till the last minute to get rid of them. He telephoned Gerry this morning, boastful of the Easter godsend.'

The Chief would never have spoken so freely with Cormac. It was as if the night air and the waxy ears of his harmless youngest son were the particular conditions for talking. But I would've gone ignorant just then. Like a gomey, I said, 'I'll do an hour for you now. I'm used to doing lines.'

He didn't smile but threw the thermos into the tractor and hauled the new weight of himself up onto the seat. 'What ye lads don't understand—' He stopped himself. 'But sure, why would ye? Who'd have taught you?'

The engine coughed up, and off he moved in his tired machinery, making lines as straight as humanly possible into the unknowable night.

9.

Twenty-five percent of potatoes are rejected from supermarkets for being too ugly, so we only ever ate hideous ones. The tuberous things got to be an affront sitting visceral on the kitchen table when the Chief had been diagnosed and had decided against the low odds of successful treatment. He'd spend what time he had left doing what he could to salvage our finances, to keep the farm in a workable condition so its sale might settle the bulk of the debt—though lowland wasn't what it used to be. No such thing as a stronghold.

Cormac had got first class honours from University College Galway and had moved into a flat with the lads in Roscommon town. He was working for an engineering firm that made humongous air-conditioning units or something. I'd stayed at home that long while, on the dole—a thing I wasn't doing to plump out my sculpted arse but on account of my obligation. So Cormac never saw the worst of it. Only at weekends when he'd call round and hear the Chief's slow breathing and see him go green over lunch, or they'd meet in a café when the auls were in to visit the bank manager, returning home without pigment in their skin.

Cormac didn't hear what I heard. The disgusting bathroom coughing. The bickering with inanimate objects. Worst: the whistling. At first he used his two fingers, but when his lungs became more plastic bags than bellows, it was a Christmas cracker whistle he used for summons. (Nóra didn't want the irony of him sounding his own bell.) *Whewwww*. 'Hart!' he'd call. 'Would you take the ashes out of the hearth before I'm among them myself.'

What else did Cormac not hear? The night sounds. The night I went for a lash and saw the bathroom door open and the light on. There the Chief lay exposed and stark in a bath of ice, submerged to his chin in the Arctic shock—legs jutted out the far end like an old man trying to sleep in the cot of his boyhood but life not allowing him the retreat. Humpback whale sounds as weren't meant for human ears. I wanted to lift my head out of his ocean so as not to have that raw calling reverberating through me. What I would've given not to be afeared of dogs then, to throw on a coat and runners and tear out into the night, abscond all places interior, on and on away off to the coast, the island's end, eyes adjusting to the bleakness eventually. The Chief announced he'd sleep downstairs from then on and there was no conversation. Nóra called the relatives round for moral support under the guise of helping convert the living room into a dying room. Cormac came too and brought a *Farmer's Journal* and a pack of chocolate digestives, at which Nóra beamed. 'Isn't that manners to make a mother proud of her rearing.'

Then Cormac was awakened to it. The strangeness of a patient man, composed as a pillar, now irritable as a teenager. The side effects of chronic opioids: nausea, itching, slow breathing, tiredness, constipation, low tolerance; cumulus, cirrus, cirrocu-mulus, altocumulus, altostratus, stratocumulus—the ways of the clouds were the ways of his condition. You could see there was rain in him, but would it arrive before the washing was in off the line?

Despite his exhaustion, he was staunch in the work getting done. Even with visitors, he wouldn't be called in from the field or away from his bookkeeping in the study. He wouldn't arrive till the table was set and hands were full of drinks. (They'd brought brandy, *buíochas le Dia*. Thank God, they said, *le Dia, le Dia. Dia leis. Dia i ngach áit. Go mbeannaí Dia is Muire dhuit.* God be with ye. God everywhere. What if we don't want God with us? We don't want God nor Mary neither. Go away with your *Dia is Muire.* Get them off us. Get them off.) Uncle Mitch and Auntie Bridie didn't know where to lay their eyes, but I was glad for the witnesses. If they could have reduced the cornea's aperture, they'd have made it a pinprick. *Enough* came in different measures for every person in the country, even if—on the whole—we were beginning to abide larger portions of it.

A casserole was simmering in the oven, a half-hour off, so Nóra paraded her vegetable patch, tearing a miserly bit of dill for Mitch and Bridie to take home. Inside, Cormac was doing chin-ups on the bar he'd had affixed to his bedroom door frame since he was fifteen. This was 2014, and he was a twenty-six-year-old fucken chin-up. In his work shirt, he counted loudly. 'I'll leave you to it,' I told him. 'I'm going to check on the small bucks below. Make sure they're not practising arsenic.'

'Arsenic?' Cormac dropped down.

'What? Arsenal, whatever.'

'Arson, you gobshite. Arsenic's a chemical element. Arsenal's a soccer club.'

'Call me a gobshite again.' I was tired and didn't want hate to overpower the other more complicated feeling I was having but couldn't yet name.

'Holy Joe, she's touchy today,' he said. 'Touchy as a bishop.' He lay his arm horizontal across the wall and pressed his chest in to stretch his pecs. He smelt sour. He didn't bother washing himself for this rough house.

I thudded downstairs, but when I got to the kitchen, my mood did another turn. The two lads—our red-headed cousins Neil and Thomas, nine and eleven—were sat in front of tumblers of clear liquid, in fits of giggles. Vodka it looked like. They were red-faced and glassy-eyed. I couldn't tolerate any more sickness or cleaning up after people. They were wild giddy, though. Shouldn't they be afeared of me? To be so blithe-like, caught not only drinking but *stealing*? I didn't want to scold them. Though I couldn't give a crotch louse about adults, I preferred to be on a child's good side. But what could I do? 'What the hell, lads? It's four in the afternoon. Are ye trolloped?'

That only burst the seams of their laughter. Tears canyoned down their freckled faces and their chins showed cellulite. I went to the table for the bottle to make sure it was only vodka and not *poitín*. 'Ye know the saying *blind drunk*'s no joke, lads? Ye'll blind yersels, drinking straight spirits. The hip flasks of ye couldn't hold a pint.'

Thomas tried to calm himself to get the words out: 'We're not drunk, Uncle Hart.'

Neil was ruined and couldn't face me, but he told off Thomas: 'He's not our uncle!'

'Well,' I said, 'if ye're not locked and ye're not liars, what are ye?'

Thomas glanced at a bottle on the counter. The penny dropped. One stubborn experience of every patient on chronic opioids is constipation. Thomas had eyed the Chief's half-filled bottle of Peri-Colace. The boys were doing shots of liquid laxative, to see who could keep it in the longest. I hadn't seen laughter like it since I was a boy myself, and it a prescription Hamlet might've come right with. I bent down and put my ear to Neil's belly for the symptoms, then rose with a stolid face.

'Nothing's happening, Hart!' Neil whined. 'I was on to win a fiver. I could've held it in. But neither of us have the shits at all.' This coming from a nine-year-old.

'Ah, my half-sized tyros. This here is one of life's great lessons. Ye're digesting it early. This here is what you'd call an anti-climax.' The boys glanced at each other, almost comforted. 'But there's another thing ye may or may not learn from this.'

'What?' Neil asked.

'What is it?' Thomas piped in, the colour of his face slowly differentiating from his hair.

'The long game,' I said.

With that, Nóra came in, the boys' parents in tow, and went to the oven to check on the casserole. The savoury smell hit the boys' nostrils and they looked at each other, what I'd said clicking. I sleeved the bottle and gave them a wink.

'Do ye want another sup of lemonade, lads, for the big feed?'

They paled and nodded. Their parents sat down opposite and began fussing, taking relief from the weighty atmosphere of our house in trivial ordeals. ('Have you washed your hands?' 'Were you pestering cousin Hart?' 'Don't nag.' 'Stop fidgeting.')

'You might have set the table, Doharty, knowing the amount I have to do,' Nóra said. 'When you've that mountain climbed, you can freshen the guests' glasses and call your father down to civilisation.'

The relatives had freed her tongue, normally glued to her hard palate—how I preferred it.

''Tis hard, all right,' Uncle Mitch said, grinning at his boys. ''Tis hard to drink from an empty glass.'

'Cormac's doing chin-ups,' I said.

'*Good*,' Nóra snapped. 'He'll be fit for pall-bearing so.'

Only the day before, I'd felt sorry for her. The whistle-blowing would've been hard on anyone, but especially on a self-strict woman whose time for taking external orders had long passed. She'd begun closing every door in the house, as if that might contain the awfulness. It made it harder to hear him at least. You'd lose a chunk of flesh if you didn't push the hall door shut to a click so it wouldn't open again with a draught. Her cooking had gone to shite. Everything was underdone. Raw. As if she couldn't bear to have anything softened, for it wouldn't be true to our lives. Carrots to break your teeth. Lettuce with the muck and maggots left on. Cold, squidgy meat. I bore the brunt of her bitterness, since she'd no one to gossip and gripe with. The phone was a month off the hook. (The Chief said it set off migraines. More like the messages coming through did as much.) To own a mobile would be to suggest her availability. As she put it: it would be one more thing to ill afford. So, with the landline off-limits, she'd been deprived of her intermittent whinge, and all that poison had collected … and was eroding some part of her, though none of us was to know which part, just yet.

Once the table was set, the eight of us jammed around it and the auls had gabbled Grace, we were relieved to find she'd spared us the bellyaches of a crunchy casserole. Maybe it was fear of word getting round the parish that 'Mrs Black has forgot how to cook a stew and, sure, no wonder her husband's poorly' that made her leave the crockpot in the oven for the full length of time. Nevertheless, the Chief—sunken-eyed, frayed—tilted the contents of his plate onto mine and said, 'Get me a bowl of warm milk and a few slices of white bread broken up in it.'

Everyone went quiet. Nóra regarded him with a look of injury.

'Do you not have the stomach for it, Dad?' I asked.

He made an involuntary face as if the smell of the food was sickening. I got up and fixed him a bowl of heated milk and bread while cutlery clicked. Eventually, out of awkwardness, Uncle Mitch declared: 'Neil and Thomas have been making model aeroplanes. Haven't ye?' Mitch had swallowed his plateful before we'd even begun and was ladling seconds.

'Have ye, boys?' Cormac asked. 'World War Two aircrafts, it is? Fighter planes? Hurricanes and Spitfires?' He looked genuinely excited at the prospect of war talk.

'They're Ryanair planes Dad got off a flight,' Neil said.

Cormac took in a quick mouthful of mash.

'They make you pay a euro for each appendage, is it?' the Chief asked gruffly. 'Even the toys are robbing the children these days.'

The bald arc of Mitch's head reddened. They'd lost half their savings from collapsed shares, but they hadn't been ruined by property like we had, by leveraging a house that had gone up in value by three hundred percent in a decade and dropped nearly that again in a year.

Auntie Bridie to the rescue: 'Isn't it *desperate*. All we can hope for is to have learned our lesson.' Mitch shifted in his seat. She quickly added 'As a country' then blathered on to make her words forgotten: 'Cáit is still on the dole, the poor pet. No redundancy package to tide her over. She's searching tirelessly but she hasn't the experience and it's a *nabsolute* catch twenty-*two* to have no experience when the most *lauded* barristers in the country are twiddling their thumbs. She'll have to do something *way* below her grade before long. Did you ever hear of qualified barristers driving taxis but in Ireland?' Though her head moved about like a bobblehead Jesus figurine when she talked, her bonnet of beige hair stayed perfectly still. Not a strand out of place. Better than Jesus, she was like the hens out back: if you held onto her body and twirled her in Os, the hair would stay perfectly still in the centre. 'But she's thinking of going abroad as a *nalternative*. She could do very well in Canada being so gifted and accomplished and *polite*, if she could put away the pennies for the flight. It's not unlike the passage to the USA long ago, when you think of it.'

'It's a passage like the coffin ships of the famine?' the Chief asked. Bridie suppressed her response. She didn't know what was being implied: the head didn't yet know if the body would be thrust upwards or down. 'The same way as we were burnt out of our houses by the lessors?' the Chief said. '*An Drochshaol.* There's a difference. Can you *páistí* spot the difference?' He asked the boys, who looked back dopishly. His pace of talk was half that of the auntie and it made you hear each sentence distinctly. 'The difference is that back then, we were burnt out by opportunists. This time, we were burnt out by ourselves. Alit our own arses. And not the first time in our history to do the same.' To stave off a coughing fit, the Chief swallowed a spoonful of soggy bread mixture. It seemed a lumpy white baby food in the bowl. Nóra took this row out on her eczema'd palms. Discretion had been her lifelong aspiration, and here she was being commingled with the nation, and denied virtue's achievement. Had her stag efforts been for naught?

Cormac stepped in. 'Here, Tom. If you ever want to learn how to build a model aeroplane, call into me on the weekend at the flat. I'll show you my hand-painted war birds. The RAF trainers were my favourite, but I've them as ornaments now so they're just for looking. But you could have a go of the plastic models that aren't in their boxes. There's a de Havilland DH98 Mosquito, Gloster Gladiator, Hawker Tempest obviously, a Supermarine Spitfire, and I've a P-26A Peashooter … that is, if you're very good for your mammy, ha?'

Nóra took her first breath in half an hour and looked ardently at her son. The only one among us who didn't make her wish she'd put cyanide in the casserole.

'Class,' Thomas said.

'A peashooter!' Neil called. 'Is that for shooting peas?' He fingered a pea out of his casserole and flicked it at his brother.

Cormac, Nóra and Uncle Mitch laughed and Bridie clipped Neil's ear, feigning admonishment.

I looked at the Chief, who was deep in thought, miles away from us. Bridie made the boys put their knives and forks together on their plates to indicate they'd had 'a nelegant sufficiency'.

'Can we go outside, Mum?' Neil nursed his ear.

'You'll wait for the dessert,' Bridie said.

I looked at Nóra and by her expression, I knew. I said: 'There's no dessert, sorry.'

The boys made clownish frowns.

'There's biscuits,' Nóra said. 'We have tea and biscuits.'

Bridie smiled thinly. She watched the Chief opening the Saturday of his seven-day pillbox and spilling its United Colours of Benicar onto his palm.

'How's the health at the minute, *a grá?*'

Ohgod.

The Chief looked up at her. So it was true that siblings could live the same trauma and one can come away with third-degree burns and the other with a sponsor for a sprinkler business. 'Did Nóra not say? I'm fixed. Bailed out.' He coughed.

Silence. Everyone's eyes scanned the room, their voices faltering. That was the first time I'd heard the Chief use sarcasm. I couldn't help but smirk. Yes. That's the answer. That stupid woman had no idea of the pain of saying, 'Fine. I'm grand. Thanking you.' I burst out laughing.

Nóra snarled at me, pronouncing both of her Ts: 'Get out.'

'You may leave the table now, boys. Go outside,' Bridie said.

But I stayed there and continued laughing and soon the Chief joined in with his maracas. After a minute of absolute bafflement, the cubs added silent hysterics. Their stomachs gurgled. Their parents didn't stop them with words, though they tried to with eyes. Cormac frowned, picked a splinter from the table with his knife. Nóra cleared away the plates, the ruins, and prayed to our father who art on sick leave.

No. There would be no dessert, only wild laughter. We laughed until there was the threat of dying from it—of never being able to stop. Those were the days for laughing and by golly we would let it out.

10.

A few weeks later, the Chief told me to phone Cormac and ask him round for tea. It was a Wednesday. There was some research he wanted done for the weekend. I didn't ask what it was. He'd have good reason for wanting Cormac's help, though Cormac would have his gloat about it.

'Post-nominal letters are what you need,' he said, 'to do the Chief's research.'

'Yeah, right, are you coming or not?'

'Lighten up, Doharty. You sound so *serious*.'

'I am serious. I'm very fucken serious.'

Cormac was quiet and there was just the phone static.

'He's taken a turn for the worse,' I said. 'He's no spirit left in him for a temper. No tolerance for ice baths either.'

'That'll be the meds.'

'It's not right,' I said, 'how it's happening, swarming in him like flies, and no one allowed to swat them. Blowing his whistle night and day, but not for help, not for real help. Yesterday, he couldn't make it outside so he called out the window, directing me how to hitch the tractor attachments, as if their being on *hire* meant I'd to curtsy before touching them. "Slide the linchpin through the link holes and blade," he's shouting, "and connect the clevis pin. Get in and start the engine. Raise the blade careful, see it doesn't interfere with the drawbar. Watch the tyres, Hart!" Then he halts his roaring to heave up a lung.'

'Look, I know, Hart. You don't need to—'

'*You don't know the half of it!* Shitting in the downstairs bed 'cause it's easier on his lungs than dragging himself to the jacks. Some days he can't swallow the tablets his throat's so swollen and he won't go near the doctor no matter what I say, what anyone ... so he goes without them and those are bad days, the worst days of his life, they are, the worst days of mine, if it's not wrong to say.' I was sobbing and Cormac waited this time. He wasn't even tapping or fidgeting, or if he was I couldn't hear it. I wanted him to suffer the knowledge in a way that might've been vicious, but I needed his company in the knowledge too. If he didn't know it, there'd be no one that knew, no one to tell, and I'd never be like that. That mute cast of a man. The rural, angered bachelor. Friel's Public has the self-same balls on him as Private. I'd not have any private fist ghouled around my throat. Fuck away off to Philadelphia.

Cormac arrived at six in the company Skoda estate wearing a plaid blue shirt, a North Face jacket and straight-legged jeans, pockets bulging. He resembled a building inspector, chin for a hard hat. I'd have suggested disguising the chin in a bit of stubble but then he'd shave twice a day out of spite. In the front door he came. Rang the bloody doorbell! The garage entrance and in through the utility room was no longer convenient. He was a guest, henceforth, was the message.

I was sorry it was one of the Chief's good days. He'd been well enough to stay out in the field from six in the morning—despite the sea-spray weather—as hadn't been the case for a week. Maybe it wasn't a good day at all and the Chief was gritting his teeth because it was reaping season and there was literally tonnes of work to be done (there being the best part of forty tonnes of potatoes to a hectare and ten hectares of the laden muck to turn). The Chief insisted on powering through the grim conditions. His friend Gerry lent a hand. I'd been out too and felt a sore-muscled wharfie. It was a lot of driving machinery, excavating, cleaning elevators and unloading in the shed. I drove the hired tractor-towed container alongside him in the harvester. A line had fixed between my brows from peering through the drizzle, but I don't know that it lent me any wisdom.

Nóra answered the door to Cormac in her apron (an Egg-Egg-7 'Time to Grill' apron he got her a few birthdays ago, which she was wearing inside out, in case she'd give anyone a laugh). She beamed at the Lidl lemon cheesecake he gave her.

'We'll have proper dessert this time,' he said, 'so we will. None of them biscuits.'

'*Ní raibh aon ghá, a stór.*' Her Irish was more synthetic than the Chief's. Holding the cheesecake close, she lowered her eyes at me as she passed in the hall, then pulled the kitchen door so it clicked.

'You've some shite on your nose there,' I said.

Cormac schkelped me on the shoulder and my tired back gave a whinge. 'Here, what're you upta Friday night?'

'Why?'

'Nothing? Thought so,' he said. 'Come into town. Flee the quarantine for a night. I'm seeing a Galway girl who's only local for the month and she asked me to watch her in a play. I won't sit on my own like a spanner and I'm not asking any of the lads to a fucken play, like. But you'd be half into that kinda bollocks anyways—stories, fictions, woe-is-me jeremiad shite—wouldn't ya? You can perfect your act. The throwback spud farmer who thinks software means his limp cock. Good luck installing that!' To limpen my fist, he added, 'She'll bring a friend out after. The stage manager … I think she said. She's female and single. She'll do the job. They come with their own instructions these days. You need to get out the house, so you do. Get some fucken notion of what's going on in the world, ya nun.' He clicked his fingers in front of my nose and I batted him away. 'Latvia's part of the Eurozone, like.'

'Stage manager'—I gave him a wary look—'means *backstage*. She'll be rough as a dance hall in Dingle.'

'You're coming.'

I stroked my chin. 'What's the play?'

'*What?*'

'What is the play?' I enunciated.

'Who the fuck *cares?*' Cormac said.

'*I* do.'

Here's what I'd've said to my brother if I knew then what I know now: 'Because the only reason to step out the door is to hear tales of people worse off than ourselves. So if it's Noël Coward or Wilde on about pomp and circumstance, celebrities with silken skin and trust funds, I've no interest. But if it's Beckett on about some poor sod getting stuck in a mound of earth for the rest of her life for she couldn't be bothered digging herself out, or about a disembodied head, or about a man listening to tapes of his youngster self, appalled at the twat he used to be, or an aul legless couple living out of bins in their blind son's flat, all of them routine addicts, unable to leave the room they're in nor stay put, then I might be interested.' That would've done it. Would've drove him spare. Only I didn't have that power of knowledge, then.

He wiped his nose on his sleeve. 'Look it up online. I don't give a fuck.'

'I'll come if you'll buy me early-bird dinner. There's full carvery with ice cream and jelly and coffee at O'Sullivan's for a tenner.'

Cormac clicked his tongue. 'Early-bird dinner's false economy. It means more drinking hours and drink's taxed more than food.'

'We'll eat out early, then go back to your flat for a sup before the play.'

'We will to fuck. Have Mam feed you and I'll swing by at six. We'll get our Vitamin G at Fox's.'

The whistle went off somewhere in the house. Nóra opened the hall door so the *gongggg-gongggg* of the six o'clock Angelus extolled from the kitchen radio. The soundtrack became her. Her untalked-of years in the Sisters of Mercy Convent before she left to play housekeeper to the parish priest. A queer step downwards, but there was no asking why she took it. It was quite impressive, actually—the convoluted infrastructure she'd built around her so she couldn't be approached head-on, even by her own sons. I got the feeling her gods were all part of that scaffold, left up around her long after her structure had been weather-sealed. Watching the ungraspable spectre of her in the doorway, I wondered had I ever seen her hair down. It was in a low bun like a half-used ball of yarn, enough to knit a balaclava. She was taller than me standing there in her shoes and me in my socks. But she still had to look up to Cormac, who had the Chief's tall genes.

'He's in the study,' she said. 'Would you try and talk sense into him, Cormac? He might listen to you, with the education. I'm no use to him. An ignorant skivvy poltergeist.'

'Mam,' Cormac said, shocked.

She inhaled and shifted her gaze to me. We had the same deep-green eyes, though Nóra wore them like wreaths. 'And would you ever close the doors after you. Keep the winter from following me around, *le do thoil.*'

Le do thoil means please unless a woman like Nóra says it. Leh-tho-hell, she says. *With your hell.* What would she have me do with my hell? With my hell *what?*

In the study, the whistle hung from the Chief's neck on a noosey bit of twine. He sat on the swivel chair by the PC. One of the small bucks must've lowered the chair when they visited, for the Chief's knees were daddy-long-legged up at his chest. He wore a soft-collar shirt beneath an old vector-patterned maroon jumper and he had his quilted jacket on over it. Filthy work jeans. Threadbare socks, no shoes. He had his wool cap on still. The ceiling bulb in the study needed changing, blinking its measly watts. The murky light cast all sorts of shadows. Paperwork was strewn on the table. Petals from a forgotten festoon.

'Are you not hot in that?' I asked, to stir him.

'It's cold.' He looked up, saw Cormac. 'If it isn't the man himself. *Mo mhac caillte.*' My lost son.

Cormac's Irish was dog piss.

'*Mo mhac cliste,*' the Chief revised his wording. My clever son.

'Smart, is it?' Cormac asked me.

'We'll see if it is now,' the Chief said. 'Do you still read books?'

Cormac shifted his weight. The room was too small for him. The whole house was a farcical set design to him, by then. He endured it out of respect for the auls. And it was useful for toilet rolls and eggs. 'The odd one, yeah,' he said. 'But not in Irish.'

'English will do us so.'

'*I* read more books than him!' I said.

'I'm not talking thrillers or spy novels, Hart,' the Chief said. 'Not *The Barracks* or *Ulysses.*'

Cormac prevaricated: 'I only read non-fiction, though.'

The Chief shook his head. 'It's ... a philosophical thing.' He packed a frown as if he was trying to recall the year of some battle. 'It's ... maybe ... remedial.' He gave up and shook out a cough.

'Is it medical?' I asked.

The heavy lines of the Chief's face skewed. I scanned the books on the shelves. There was one on Mao. Maybe he was looking at mystic tomfoolery treatments. Or maybe he'd a bucket list to run by us. Maybe one of the items on the bucket list was to read the best book ever printed and he wanted recommendations. Maybe one of the items was telling his sons he loved them. He loved them equal.

'Is it metaphysical, Dad?'

He looked up at me and took off his wool cap. He stuffed it in his jacket pocket and lifted his unworkable body from the chair. He staggered to the shelves and pulled out a red cloth-covered hardback from beside *Magner's Classic Encyclopaedia of the Horse.* There were a lot of single-use books in the house. He dropped the red one on the table before us. *Holy Bible.* Pressing his thick fingers on its linen, he said: 'Will you read that for me and find the bits that reference suicide.' Our eyes rested on the book and his muddy nails. We didn't look up for a while. He allowed us the time to understand. Then he said: 'There's spraying to be done before the dinner.' He left us standing in the puddles of our own shadows. But Cormac wouldn't let the moment absorb fully. He grabbed the book and stormed out. I had to let the blood that was pooled in my feet rise back up to the rest of my body before I could move anywhere, or step away from the question. If he's that far gone, why wouldn't he read it himself? Why couldn't *he* do it? There must have been another reason. Fear of fire talk?

11.

I perched on my bar stool sideways, watching his chin go. Brian the barman was an old classmate of Cormac's. They were shooting the bullet points of their adult lives at each other, hoping one of them wasn't a blank. Brian had no hope, his weapon banjaxed to begin with.

'You've a woman?'

'I do, yeah,' Brian said, towelling a pint glass. 'And a wain.'

Cormac squinted into his Guinness as if into the shotgun's eyepiece. I felt my blood quicken, seeing him limbering up to destroy that poor caffler. He opened his throat like a chamber and swallowed the Guinness in one. It practically clunked. 'She's *old* ... says the fellas. Forty anyways?' Cormac clicked his tongue. 'Sure, isn't your mammy younger than that!'

Sweat twinkled on Brian's far-flung hairline. He was casting about for a comeback. Your mammy is—

Cormac prompted: 'Ha?'

Come on, Brian. Tell him: your woman might be old but your

daddy's not a walking corpse. Your mammy's not a nunnery reject. You're not a big-chinned dryshite who wouldn't know a girl from a go-cart. Fuck off to that apartment in Bulgaria that the bank owns, tell him. *Tell him.*

Brian made brave sounds that were beyond the human register—beak agape, Adam's apple pulsating, before shrinking away. I thumped Cormac on the arm, though I was glad he'd spent that bit of rancour on someone else. I moved off to one of the wooden booth asylums we're so drawn to—them being alike confessionals. The pints would act as the bit of curtain between us. Now, to determine the dirty sinner. Cormac set both pints before himself so I had to reach out for mine. 'You ate?'

'Watery chicken and spuds hard as apples,' I answered. 'I'll get my iron though.'

'Not like back in the day, we'd lamb every night! 'Member? A month o' the stuff. Rack, shoulder, loin, shank—'

'Lamb pot pie, Barbados black-belly lamb—'

'Cutlets in eggy breadcrumbs—'

'Pan-fried kidneys, lamb casserole—'

'Lamb chops for mopping up the lamb gravy!'

We smirked and our eyes met. Then, out of awkwardness, we watched a game of Gaelic playing on a television small enough and high enough in the corner to be a CCTV camera.

'How's Mam holding up anyway?'

'Wojous,' I said.

He tutted. 'Ah, it's tough on her. Sure, the whistling'd have Mary chewing her halo.'

'What gets her is the quiet. The phone's off the hook so she has nowhere to projectile her poison. The griping's stored inside her like battery acid. She'll leak soon enough.' I lifted my glass. 'How d'you get rid of spoilt batteries again?'

'Shut your gob while it's still on your face.' Cormac looked deadly at me. 'You couldn't be more wrong about her if you tried.'

'Fill me in so. On all the wrongness.'

The bridge of Cormac's nose bunched, as if he'd been given an offer of advice. 'That's none of your fucken business. And why d'you need to know her trauma to have some fucken sympathy. How the hell you got your sensitive reputation with the girls is a fucken—'

'In my arse, trauma! If the ruler really stung her, from that place and from her rearing, she'd be a bohemian now, smoken hash and picken flowers, and not Luthering herself bloodless. You know, I've a feeling ...' I shook my head. 'I've a feeling she had the time of Riley in with the nuns, and—'

'AND?' Cormac laid that syllable on the table like a knife, the 'D' misleadingly blunt. He waited until my eyes went to it. 'Feelings, Hart. 'Twould convert an atheist, the impossible range of feelings piled into one man. Can't be science, did that.'

We settled down then and Cormac took a page he'd torn from the Bible from the breast pocket of his jacket. 'So,' I said. 'Is it acceptable to hang yourself, if you do it with a string of rosary beads?'

Cormac took the drink mat from under his pint and began tearing it. 'Brutal thing to ask me to do.'

'Would he ask if he wasn't desperate?'

'The fuck do I know if Heaven lets you top yourself? The fuck do I care?'

'Don't waste your time with it,' I said. 'I googled it and there's only a few vague things in the Bible to do with suicide, so we'll tell him there's fuck all. The point is, you know as well as I do, he wasn't asking for an essay on holy allowances. It's him warning us, of his mindset.'

Cormac downed a quarter of his pint. A silence went on long enough for us to make out the music playing. It was your man from Led Zeppelin talking bollocks, singing about a train *rolling* down the track. Sure, trains don't roll down tracks. They're moved by way of energy transference. They're pushed.

'You think he was warning us?' Cormac said, flicking his pile of shredded cardboard. It was strange having him vulnerable to my knowledge. I swallowed the rest of my pint in one.

'Whether he was or he wasn't—' I caught my breath '—that's no ending for our father. Neither is vomiting the content of his bowels, which is the way it'll go, with the secondary. Vomiting faeces or coughing up a lung in bits and pieces. Neither of them are options for the Chief. Nor is stringing himself to the shed rafters.' Cormac looked up at me. *What's that you're saying?* I gave him a minute, then pulled a wad of paper from my pocket and laid it down. 'If he's away off, we'll help him leave standing up. We'll administer euthanasia.' I had practised that line many times, but the words still felt extreme. They were culpable words fit for the booth we were tucked in. The probability sums of the universe threw us an eight ball then, and Zeppelin belted out a plea to the hangman to hold it awhile. He offered all kind of bribes to fend off the gallows pole, including sex acts with his sister, which was fucken odd to say the least and ruined the vibe, to be honest. Brian arrived to clear our glasses. I thought the song might give us away.

'Will I repair these for ye?' Brian meant the pints, though he was eyeing Cormac's beermat flitters. Cormac was leafing through my paperwork on the Swiss laws of euthanasia.

'No, thanks, Brian. We're off.' I stood up.

'Ye are so.' Addressing Cormac's rusty head, Brian delivered his own lines: 'You never could sit still, sit the fuck down. Al'as somewhere be'er to be. Al'as some'n to say on your way out. Schooling us all, ya wiseacre. You were that way long ago, you're that way still, by the looks of it.'

So that was his long-considered comeback, and Cormac heard not a word of it. I looked at the dancing nerves of Brian's face and tried to seem regretful on my brother's behalf. 'Come on,' I said. Cormac grabbed his jacket and got up without lifting his eyes from the pages. We left Brian to gather the beer mat confetti and the singer to suffer his raspy fate.

12.

There wasn't a play in all the countries and all the centuries that wouldn't have represented some part in the drama of our lives that night. Every statement and act and interrogative spoke to the melogent hand we'd been dealt, the responsibility we'd been given like the sole torch in a district blackout.

The play that was on was a home-grown thing called *Bailegangaire* by a Galway sham, Tom Murphy. *An baile gan gáire* means 'the town without laughter' and what a title that was to make a man hold his breath. What a national Christening was that. The *town*, for we were only ever a town and nothing larger; the town *without*, for we were defined by what we weren't—not married, not fertile, practising, prosperous, no longer political, no more brave rebels; the town without what? Without hope? We never needed hope to keep us going, keep us drinking. We never needed promises or prospects like the Yanks. No, no. What we could not be without is *laughter*—the thing austerity couldn't touch. O-ho, the wild laughter! And what would we be without that but a grassland blackened by scarecrows, hoping the hooded game might hold off and not circle down on us as they'd done long ago, hoping they'd stay in the sky like old-fashioned film credits, gliding an eternal acknowledging script.

'The town without laughter is close to home,' I whispered to Cormac in the dim auditorium.

'We'll see, so we will.'

The story was about two long-suffering granddaughters attending to their bossy, bedridden Mommo, who was losing her memory if not her mind—a vicious but fervent, tragic type that brought a pang to the back of my throat. Maybe that had to do with the acting. Maybe it was the writing. I wished the senile Mommo was my own mother, even with her grief and misery. She wanted heeding—her epic tale of the village laughing match. Dolly and Fidelma were fine white-armed daughters: honey-haired Fidelma in tight trousers and leather jacket and Dolly in a homely layered skirt. With all the layers that covered her, the under-layer was surely crushed velvet. She was fleshy in the right places and she'd a mole high up on her chest that made the rest of her a white canvas. Her hair was black as space. She'd be Cormac's date, the fuck. If I caught her eye, I'd have given her a look to make her thighs quiver, but she couldn't see me in the stalls and the blood with Cormac was never worth it. Besides, she was a bit plain in the face. I planned on peering into the shadowed wings to catch a glimpse of Gillian, the girl meant for me, but I was too caught up in the story being told or trying to be told that was the pain of their lives: the knowledge that once Mommo's story was narrated—once she was purged of it—the past would be separate from her and the present would peel itself away too before long. Murphy's words doing the paring—jaypers, they were forceful. The primeval way they came out of the women's mouths. The whole thing made me horny and doleful at once. Being pulled into Mommo and Dolly's world and away from our own was some kind of relief, though their world wasn't in the least comforting.

After, I sat in the stalls watching people leave in pairs and groups, listening to their chatter and impressions. Then I followed the route Cormac had taken backstage. A small blackboard hung from one of the doors with *Green Room* writ in blue chalk. I saw the Fidelma actress first. Costume racks compartmentalised the room, so I couldn't see Cormac. Fidelma was wiggling her hips to hoist up her tight jeans with diamanté pockets. With the water-balloon tits on her, I couldn't help imagining pinning on a brooch and bursting one. In her V-neckline, they were squeezed together unnaturally so the liquid of them was towards her chin. The stage make-up was still caked on and she'd an orange stripe on her jaw. But she was all right for a go. A bit old—she'd ten, fifteen years on me. I gave her the narrow eyes anyway. Why not? She lifted her brows, setting off a chain reaction on her forehead. She rooted in her handbag and found what she was looking for, then held her left hand up, and slowly, seductively, lowered the gaudy ring onto her wedding finger. So I gave her permission to go to the toilet: '*Tá cead agat dul go dtí an leithreas.*'

'*Tá cead agat dul* back to your favourite sheep,' she said. 'Muck snorkeller!' Her adenoidal Dublin accent was a far cry from the west-country lilt of her character. She pushed past me.

I took a look around once she'd gone, pleased with myself. I saw the old Mommo pulling on a pair of skin-coloured stockings over varicosed shins like blackberry ripple ice cream. The tights were opaque enough to make mauve of the worrying purple. I supposed all actors were deceiving like that. 'I enjoyed your performance.'

She looked up, dropping the stocking. Her face was gluey. 'It felt middling. I didn't do it justice.'

'There was nothing middling about it, 'twas powerful. *Powerful.*' That was the only word I could come up with. So I said it a third time. She must have been disappointed, as she got going on the stocking again. She seemed older and wearier in that fluorescent lighting than on the stage. The clothing racks grew around her, boxing her in mustiness. She panted with the effort of dressing, prodding her foot into a maroon patent shoe, though the stocking wasn't fully up. I wanted it to be easier for her, but I was mildly repulsed. 'You all right there, Mommo? You seem feverish.'

She stood up lively and said: 'Oh, a fever, is it?' She held the back of her hand to her brow. 'A fever. Give me a second. Let me think. Yeah … Go alone to a crossroads at night and when the church bell tolls midnight turn around three times then drive a hefty nail into the ground to the head. Walk backwards from the nail before the clock is finished with the twelfth kneel. No. Knell. The ague will leave you directly but 'twill go to the person next to step on the nail, so you best be able to live with that fact.' She leaned in discreetly. 'Passing it on.'

I pulled a face. 'What's that from?'

'What's that *from?*' she baulked. 'It's from *life!*' She became purposeful suddenly and finished clothing herself with greater success.

I stumbled back and tumbled through a clothing rack to where Cormac was chewing the face off the black-haired girl. 'Dolly, is it?' They pulled apart and she turned to me with sucked lips.

'Aleanbh.' When she made the 'v' sound at the end of the name, her teeth caught on her bottom lip and stayed like that for a second, until the lip slipped free. It had been too long since I'd breathed in non-menopausal women. This realisation came as a shock: no wonder I was out of sorts. I got half my confidence from the gee-box. The other half from the fact the owners of the lovely contraptions seemed to like my company.

'We'll stick with Dolly, so we will,' Cormac cautioned, standing tall. 'Keep it simple for him.'

I caught her giving me the once-over. 'Your performance was powerful,' I said. Practised, this time. A dimple sank into her left cheek. She did a small bow. She wore a navy dress with tiny white polka dots, short sleeves and a collar. The skirt went out like a swing dancer's. There was no doubt that her shape was mighty. She turned to the bulb-ensconced mirror and put on an oval of cherry lipstick, which gave her face the definition it lacked naturally.

'Gillian's the name of your girl tonight,' Cormac said. He flashed the underbite.

'Your *date*.' Dolly side-eyed Cormac, then addressed me. 'She's good company, don't worry. Just don't bring up Fine Gael and you'll be grand. Gill gets very heated on politics.'

'Heated's not a bad state to be in, babe,' I said.

Cormac pummelled my shoulder. 'Do you want your tongue cut out?'

Dolly laughed.

'*What?*' I said. 'Her name's babe!' I nursed my shoulder. '*Leanbh.* Means "baby" in Irish.'

Cormac looked at her for corroboration. He relaxed a bit then, but she'd seen his temper. She'd seen my wiles, too. 'Old Mommo there,' I said to Dolly, 'is she all right? I was just having a chat with her about Murphy's genius take on regret and ageing, and she suddenly lost her lid.'

'Yeah,' Dolly said, seeming to let her eyes unfocus. 'Could be she's *taking on* a bit of the character, d'you know the way? Just to stay in the frame of mind, for the run. Or it could be serious. Half the time she thinks it's the sixteen hundreds and she has the plague. Writing "ABRACADABRA" in a pyramid on her mirror in eyeliner. Stuff like that.'

'A triangle, d'you mean?' Cormac said. Dolly puckered her brow. 'You'd want to be an artist to draw a pyramid on a mirror, is all,' he said.

Dolly continued: 'Just as well she *is*, an artist. She hasn't stalled on a line or missed a cue to date, so. We won't interfere for the minute. So long as she keeps her monologues about the printing press saving us from British Rule for backstage!' (We looked at her, hungry for her mouth to keep moving.) 'She's been yabbing on about the printing press coming *late* to Ireland, which meant Protestant ideas weren't properly disseminated, and by the time they *were*, we couldn't be budged.'

'Fascinating!' I said.

'Well, it is, yeah. It's 'cause she's a Fitzgerald from Kildare. The Fitzgeralds were a dynasty back in the day.'

'Right?'

'Ran the country till they were ousted by Henry the Eighth and his lot. Once the planters arrived in the sixteen, seventeen hundreds, we were ruined. Just biding time then, really, as Ruth said. Writing aisling poetry out of blood on one another's jumpsuits, locked up for speaking our own language.' She caught her breath. 'What do you think, Cormac? Do you think *Bailegangaire* is a kind of modern aisling? Mourning the loss of our nation's stories— the ones we can't recall? Or is it a kind of wake for Kathleen Ni Houlihan?'

Cormac blushed. A lot of declarative statements had been made, as were his sore spot. 'I wouldn't say it was biding time for those hundreds of years, no,' he said. 'That's a bit simplistic, so it is. There were civil wars as good as genocide. Do they teach ye about the freedom fighters in Galway? The hunger strikers—'

'Dolly,' I interrupted loudly. 'You said it was Gillian gets hot on politics. It seems as if we're getting warm here too. And the problem with heat is that it disperses. That's what my engineering brother taught me.' I clapped a palm on Cormac's shoulder. 'A bit of heat is being lost with everything we're saying now, and, if you don't mind, I'd like to store a bit of the stuff for later. So I suggest we go and whet the backs of our throats with the black stuff, if not the brown stuff, if not the clear stuff altogether.'

'Oh?' said Dolly. Cormac looked at her for a reaction. I put my arms round the two characters—Dolly clicking in her heels, Cormac's tail unstiffening, slowly but surely—and off we went down the yellow brick road ... or the famine road ... which of the two, it had yet to be decided.

13.

The girls were happier with off-licence prices, being poor thespians, so we went straight back to Cormac's gaff. His flatmate was gone to Athlone for a match and I was let kip in his room. We'd limbered up with a few Jack and Cokes and yakked with the ladies about films we liked and didn't, what life was like as a part-time actress, how the country had become more self-reflective for having a poet-president but that if he'd been a playwright the banter would be brilliant; which airborne diseases you could catch in the midlands if you yawned too wide (manic depression or SARS). Dolly liked my self-deprecation and the way me and Cormac one-upped each other. Like the bottle of Johnnie Walker Black Label drained and filled up with Bushmills, we were showing misleadingly good spirits. Cormac even went soft on the facts.

Gillian would've been a better match for him. She'd earned herself a restraining order by hosing a water inspector's garden with Coca-Cola to protest water charges. She said things like 'fiscal rectitude, my arse' and meant nothing fucken kinky by it. She wasn't near as handsome as Dolly. Skinny in the body and pointy in the face. Nut-brown hair was braided down her back. I made her my horsey anyway, used her plait for reins. *Up up a chapaillín, up up again, you couldn't sell this chapaillín for five pounds ten,* I hummed over her yelping. She had an eternity symbol tattooed on her shoulder. Idiotic thing to put on a lump of flesh that's doing nothing but perishing. I tried to rub it off. She wiggled the shoulder blades and I wondered if something might come out from under them, like beetles from a cleft stone. To override that image, I thought of Dolly, who wouldn't be stiff like this one. Whose black hair would be slinking across her neck to the damp-skin slapping sounds. Who I could make tremble. Fuck him, getting her. It was one thing I'd always had: first dibs on the women. 'Are you bored or what?' I tried to grab her buttocks but they were strapped to her. Her skin was cling film wrapped around her bones. The whole of her was tight, I'll give her that, but there can be too much of a good thing. I reached round and grabbed the front for something to hold on to. She howled. 'Do you like that?'

'No, not so hard.'

I slapped her bony arse very hard then. Air whistled in through her teeth. Hardness was the only way with this one. For all her hardness, I'd give her hardness back. She was wet for it. I slapped her again on top of the red hand mark. She screamed. Not the right kind of scream. *Fuck.* There was a knock on the wall from Cormac's room. I wanted her off. I pushed her forward. Her head whacked the headboard. She wailed. A rush of footsteps shook the apartment's cardboard walls. Dolly opened the door, holding Cormac's chequered shirt in front of her. A swollen nipple was exposed. Redder than it should've been. He'd been sucking on it, the gimp. Of course he had. Gimpy mammy's boy.

'Jesus! Gill, are you okay?' Dolly stayed in the doorway.

Gillian was holding her forehead in her hand, fake-snivelling. 'Should've left him to his livestock,' she said to Dolly, who mumbled something back. I was hard as a fresh-pumped tyre and made sure Dolly saw it. 'Copper-nobbed fuck!' Gill picked up her jeans and top. She stepped into her high heels and looked the right scanger walking out on tiptoes with her bare, slapped arse not even giving the slightest wobble.

'What's going on?' Cormac called from the adjacent room. He wouldn't come out and risk comparison.

Dolly was talking with Gill in low voices outside my open door as the latter pulled on her clothes. Keys. Phone calls. Taxis. 'It's fine,' Dolly called to Cormac. 'Gill has to go. It's fine. Back in a sec.'

A minute later, when the front door had clicked shut, Dolly reappeared at my doorway. Her red lipstick was long gone, but she no longer needed it. I didn't find her face plain any more, not after the things I'd heard her say. It was a devastating face. She looked at me seriously and said: 'There's rough and there's rude, Doharty Black. Some girls don't like either.'

'I don't like some girls.'

She raised the decisive black brushstrokes of her brows. 'You're very harsh.'

'Maybe I am. Maybe I need improving. Like what's-her-name. Pygmalion.' I gave her the narrow eyes, but I needn't have. She could see my scouring-pad chest and she struck me as a woman who'd want her supple white body scrubbed raw with it. I know where I'd start.

'Dolly?' Cormac called.

The dimple sank into her cheek. She dropped the shirt and gave me a moment before she turned and left.

14.

'"A" is for Asphyxia.' Each day, I phoned Cormac with the findings. He came around to the idea fairly quick, so then it was a matter of researching the best itinerary out of this life and presenting it to the Chief conjointly: a mortal holiday brochure.

Option 1: A snapped neck. Twist that substantial chin he passed on to you.

Cormac hung up.

Option 2: A pillow in a deep moonshine sleep, once he's consented, like?

Mind what you bring to these phone calls, Hart, if you value your bollocks.

Option 3: We could drive to the Cliffs of Moher. I know it's County Clare, but we could avoid the locals, keep a hurling stick handy. We could wait till all the tour buses have fled for Galway.

We could have a picnic. That'd be peaceful and honourable. Might even be beautiful, watching him plummet like that Red Bull boyo who skydived from space.

Bickering erupted then about the force of gravity and *terminal velocity* (which Cormac saw no humour in) and whether or not a big man would fall faster off a cliff and Cormac shouting: Gallileogallileoyoufeatherbrainedfuck!

Option 4: He could pull a MacSwiney.

Terence Joseph MacSwiney starved himself to death over seventy-four days in the War of Independence, bringing the concern of the world to our wee struggle. South American countries were appealing to the Pope over us. Not only that kind of martyrship, and he a mayor, but he wrote *plays* while he was at it. Why wouldn't you pay homage to an activist man who wrote a play called *The Revolutionist* and died as loud a death as can be drummed.

And how would starving himself be *less* painful than the way he'll go naturally? Cormac asked.

Option 5: Drugs. We didn't have access to the death-by-sleep pill, pentobarbital. But a decent percentage wake up from a supposedly lethal dose, gasping and vomiting. Well, that's not fucken on, Cormac said. I read out: *To reduce the chances of the euthanasia drugs being vomited up, an anti-emetic must be given.* His flatmate had access to P, E, a bog-load of hash and a nugget of crystal meth, but we decided that kind of ashen cocktail would make for a very bumpy journey out that wouldn't be at all ideal. The only doable drug was diacetylmorphine hydrochloride. A stocktake of the Chief's medical cabinet showed he'd less than sixty milligrams of morphine in capsules. He'd need four times that, given the hulk of him. We formulated a plan for obtaining the additional quantity: he'd been contending with a sore throat. He'd voiced that complaint in front of various people. The whistle was evidence enough. I'd caught Nóra filling the Chief's glass with holy water from Lourdes and setting it beside his pills. (What she thought would happen is beyond me, besides the stale old water giving him the scutters.) He could make a simple phone call to the doctor for liquid solution or morphine sulphate suppositories instead. We'd collect the prescription for him. The doctor would hardly ask for the old pills back.

The truth is we feared it would be traumatic. The research mentioned flaccid muscles, pinpoint pupils, fading pulse, stupor, fluid in the lungs, the slow onslaught of breathlessness. Finally, death by respiratory depression. Since the lungs were the main culprits to begin with, we expected a choked end. We'd have to warn him, so he knew what he was in for. He'd be courageous, but I couldn't vouch for the rest of us. I couldn't promise I wouldn't try CPR after. I couldn't promise anything.

When? Cormac asked. He's not sick enough yet, I said. You had to be fierce sick for euthanasia, for it to look forgivable. When either of us had to digest a thing like that, there'd be long silences. My mind would fill them with imagined exchanges: Nóra imploring of Father Shaughnessy, 'He was *hours* from dying and wanted to speed up the journey to Heaven. *Ar dheis Dé go raibh a anam.*' 'Lord save us, of *course* he did.' The priest would convene his palms. ''Twas a *bad* dose he had, poor craythur.'

What room would it be done in? One with enough chairs for the four of us. Not the kitchen, with its smells. Strung up in his shed, like the aul lambs? No. Not his bedroom nor the living room with its fireplace and crucifix. There'd be no kneeling. No counting off beads or blessings or minutes. No one would sing 'The Well Below the Valley' or 'The Dawning of the Day'. There'd be no music. I hadn't learned the fiddle, after all. Though I'd never asked my father for lessons, I got them anyway.

15.

Me and Dolly thrashed out our differences in Cormac's shower the morning after *The Town Without Laughter*, and I absented with the steam through the window. We didn't get it out of us on the first wash, it turned out. No matter: we'd have a few more goes at it. Nothing perseverance wouldn't solve. Being needed day and night was a new, nervous experience and I felt a man for it. Cormac started pestering me: why had my research dried up? Why did I sound so zonked? Why hadn't I helped the Chief out of bed this morning? Was I hiding out in my room? Nóra phoned saying she near made a wishbone of her back. Couldn't I find the Chief a bell from the attic forfuckssake instead of that whistle? Didn't I know he could barely blow the clock off a dandelion?

'How did you sleep, on a scale of one to five,' Dolly asked, 'one being extremely well, five being extremely shite?'

It was our fifth night together, in her house-hotel. We were head-to-toe on the bed, drinking Jack D from mugs. She had on a silky black slip with wet patches drying to shadows. I could have sold her for an estate in Spain, or a car park in Dublin.

She worked part-time in a call centre forcing questionnaires on people at ungodly hours. Market research in such a maimed decade is not for the thin-skinned. 'You've to be very self-effacing. You've to tut a lot and inhale every other word. Do you know the way? *Empathise*.' She'd scythe the grass of my chest with her fingers, telling me how many people out of every ten are Polish or Nigerian in different counties and how that's not represented in popular culture. She couldn't think of a single Irish play with a character called Piotr or Dorota. I started to get the feeling her knowledge was unreliable. That it came more from the stage than the call centre. Feminism by way of Caryl Churchill, socialism via Seán O'Casey and George Bernard Shaw, cruelty according to Antonin

Artaud, sexuality à la Marquis de Sade, disenfranchisement via John Osborne, strangement from Bertolt Brecht. I absorbed what I could and said I liked the sound of her theatre. She asked if I'd move to Galway and live in a flat on the docks with an electric piano and book stacks for divider walls and beanbags for chairs and no television to be sucked into or clocks to be whiled away by. There'd be a circle of friends to join like some kind of ring-around-the-rosie and me going '*A-tishoo!*' with my culchie plague. Had I no friends at all in Roscommon? A cousin and brother were no good for friends: blood ties can putrefy like an umbilical cord left hanging from a child's belly. They were never meant to hold. I could go to college a mature student. I could do anything I wanted. Didn't I know I was full of potential? If I turned out a cunt, I'd be out arseways, but she suspected I wouldn't. I hadn't the makings of a player.

'Are you a lassie for your father?' She watched my reaction to this closely, no doubt to add to her play-text understanding of how fathers and sons keep the real meanings of their sentences in asides. 'Why are you at home still? Not out living your own life like your brother?'

'What if I like having my bed made for me? And my sandwiches.'

'Go away with your sandwiches! I know a daddy's boy when I see one. I'd suppose you were staying on to take over the farm, but you just don't seem the farming type.'

'Oh? What type do I seem?'

She tilted her head so her hair closed around her face, then she brushed it back. 'Like the type that lets others ascribe a type to him, without seeing that's what he's doing.'

I looked at her legs: the muscles that proved her venturesome, the flesh that proved her desirous. 'I'm at home, waiting for my father to die. He's dying, I'm waiting, that's all there is to it.'

I felt her eyes search me as I traced the ins and outs of her shin, like roughly sawn but smoothly sanded oak.

'And then what?' she said.

'Then? I'll sell the lot to settle our debt, lock Nóra in a shed with the unsellable potatoes, and see if I can't live some kind of life. Penniless. Fatherless. Cursed.'

'What's wrong with him?' She wasn't polite in asking. She was hungry to know.

I clutched her ankle in my fist. 'Wrong?' I said. 'What's wrong with the best of us?' I dragged the heat of her towards me and pushed up her satin, slipping my fingers into her, like a gorgeous greasy tractor axle, thumb on her clit. 'He won't let a doctor take the wrongness from him. Won't let anybody lay a finger on him. Doesn't think he deserves repairing.'

'Fingers,' she said, like a curse word. First I thought she was mocking my accent but then she tightened around my hand and repeated the word in a spiteful old person's voice: '"Who's talkin' about fingers when the whole world knows ya can kill a body just be lookin' at them if you look long enough and you look wrong enough".'

I felt her skin texture where my other hand rested on her thigh. She'd given the both of us goosebumps.

'What's that from?' (I recalled the batty actress scolding me for the same question: *It's from* life!)

'*Portia Coughlan.*' Dolly spoke her other language. I frowned, still holding her glut. 'It's a Marina Carr play about a woman haunted by the ghost of her dead twin and ex-lover. I played Portia a few years back. That wasn't my line to deliver but it's the one I was there for. Haunted me more than the ghost twin.' She leaned into me, compressing my fingers with her pelvic bone so it hurt a little and she delivered the line again, more slowly, darkly, forbidding.

I thought about asking what it meant to her. Instead, I pushed up her skirt fully to regain command. 'That's some line,' I said. She looked at me like no girl I ever dreamt of. White flesh, black silver-threaded hair, her gall and her vigour and her nerves in all the right places.

'I think you have something unique to say with that silver tongue, Doharty Black, and I intend to draw the words out of you.' Then she drew me into her and we both got very fucken eloquent.

Those were the ways we spent our nights together. Her teaching me the dramas of her life, which weren't her personal dramas but ones borrowed. She'd have her own woes too, I was sure, but right then, she was the one star that shone through a clouded night. The only thing better than a fresh batch of *poitín* from the bathtub. The next best thing was the Chief being too breathless to blow his whistle for a whole afternoon.

16.

I wasn't plying facts earlier when I said the Chief worked his dying day. He could barely make it to the kitchen by the last, but I wasn't ready to say it as it was and we only in the springtime of our story. I couldn't tell how it happened, the scent still hanging in the air.

In a conversation that was mostly silences, the Chief indicated he wanted to go sooner rather than later. Could we have one last family trip to see him off? But to the coast, for once, for scenery he could take with him on his way, as a kind of reverse honeymoon, to a lucidness that can only be reached by way of cobalt sea. If there were seals, they might help him come to terms with the cold blubber self. If there was a bottle shored up on the strand, he might find a prayer in it.

We'd make the trip on Sunday, then back to do the job Monday morning. Monday would be the day for putting him down, gentle as we could manage. That gave me a tight schedule for coaxing and confessing.

17.

We'd found neither allowance nor consolation in the scriptures for the Chief. Though he hadn't brought it up with us again, I had the sick feeling he'd beg for holy orientation just before the whistle fell finally from his lips. After seeing Dolly eight or nine times, I told her. Well, I told her we suspected he'd top himself and that we'd let it happen. I didn't say we'd go so far as to pour the toxin down his gullet and pinch his nose for him. I said he'd asked us to search the scriptures—for lines, of a kind, to learn by heart. 'Oh. Well, in that case, ask the director can you alter the script,' she suggested, meaning a priest. But priests aren't GPs, held to privacy: there was no way of asking for sweet sacred nothings without condemning myself. They mightn't be allowed to disclose your dark enquiry outright, but they could phone up your auntie and talk around it in that transubstantiative way.

Dolly went to her closet and began rifling, mumbling that none of it would do. She shut the closet, put her hands on her gorgeous wide hips and said: 'We'll have to break into the theatre.' It was a curse to be around her altogether. I was halfway to rigor mortis myself. 'All I'm saying is, if you're worried about incriminating yourself by asking the priest for a pep talk for your dad's soul—which is ludicrous by the way—then remove the risk. Go in costume. Are you any good at accents?'

'You bet your ass,' I said, in my best generic American.

'Hats!' Dolly announced, ignoring me. 'I've a pair of hats that'll do, in case you take the wrong angle first time round, or you get the willies. You've to look like a visitor. Talk like a visitor. Not a local. Else he'll place you. The shoebox town you're from. Don't address him by name. Just "Father".'

'Hats it is!' Her giddiness was infectious. I wanted to pull on the costume immediately. But first, I wanted hers off. It was beginning to get painful. 'What's this about breaking and entering?' I swung her onto the bed.

'Ah,' she said, one leg bent in, fingers flexing in her lap. 'What's one more sin to be sorry for!'

Later, when we hadn't a usable muscle between us, she said: 'You know I've only a week left?' She stared at me, unblinking. Was the look to say: is that us? Our energy spent? I found it hard to meet her ransacking gaze.

'Oh.' I hadn't calculated it. 'You're back to Galway then? What day?'

'Sunday.' I must have scowled in my calculations, for she asked: 'On a scale of one to ten, one being absolutely overjoyed, ten being downright ruint, how do you think you'll feel come Monday?'

I felt the blood rushing to where she rested her palm on my cheek—my still-young, bristled cheek that hadn't yet totally vacuum-packed to the skull—and thought: *Will I be relieved?*

18.

'I lug it round with me ... like a bindle on my shoulder,' I whispered in a lilting Donegal *blas*, angled out of sight in the dark oak snug. 'The hate.'

'You're not confusing hate with dislike?'

'I'm sorry, Father, but it's hate.' Hushed, the haitches came out like a gas. Only a long brown curtain hung on my side—no door— and I hoped my words wouldn't carry out to the pews. The curtain was thick flannel: a fabric that thwarts all manner of advances. Father Shaughnessy's robes made a dry chafing sound as he settled. I knelt, head down, hands pocketed.

'You want to repent to the Lord and honour his directive that you shall not take vengeance or bear a grudge against the sons of your own people, but love your neighbour as yourself?'

'I'd go on bearing it—the hate, Father—only I've a feeling it's sinking into me. Splinters from the old bindle stick are nesting in under the skin.' And it came to me like that, only a few lines into the role—an understanding of Dolly's calling. The mad release, and possession.

He responded gently through the grille: 'The longer you let hate sit on your shoulder, the more embedded its talons will become, the more you'll be bound and pressured to do its bidding. Explain now to the Lord what's driven you so far from his bright and temperate skies and so close to Satan's underworld, whose fires your hate fuels?'

Who else could I pin the blame on? Flan-flavoured Clara at Spar, for charging the full €9.20 for Benson and Hedges, back when I could afford to kill myself slowly? Morrigan, for absconding in his daughter's 2007 Alfa Romeo and returning in 2009 through his cast-iron gates to live off caviar in the panic room while the rest of us were pulling out our teeth in a tribal effort to seed the desiccated soil? Mr Lyon the bank manager, for the warped press-stud of his wallet in the sunshine and his dry hands come the rains? *Rainy days are no good for harvesting, I'm afraid to say, Mr Black.*

'It's my brother.' I blurted this out, annoyed I'd not started with the real subject. I had no stage fright. I'd needed no warm-up.

Father Shaughnessy sucked in air through his teeth. 'Your brother. Your own brother that you hate.' You could hear the sieve straining lumps out of his crude judgement. 'What despicable thing has he done to be the victim of your hatred?'

'*I'm* the victim. *He's* the aggressor. That's the way.' I pulled my flat cap down and tried to stay anonymous. 'He's a vainglorious, conceited c—'

The priest made no sound for a while, other than involuntary body sounds. The whistling of air finding its way through a shaggy nasal passage.

'It might be only small stuff, Father, but it's built up. You could build a pyre from it. I could set up a stall selling bangles from the Chinese burns he gave me. Oh, and when we got a new car, he told the whole school it was from saving up the disability allowance we got for *me* being Technically Retarded! All sorts of … Like, I'd a terrible fear of dogs … as a child, so when he found a dead dog fresh kilt on the road, he ran off to get a neighbour's wheelbarrow. He pushed that carcass all the way home, waited till I was asleep, *broke* its rigormortised jaw to affix it around my *ankle* in bed, so I *woke up* to—' Then the priest cut in to ask if I knew the parable of Cain and Abel. I didn't like that. The cutting in. 'Yes,' I snapped, without the 'Father'. 'The jealous brothers trying to one-up each other for God's approval,' I said. I felt my cheeks hotten.

'And what did the Lord say to Cain?' Then he answered himself: '"Why are you furious? And why are you downcast? If you do right, won't you be accepted? But if you don't do right, sin is crouching at the door. Its desire is for you, but you must master it".'

'Right. So that's the advice? Master your sin.'

'Avoid succumbing to it. And do you know what Cain did then?'

I didn't like the schoolteacher questions and my kneecaps were beginning to ache on the miserly cushion. 'I'm not jealous of my brother. He has a good job and brains—a right know-it-all cut-jack mammy's boy—but he's nothing to envy. Hasn't a funny bone in his body. Not a funny knuckle on either fist. And God forgot to do his face. There's textbook rivalry right enough, but that's not it. It's more …' I trailed off in my performance, but Father Shaughnessy had been listening.

'If it's not jealousy, are you trying to prove yourselves to someone else? The way Cain and Abel tried to prove themselves to the Lord with offerings.' I could hear the click of heels outside that might've belonged to one of the local gossips who can detect the agnost in the church just by sniffing. How the hell would I get from here to the suicide question? 'Listen to me, son. For your confession of bearing a grudge, I can absolve you through the Sacrament of Reconciliation, but it's the Samaritans you need to talk to if you fear that you yourself or your brother might become violent.'

'I'm not going to murder my brother, Father. I might dream of him drowning in a slurry pit, but I do *not* dream of pushing him in.' This was a waste of time. Dolly only encouraged it because the drama roused her—it was never going to help.

Father Shaughnessy made a horrible gulping sound that had me peering through the lattice gaps to see he wasn't choking on his collar. Doubled over in his chair, his elbows were on his knees and his palms were convened in prayer, fingertips pressed against his forehead. Then he sat upright and asked me to come out to the church and have a talk, 'as two fellows rather than as priest and penitent. There's something you might benefit from hearing, but outside of the confessional.'

I pulled my cap low and stretched the cuffs of my sleeves over my hands. 'No, Father. I'll not.' I could feel him gape at me then, as I inspected the kneeling bench. The wood smell became sharp and thick as if it was sighing.

'Well, may I speak to you as Declan Shaughnessy in here then, and not as the representative of the Lord, just for a moment?'

Jesus Christ. Fine. I'd tolerate that. His breathing whistled through the congested nasal tunnels. It was a sound I was used to hearing through a microphone, but it sounded louder without one. 'I had a brother myself,' he said. 'But he wasn't for this world. Original Sin didn't sit well with him. So the Lord took him from us early. Jason, his name was.'

'Younger or older?'

'He was my twin. My only sibling. Our mother suffered complications birthing us that put an end to her childbearing. And the fact is, we treated each other brutishly. We harassed one another from the outset.'

'We were the same. That's normal, Father.'

'It's natural for siblings to prod and provoke—particularly boys close in age—but our rivalry wasn't *normal* brotherly competitiveness, as you say, though our parents dismissed it as just that. No. It was the Devil pitting us against each other. And one day, with the Devil perched on his shoulder, Jason made me swallow down a shell with some sour milk.' Father Shaughnessy took a deep breath and didn't seem to let it out. 'When he saw the pain on my face and the little flecks of blood that came out on the handkerchief as I tried to cough it free, he promised to swallow something in return, so long as I wouldn't tell. As if it had been a test of machismo all along and not a deliberate injury. Rather than going to our parents or to a neighbour or to our Lord, we went to the garage so that I could choose something for my twin to swallow. Dad was an electrician, so there were lots of gadgets and appliances. I opened a box marked "Neodymium Magnets N38–52". In it were small magnets the size of copper coins, kept apart by thick slabs of plywood. I recall the sharp pain in my chest from the shell. Jason joked that the sphere magnets looked like Christmas cake decorations and said they might be tasty … so I chose the less festive discs. I pulled one off and told him to kneel before me. I placed the magnet on his tongue like the Eucharist, and … Lord have mercy on me … I said to my brother, I said: "One for God the Father".'

His words began to break up and I thought I should stop him there, but the place was so dusty my chest felt like an hourglass too tight for its sand—stucking us both in the moment.

'Jason swallowed it with a gulp of flat 7Up and pulled a face,' he said in one go. 'When we were sure it had gone down and wasn't coming back up, I took another magnet from the box.'

A kind of closed sound came with it too—the dust—the weight of sand over our heads so that everything the priest confessed was a record playing in another room of an unfamiliar house, with the notes all out of true and not loud enough to dance to.

'Jason gave out … but I said that if he didn't do it, I'd tell on him about the shell. The Devil then crept off his shoulder and climbed onto mine.' All there was for it was to cover my ears and wait for him to skip. He spoke right into my ear through the dust and all, and it must have been my penance in there, and his own, when he cried: 'Lucifer couldn't believe his luck! To my brother, to my twin, I said: "One for God the Son".' Ohmygod ohgod ohmygod. 'Jason uncrossed his arms from his eight-year-old chest,' the priest said, 'all ribs … and swallowed. I recollect feeling some powerful change in the world—something altering irreversibly in the constitution of myself, akin to what a girl must feel when first she bleeds. Scared, forbidden, perversely … thrilled. It was a kind of trespassing. After enough time passed for the wrongness to catch us up, I looked straight through Jason's watery eyes and placed a third magnet on his worming tongue. "One for the Holy Spirit".'

There followed a gasping like a dry kettle switched on, and I pressed my forehead to the grate, tasting its bitter varnish. Tears wrung from Father Shaughnessy's close-set eyes. Though he faced me, I needn't have feared he was seeing me at all. He was seeing the inside of his twin brother—the powerful disc magnets attracting to each other, taking a shortcut through the intestine, perforating the gastrointestinal tract. He was seeing the buckshot through an abdomen, with no evidence or trace of a bullet from the outside. He was hearing the screams as Jason clutched his gouged stomach. He was imagining his younger self—hearing, seeing, wondering whether to get their father or mother or to leave his twin in the hands of the Lord.

'I have to go.' I pulled aside the curtain, and the priest started.

'Not yet—'

'I *have* to.'

'Let's complete the Act of Contrition,' he pleaded.

'I can't, Father, I'll miss—' It was all I could do not to run. But the curtain stuck to my clothes and Father Shaughnessy caught me by the wrist. I looked back at him, but he kept his gaze directed at his own hand, sparing me. 'How many Hail Marys will I say, Father … for hating my brother?'

The priest tried to clear his throat, but it couldn't be cleared by will alone. A nocturnal, songless bird with not one fellow creature to witness his endurance. 'One Hail Mary,' he said, tender as you like.

'*One* … Father?'

'And I'll fast for you for thirty days.'

19.

Friday night, I woke to an explosion. I took the stairs four at a time and skidded into the living room where the Chief's bed sheets were straitjacketed on the floor. The puncture-headed image of him threatened to take shape in every unlit space. The mess he'd have left for us. No. The kitchen was empty. That wouldn't be the way he'd do it. No mess. The study was empty. He was a tidy man. He'd spent the last six years hauling his would-be capital into as compact a settlement as possible so as to leave us less mess: a failure neat as an own goal. Lavatory. Utility room. The shotgun was gone from the closet. The garage door was open a sliver and the cold sucked in. '*Get.*' The Chief's granular voice milled to powder on the night air. I ran out to see his figure wobbling towards me from the newly seeded field. He wore slippers, a dressing gown and Y-fronts, washed grey. He dug the muzzle of the shotgun into the grass for a walking stick. A plume of smoke settled lazily beyond.

'Jesus!'

'Back to bed, Doharty,' he croaked.

'The hell, Dad?'

He suddenly twisted to look behind him, leaning dangerously. Peering at something. 'He's a brazen fella, that one.' He sounded winded. 'I won't shoo him off gentle any longer. The country's in no mood for manners.'

'What are you on about, Dad?'

'I ask you! What protection has a father to give when *gunpowder* won't hold them off?'

'Let me take this from you. Save you carting it.'

The Chief held onto the stock for a minute and I was alarmed by the strength of his grip. I clapped eyes with him until he let go, panting.

'You might have to use it yet,' he said.

'On *who*?'

He turned round again and scoped the field. I tore my gaze from his wilting chest to the gloom he squinted at. I wanted to tighten the belt of his bathrobe. My teeth clicked like a frigid engine. He thrust his arm out. 'The watchdog. I'm not at all sure that sins matter. Though not a word of that to your mother.'

It was then I made out the black spot of the scarecrow in the distance. 'Dad, are you well?'

Looking at me, the charcoal lines of his cheeks compressed. He took a firm hold of my shoulders so the shotgun's warm barrel pressed my thigh. 'I'm so sorry to have caused you this.' Tears glinted in the ruts of his face. '*Tá brón orm.*' I braced myself—one foot behind—and let him lean into me. *Tá brón orm.* Not 'I'm sorry' exactly ... but 'sorrow is on me'. The sorrow weighed of two grown men. Rubbing his back in large heavy circles, I warned him to calm down before his lungs gave in. The hiccuping slowed and he managed to swallow the fit that might well have killed him then and there in his stained Y-fronts.

I wrapped a hot-water bottle in tea towels and took it to the living room, where my father lay shaking, to tuck it under his thick back. I thought it might feel natural, inevitable, hormonally programmed to be nursing a parent and putting him to bed.

20.

Sunday morning at ten, through the kitchen window I saw Cormac tear up the drive in his estate. 'Let him in!' Nóra called from her utility chamber.

'He has someone with him,' I found myself calling back. 'A woman.'

'What?' The iron thudded and sizzled in my non-response. Nóra came in with lips like washers. For Cormac to have brought a *girl* along to his father's farewell! Not one additional dark deed could our home accommodate. Not the rind of a noxious lemon. She shut herself into the hissing-iron environment for the next half-hour and I wondered might she do herself an injury, scald a stigma out through her skin.

I took the stairs by threes and changed my clothes. Pushed away all thoughts besides the impending greetings. What would I say to a girl I'd met just the once (as far as Cormac knew) versus a girl who'd rudely, unconscionably turned up on the day we were due to say goodbye to our father for good? Was Cormac dragging her along to pad out the experience from himself? Maybe she wouldn't stay. Maybe she'd just be dropping him off. That was more likely. But she was stood at the door with him when I opened it.

'Hawaii, Barbie?' I leaned on the door frame. 'What's the craic?'

Cormac scowled in his shiny grey suit. 'Dolly,' he corrected me. As usual, he'd brought his mammy an offering. A wad of salmon-pink lottery tickets.

'Cormac says ye're headed west,' Dolly said. 'I'll grab a lift, if ye'll have me. The bus smells of puke.'

'Oh?' I tried to look at her innocently. 'I suppose a second date with this fella beats puke.'

Cormac whacked the back of my head. I felt the dig of his palladium ring. A new chunky thing he bought himself online from Dubai.

'Unless ye'll be *at* each other all day?' Dolly frowned, stepping in. 'All day?'

Would she be around all day? Was she coming to Connemara? What had Cormac said about tomorrow? A mighty one for the backstory, she'd've been asking curly questions. How much had he let on? He ballooned his chest and said: 'Sure, sand tiger sharks eat one another while they're still embryos. Intrauterine cannibalism. If he's not dead yet, I'm going easy on him, so I am.' Dolly rolled her eyes, somehow not disparagingly.

When Cormac demanded the Chief's whereabouts, I said he'd been on the phone since we came back from early mass. He was on to Gerry, consolidating his dues. He said to leave him be till we're for the road. Nóra was ensuring the coop and the crucifix would survive a day's forsaking. Egg-and-spinach sandwiches were parcelled in tinfoil. Our overnight bags were packed and lined up by the door. There'd be no time for saying the things I needed to say to the Chief or for hearing the things I needed to hear said. He was on the phone and then we'd be in the car and then we'd be at the ocean, where Nóra would sequester him for prayers and whatever else were her priorities and then we'd be in the mobile home and I couldn't disturb the final processings of his whiskeyed head. Twenty-four, thirty, thirty-six hours was a short time left for a lifetime. A hangover's worth of time. Cormac was scanning me like the World section of the newspaper—wanting to see how the Syrian Rebels welded their home-made missiles, but squinting to block out the aftermaths. He wouldn't worry after me for a second—he only wanted to know roughly what was on my mind. What was on it? Something the Chief said when I was putting his shoes on for him that morning. *Ní dhíolann dearmad fiacha.* A forgotten debt is still unpaid. No matter how often I replayed it,

I couldn't make head nor tail of it. He wasn't leaving some huge debt; the bank had the foreign properties long snatched back. What did he think could be forgotten?

'You look a bit shook, Hart,' Dolly said. 'Come here and sit down beside me.' She patted the wooden chair at the kitchen table. She shrugged off her red wool coat so it spilled around her like a pool of blood. In a sexy way, though. Underneath was the wrap-around polka dot dress from the night I first met her at the theatre. She didn't have on the lipstick and her hair wasn't loose but was pulled back in a plait. Her earlobes were white downy disks, weightless as Eucharists or Disprins. I'd never had them on my tongue. I wondered if they'd melt or, if I bit them off and swallowed them, if the lobes would draw towards one another in my brain, taking a shortcut through my consciousness.

'I have to bring in the planter,' I said. 'The tarp won't do, with the forecast that's in it. It'll rust.'

'Just sit for a minute—'

'I won't sit and drink tea. Not today. Not tomorrow.' I faced my brother, but Dolly lifted a few inches in my purview—her pelvic muscles contracting at the monologue she knew I had in me to deliver. But where was the curtain to be drawn down after, to mark the heroism concluded? How would I straighten up if I bowed? To play the bottle-stoppered countryman was second nature: nature's understudy. I was good at that, line-learning and knowing where to stand. 'There's jobs to be done. Call me when you're ready for it, Cormac.'

21.

The time Father Shaughnessy sent you and Gerry to buy the church Christmas tree before mass and I got to tag along and the three of us towed a twenty-foot Scots pine in Gerry's trailer with barely a score of branches on it. It was the uncommon thing you were capable of, to choose that tree. The unlikely thing stood scrawnily up in its glorified bucket by the altar, draped in tinsel and fairy lights.

That Christmas Day listening to the mixtape I made you called 'Farmtastic'. You using me as a guitar on your lap.

How you'd wipe my face with a kitchen towel.

The time I found you polishing Grandad Black's silver ploughing trophy from 1938 in the garage, your back to me. I was scared you were crying, remembering your two uncles taking off for Tasmania on the boat for eight weeks and your mother weeping for a month knowing she'd never see her brothers again and how you watched her lament, perched up in a tree. I've never seen my mother crying and I have no mind to.

The midnight you came downstairs for a hot whiskey for strep throat and found us red-cheeked from grappling and raiding the cupboards for sugar, fed up with our healthful country diets. We wanted biscuits to suck our tea through like straws. Penguin bars, we wanted. You shook your enormous head, saying Penguins were in short supply, pulling Darina Allen's cookbook (a birthday present from Auntie Bridie to her sister-in-law) from the nook and announcing the ingredients. Me and Cormac knelt staring at them cookies rising in the oven, rising too much for we'd used self-raising flour on top of baking soda and baking powder and eggs but we three ate the whole batch of them anyway—the puffy muffin-biscuits dripping butter and honey—so there was no trace of them in the morning, till Nóra did the laundry and found our trousers with flour handprints on the pockets.

The time you taught me to ride a bike. You on a bike that had been bought with a different currency, in a different century, sporting your Donegal walking hat, your knees knocking your armpits. Me wobbling on Shane's Raleigh with the ball-breaking crossbar and the bottle cage clattering. It was to see if I liked it and wanted a bike for my birthday so I wouldn't have to take the school bus with Cormac and his boyos always handy with wedgies and noogies and slagging. We got to the Qualters' bungalow and the turn-off for the boreen was soon, but even though the Qualters' gate was locked, the wolf-dog mongrels went wild on our approach and I could see two of them haring the length of the field behind the house to get round to us. I did a clean U-turn and raced the road-length home. That was all I needed in the way of lessons, you said.

Those were some of the things I wrote for the Chief to show how he'd be remembered. The measure of love I had for him was not unlike the riz biscuits, in the awkward uncontainable way that made it wise to push the batch of it aside and start over for fear of being poisoned by too much swelling.

22.

Cormac belted my name across the field with such urgency I near capsized the tractor diving out of it. The copybook clutched in my fist, I sprinted across the fields, hurdling stone walls, so my heart was in my throat by the time I skidded to a halt on the drive and found them all packed into the Land Rover—Cormac languishing against the driver's door in his suit and sliotar cufflinks. I doubled over to control my heart and my temper. 'Hop in,' says he, 'and don't be holding us up with your antics.'

The Chief was fine. He was fine. Not in his glory but alive in the passenger seat, slumped as a hessian sack come loose at the seams. Despite the roomy car, he was too big for it, dressed in his Sunday rig-out: a white shirt, woollen overcoat and corduroys. I knew his socks were angling socks pulled up to his knees out of habit because it was cold in the tractor. I knew the white vest he wore beneath the shirt he'd had since he got married. I knew his wedding ring fingernail was long because it was crimped from Gerry Lardner's skewbald mare trodding on it and it couldn't be clipped but could only be filed and the Chief had no time for filing. I knew he'd a dandruff-clogged comb in his coat's breast pocket that he pulled across his scalp for the momentary relief of it. I knew his right premolar tooth needed the roots cut out from the way his tongue had been pushing at it for a month now. I knew that the biggest insult of his sickness was the inability to be totally and utterly silent. The rattlesnake lungs hissed ceaselessly.

Dolly was in the back beside Nóra, who had welded herself to the door for maximum distance from the occultist interloping townie. But I ruined that by coming in on Dolly's side, so she had to slide to the middle seat. She'd be Nóra's worst nightmare, I hoped. Somehow, though, Dolly'd managed to prize my mother's tongue from her copper vault palate. 'Isn't it well for some,' Nóra said.

'And they've the caravan sat there the year long, with not a soul in it?' Dolly asked, her consonants skelping. Cormac had the rear-view mirror angled to her snow white cleavage. Still, I had the whole length of her side pressed against me.

'They do,' Nóra said. (Dolly gave her time to elaborate.) 'They go out to it once in a blue moon, if they don't wait for a purple one. Certainly not enough to keep it free of cobwebs.' (Another coaxing silence.) 'If you don't count the time Mitch absconded for a whole month "to arrange his VAT receipts", the Lord save us. You wouldn't know what would go on.'

'And have they had it a long time?'

'Well! It's a Celtic Tiger curio. Unearned, unnecessary and neglected.' Nóra's voice was a parody of modulation.

'Showy, is it?'

'It has an inbuilt shower and it facing the Atlantic Ocean! On a campsite that has a building set aside for showering. What use is that, may I ask, with the Africans and Australians going thirsty?'

Dolly sucked in air loudly. I had to hope she was honing a character. 'At least they've offered ye the use of it.'

'Oh, they've done that much. Gone *way* out of their way. Mitch especially, with his brother-in-law on his deathbed.' Nóra sourced a tissue in her handbag where the roll of pink lottery tickets nodded. She would wrap the tissue around her eczema'd index finger, rub the end of her nose with it and keep it clutched in her hand for the rest of the day until it moulted. There wasn't a pocket in her funeral frock to put it in, just a hundred buttons up the front and a dozen buttons at the wrists, and folds from the hips down to her shins, which were plastered in baggy skin-coloured tights— hairs thorning through.

'He'd rather spend his energy planning his niece-in-law's wedding in Ashford Castle, cutting up banknotes for confetti to throw after them. That's all.'

'Ashford Castle!' Dolly repeated. 'Is she a stockbroker or what?'

'The daughter works for Yahoo or Macintosh or whatever it is. The American corporates.'

'She doesn't work for Apple, Mam,' Cormac called back. 'She's an app designer.'

'A lot of lives that must save.' She looked out the window as if there was something to see beyond the smear of stone wall and clotted cloud.

'It must *vex* you,' I said, 'that she's loaded and not the cause of our hardship. And a Catholic, too! Not even a heathen.' I tucked my chin to my chest and imitated Nóra's clipped voice into Dolly's ear: 'The brazen, privileged so and so! Working for a *foreign* outfit.' Dolly elbowed me.

'Doharty,' the Chief warned, surprising us all that he wasn't asleep. The eyes stayed closed.

We drove through miles of countryside with compatible smells coming in through the fan. Cormac relayed some crap joke he told at work about euro notes being waterproof and that's what makes them insolvent. Dolly laughed generously and Cormac clapped himself a *bualadh-bos* on the steering wheel and accidentally hit the horn, setting off a round of Jesus-Mary-and-Saint-Josephs from Nóra. Dolly tilted her head so much I thought she was going to rest it on my shoulder, and Cormac did too, going by his crossed eyes in the mirror. Then Dolly came out with: 'I'm afraid I can't give you any *credit* for that one. You're completely a-*loan* in thinking that's any good!'

'Yow!' Cormac heckled, relieved. 'I'm sorry I'm not *stimulus package* enough for you! Doharty might've liked it? He's well used to having to *do more with less*.'

The chin was going like a pokie machine handle, but I blocked them all out, *disturbed* as I was at the whole foreboding atmosphere of the day, *troubled* as I was that Dolly seemed to have held this tie to my brother. What manner of tie, I didn't know. Her sense of fun was unfamiliar. Or maybe she was doing it all for me, to show how easy it was to stage-manage such a small and knowable family— how I needn't make a song and dance of it. We were Russian dolls she was gathering up and fitting together like so many stock characters. Eventually she'd get to the Chief, who'd be the biggest figurine to keep us all safe inside, even if his woodworm would pass on by proximity. How easy us muck savages were to grasp. How basic our motives. It was an old sentimental story that went down like trifle: the struggle for selfhood, exorcising the individual from the mass; the inexpert misunderstood miserable myth-drunk countrymen, versed in obsolete statistics, stuck in de Valera's era, privately yearning for intimacy, reflexology and office jobs with casual Fridays. Also yearning for the story—however tired—to deserve telling.

'Get on with it,' Cormac said into his phone. 'I'm pulling into Mitch's.' He sniggered, hung up the call he'd been on and made circles with the heel of his palm, turning us into the drive of Mitch and Bridie's pseudo-Tudor house.

'I've a tray of eggs for them. Go right up to the door,' Nóra directed. 'We'll be a few minutes. Your father needs to … speak to his sister. Tomorrow's Monday, so. She'll be at work when we bring back the key. That's all.'

Cormac caught eyes with me in the mirror. We all sat unnaturally still for a minute.

'Take your time,' Dolly said, puzzled. 'My shift doesn't start till one, and I can always blame a travelling circus.'

Nóra fussed about in the boot for her salver of eggs. With Cormac supporting him at the elbow, the Chief rose out of the passenger seat with an invisible tambourine.

'Come and shake hands with your uncle,' Nóra told Cormac, reviewing his suit. If her hands weren't beset with eggs, she'd have spat and rubbed his lapel and done up his fly. 'It's months since he's seen you and he doesn't know the businessman you've become.'

'A businessman, as well as a boffin?' Uncle Mitch called, cross-armed from the front door. He wore a grin you might draw on a balloon. 'D'you keep up the hurling still, too?'

My eyes jumped to the tan stripe that darted between Uncle Mitch's ankles. I shoved Dolly aside, dove between the front seats and stretched forward to shut the driver's door. A rapid scuttling on the tarmac. *Fuck.* If I shouted, it'd only race faster. I hyperventilated. I couldn't close the door unless I got into the front seat proper, but he'd be in by then. He'd jump directly onto me. Dolly wouldn't be able to tear his teeth from my neck—they clamp down their jaws hard enough to fang their own gums. 'Cormac! The *door!*' Cormac swung round and cupped his ear, then he reached the same hand out to shake Uncle Mitch's. The Chief did look back before stepping into the house. 'Call the dog in, will you?' I heard him tell Mitch. 'Hart doesn't like dogs.'

'Ah, that fella's harmless!' Uncle Mitch said. 'Sprite! Blind as a bat now. So if he went for your ankle, he'd get your bollocks!' The front door shut, with everyone inside. The dog bounded into the front seat. Some unhuman noise was coming from my throat, but Dolly was taking control. 'Come here, Sprite. Come here to me.'

'Get him *away*. Please don't, please, *please ...*'

Dolly had him by the belly in her hands. He was springing and squirming like a pollock. 'Reach across me, Hart, and open my door.'

All my effort went into tucking my limbs into myself. My stomach was up in my chest and knitting all the organs together.

'Fucksake! Keep your fangs from my coat,' Dolly said, managing to contain the dog with one arm against her chest, opening the door with the other. I couldn't look. My brain was protecting me from anything that could become a memory. I would only survive if the dog allowed me to. Adrenaline served to keep me clenched tight as possible so as not to leave appendages ripe for the plucking. A minute later there was a bang, and then another. A heaving sensation. Pressure on my lap. Frenzied barking. I flinched.

'Relax. He's gone. It was a chihuahua, you realise? Or were you having me on?'

'Do I *look* like I'm having you fucking *on*?' Some of my spittle landed on Dolly's Spanish swept eyebrow. My throat smarted. My heart ached with stress. Pressed against the window, I located the hairy little radioactive rat yelping by the front tyre, as if it had some *right* to me. As if I had done it some injustice. The righteous, ferocious, parasitic cunt. If I'd the nerve to take the switchblade to it, like the lambs—

'There's worse things than the nip of a chihuahua, Hart,' Dolly said. 'If it could open its jaw wide enough to bite more than a peanut.'

'That thing is *evil*! I *hate* that evil fucking thing and I hate anyone who'd own it.'

Dolly shook her head. 'Get some perspective, Hart, before the world forces it on you.'

I closed my fist and walloped the middle car seat by my shoulder as hard and fast as I could. Once, twice, three, four, five times and I caught the top of Dolly's arm on the last two. She cried out and recoiled from me. Grimacing, she shimmied off her red coat to nurse the arm.

77

'Sorry, Dolly … I, I'm sorry, I didn't—'

She slid sideways and looked out the window at the ridiculous caucus of garden ornaments. *Fuck*. My heart let up now that I was inside and safe. I could drive off if need be. But I didn't like Dolly faced away. What she might have been deciding. I looked to where she looked and let enough time pass for a photograph to develop.

'Bridie's been shopping again,' I said eventually. There was a new plastic St Bernard dog with its hanging tongue painted pumpkin orange as the new centrepiece garden ornament, next to the bearded gnome playing the *bodhrán*, and his harpist brother. A formidable addition, holding its own among the competition. There was a ceramic dwarf with a finger up his nose, sat on a toilet. There were a dozen enchanting hares, some alert on their hind legs, some in running motion around a luminous white birdbath. Faded resin statues of a Mary and one of the bloodshot-eyed saints in sandals stood behind a brace of ducks. St Francis of Assisi. The whole jamboree was contained by a large ring of white pebbles.

Dolly began: 'Is that—'

'A sleeping pig? It is, yeah.'

'—a Friesian cow?'

'Oh, no. That's a Holstein. But may I draw your attention to the bronze fairy on the swing, and the owl who looks to be perched there gently, wisely, on her shoulder, imparting sweet nothings … and behold the three engraved slates and ceramic urns that house the ashes of Sprites departed. Two ash chihuahuas and one ash Shih Ttzu.'

Dolly glanced at me. Her chin was dimpled and she was rubbing her arm. Tears brimmed and ran down her white cheeks.

'I fucken love you,' I said.

She burst out laughing in an earnest, involuntary way. I pulled her towards me by her hurt arm and hove her atop me. I'd fog the car windows with her breath if I was good for anything. I groped the feast of her stomach, back, chest, ran my tongue around her silk mouth. She was a stealthy wave I wanted to dive into head first, no matter if it thrashed and trampled me breathless. Between greedy kisses, she told me not to return to the midlands tomorrow. To stay out west with her in Galway. She pressed into me so my stubble scoured her chin pink. 'What do you have to come back to? There's nothing for you. You could start *living*, in Galway.' I had no notion of staying with her—not until the Chief was long gone and the fields belonged to some other crofter—but I loved that she wanted me waiting in her flat when she came home from work. She wanted me alongside her on the bar stools in Sally Longs, watching Guinnesses cream and the Milky Way materialise in fast-forward out of all that bareness. She wanted my pubic hairs in her bathtub to cringe at and collect. She wanted to make me a reading list and to culture me and to hear me invert the culture. She wanted to lie against me each night, breathing in the smell of my skin she's named barley, the peculiar scalp oil smell that's some way universal but entirely individual and addictive. We'd catch fish on the weekends with two-euro nets on sticks and I'd bake trout fillets in tinfoil with garlic, salt, lemon, pepper, buttered red onions and she'd lick the foil if she wanted to because she doesn't have any metal fillings, only porcelain. It was a sin I had no fillings, she said. She'd be sure I needed fillings before Christmas. We'd make dauphinoise for a side dish and sell it in little cartons in the Saturday morning market outside the pungent cheese shop and Protestant church where the closed-lipped dead are interred under the stone floor beneath the churchgoers' hard-wearing soles. I slipped my hand up her thigh and held her stockinged fanny tight, shuddering her warm. I lifted her—

'Don't, Cormac.'

I pulled back. Scanned the front door. It was locked. *He'll kill me before we get to the Chief* ... The barking had stopped at some point. I couldn't see the dog. The light outside seemed to change from a tolerable after-the-fact ash to the thick white smoke you get from burning evergreen trees or electing a Pope. I blinked a lot. Waited. 'Have you been seeing us both?'

She sighed heavily, flushed.

'All along?' A metallic tang reached my mouth.

She brushed her dress over her knees. 'The problem with you, Hart, is you think the whole world's out to get you. Women and bitches alike.' She shuffled sideways and left the door ajar after her.

What kind of an answer was that? I slammed the door shut quick, wound down the window and said, 'The problem with you, Aleanbh ... is .., it's all a big act ...' I worked the window crank and watched her twist and turn through the garden furniture. I thought back over what I'd said. Where was the sense? At the urns, she rose to her tiptoes and lifted the lid off one. She seemed to be shivering. Her back was to me. Was she all right? I thought about going out to her and telling her everything: why I was the way I was and how I wanted to be. My ears were pinned for the dog. I searched the car for a weapon I could use against him. Maybe I could call her back. But she wasn't alone now and the dog must have found something to persecute elsewhere, for it didn't even skid out to defend its territory when Shane's motorbike tore up the drive.

One of those Italian racers, it had him leaning forward like a fly trying to hold onto the roof of a moving truck. Half of it he'd put together himself from the hardware shop's surplus stock—the other half was bought from some lad in Tyrone—so there was a bit of commotion about it. Cormac had come out to slap backs with Shane and introduce Dolly, squeezing her upper arm where I'd thwacked it. He looked confused when she flinched and pulled away. They congregated between the car and the statues: Dolly doing the po-faced wronged woman; Shane groin forward on his second-hand saddle; Cormac leaning on the St Bernard, pinstriped, cufflinks glinting—the three of them recession goodfellas. Shane caught the set of keys thrown at him with his leather-gloved hand.

When I rolled down the window, I heard Cormac say the tank needed filling but to keep the receipt.

'Spuds!' Shane lifted his chin to me. 'Don't be acting the gom and get out?' He pulled off his full-face helmet and rested it on his handlebars.

'How's the form?' I asked through the window.

'Savage. Slugger has me stalking the jungle like a filthy Black and Tan.'

'Is this the business I only learned of this minute?'

'Did he not tell ya?' Shane raised his brows.

'No need to go into details with him,' Cormac said.

'Acourse there's no *need*,' Shane smirked, 'but I'll give ye the gist of it, Spuds—'

'It's only shits and giggles,' Cormac said sternly.

Shane continued: '—in case ye've a notion of moving up in the world one day and not be always your aul fella's dogsbody. There might be an opening for ye, ye never know.'

Cormac cracked his neck and threw a look Dolly's way. Her arms were crossed in the cold—giving my brother an ample eyeful. I thought of passing her out the coat. Dolly asked, 'What is it? Are ye buying wholesale teabags and selling them off one by one?'

Shane gave her a squint and a smile. He still had the cut turf hair and the wolverine eye that would have him on ADHD pills if he lived in the States. 'One up on that, missus. Horses! We buy them from owners who can't afford feed. Rotten sodden season that's in it. We save the poor craythurs from mincing and slapping ta patties. Don't we, Slugger? Horses worth thousands we buy for yoyos. Shuffle them round a bit, fatten them, and I'll tell ye we sell horses fit for warfare. Gambling, farm work, transport, what have ye? "Colt Horse Cash. We're the answer to your equestian"!'

'Badabing!' Dolly clapped once, thrilled. 'Isn't there a lot of work in keeping horses?'

'Not enough to kill ye,' Shane said. 'It's the trading's deadly.'

'It's the paperwork's deadly,' Cormac corrected him. 'Shane has his teenage sister and her classmates mucking out sheds, so he does. Exercising the ones that won't bite off their fingers. They choose their currency of payment. Buckfast or Magners or Smirnoff Ice.' Bombastic from his own carpetbaggery, he looked like he was on yokes. Dolly watched his gurning jaw with raised brows.

Shane started up his engine. 'Listen, I've two mares in Westmeath need shiftin' lively. Though there's horsepowers enough fer it, I can't hitch them onto this thing. So I'll make like an Irish college graduate, heh?' He did a backwards crab dance to turn and took off.

What did Cormac do for this business? It sounded as if Shane was doing all the work. Dolly must have asked him something similar, for he said, 'Provide the bread.' Looking off into the distance as if surveying his empire, he fingered coins or keys in his trouser pocket. 'The fodder, the dough, the brains, the lot. Inventory management. Shane does toing and froing. Logistics and the like.'

'You've kept your engineering job, I hope?' Dolly awaited his response. 'I mean … you must be paying for feed and stabling … and land lease and petrol and *insurance*—'

'Don't worry yourself.' Cormac sauntered to the car. Nóra was helping the Chief snail towards us. 'Like Rupert Murdoch put it: "We've no intention of failing. The only question is how great a success we'll have".'

I got out of the car and faced my brother across the roof. He met my eye all right, since Dolly was there. The chill air skirred over his close-shaved face, there being no worry lines for it to catch in. 'That's the talk that ruined us,' I said. 'That broke the Chief's back and buried him with his own spade. So keep your rich talk and Rupert fucken Murdoch to yourself, till our father's six feet out of earshot.'

When they were all piled in and Cormac was revving the engine, I could feel Dolly's gaze on my red cheek.

23.

The sun was making an effort behind the glut of autumn cloud. But, much as I'd been told as a schoolboy, the effort alone wasn't enough. It had to be married with a certain natural propensity. What was that line Mr Healey used to wag at me like a ruler? 'You've got to do your own growing, no matter how tall your grandfather was.' My grandfather was burnt to the height of a dust mite. I took that personal. It can be the composition of your mind isn't arable, however you put down seed. I wanted the effort to be enough. For the sun to warm the Chief's hands on his lap. I wanted it out glaring, making an oasis of the N63. This sun-starved bogland was a national heritage site, I thought of telling Dolly … so the Chief could hear I was laying claim to it. A kingdom flat as a witch's chest—imposing in its own way, in its downright green.

It had been a long stretch of dual carriageway when the Chief's chest crescendoed, which could only have been in advance of a speech—the way the fiddler lifts her bow high before delivering a forceful ballad. That's what I imagined when the Chief took that breath: him lifting the bloody lot of us by our major chords. 'Did I ever tell you about the Connemara man and his hare?'

'It blew off with a westerly?' Cormac said.

Fuck's sake. I kneed the back of his seat. A tissuey finger inched forward in the corner of my eye: Nóra pushing down the lock on her door. Dolly lengthened the hare's ears she had for anecdotes. The Chief spoke calmly with long, susurrating pauses. His eyes were closed. His hands were willows on his lap: 'A fact our guest here might not know is that there's predators in the countryside as well as in the city. The foxes.'

'A local clan?' Dolly asked.

'The animals.' The Chief frowned, keeping his eyes closed.

'Oh, sorry,' Dolly said, almost coy.

Cormac tsked. 'You're grand.'

The Chief waited for silence. 'To protect her young from predators, the female hare makes numerous nests in the field. She moves from one nest to the other, nursing the babes.'

'Leverets, they're called,' Cormac enlightened us.

The Chief waited a good half-minute before he took up again. It wasn't that he demanded attention, but he hadn't the energy to be plough-talking and he'd decided to let this tale out so godforbid he be plugged. Meanwhile, Cormac had cracked all the knuckles he owned and some that he didn't.

'There was a Connemara man found a nest containing one tiny leveret in his own back yard. What would he think but that its mother had abandoned it? So he took the creature inside and looked after it, tender as he'd done anything in his life and he a hard-boiled bachelor. For the first hours, Séamus struggled to feed the thing, for it wouldn't touch a bowl of milk or a bit of greenery, no matter how fine he minced it. It was nowhere near solids and needed milk badly. 'Twouldn't fill the palm of your hand, it was that small.' The Chief took a moment to let the raised silt in his chest settle. 'Getting desperate, Séamus took out the old valve of his bicycle tube and used the short length of rubber to fashion a sort of teat. The pump valves of old bicycle tubes differ to the modern ones. 'Twas less than two millimetres wide and, would you believe it, the leveret took to it. So Séamus managed to feed it milk and soon enough it was lepping around, a house pet. Séamus took that creature everywhere, in his sleeve like a newborn. When they'd return from the mart, he wouldn't put it out to feed with the pigs but would sit it opposite at the kitchen table, eating a tidy meal. Before retiring to his bed, he'd work on getting the young hare to do a trick or two. He got it to stand up and roll over until eventually it could perform a sort of standing dance, you see. He got to entertaining his friends in the pub by having the hare perform his little routine to a bit of piano accordion. The whole community came to love the thing. But more than anything, they loved the satisfaction and the smile it drew out of Séamus.'

No one but Cormac was minding the traffic any longer. No one was reading the luminous roadside billboards or paying any heed to the electronics megastores lassoing hire-purchase hopefuls with their cables and covenants. We listened to the Chief wheeze awhile but soon Dolly was agitating. She couldn't cope with the scriptless characters he'd put in her head. Who belonged to whom? The hare to the human? The man to his pet? The Chief to his story? The Connemara bachelor to some inevitable brutality, to some misfortune of isolation, to trope, to deep-seated lack of motivation, to a fox that got in the cat flap after all his efforts with the valve, after all the mother hare's careful spreading of nests? 'What happened to the hare, Mr Black?' *Was he roasted for supper in a twist of fate—two bananas caramelised in his long ears?* was the tacit question.

'One morning,' the Chief said, 'he was gone. He'd left. No amount of vigils or searching the fields could locate him. When a week had passed, Séamus accepted that the fox had finally caught up with him or a tyre had done the same. If that was the way of it, Séamus could accept it as a part of nature, though it saddened him something terrible. But that wasn't the explanation. The hare turned up in the yard one afternoon a week on, out of nowhere, and life got back to normal. They were back down the pub dancing jigs and reels, magnificent. But another blow was in store when the hare disappeared *arís*. This time not for a week only. This time the hare stayed gone and Séamus began to accept that it might never return. Truth be told, he'd become too aware of his own season, no more than myself, and he shut himself up in the cottage for days on end. Then one day he heard a tapping at the front door. A kind of scraping … I wonder did he know that raven poem, come to think of it. Was that Yeats?'

'Poe,' Dolly said. 'You mean Edgar Allan Poe's "The Raven", Mr Black?'

'I do know that poem. But Séamus mustn't have, for he opened the door freely, and there at his feet was the hare looking up. Speechless, he stooped to pick it up but the hare skipped out to the front gate, looking back as it went. You see, there was another hare at the gate and the pair of them looked back at Séamus. After a moment, the two hopped off together and that was the last Séamus saw of his small companion. 'Twas as if he'd come back one last time to introduce his small hare wife, and to let Séamus know the foxes hadn't et him. *Sin é an scéal.*'

Nóra was peering out the window at the Martian oranges and reds that the birch trees had released in the distance. She must have wanted to get at them with the rake. She lifted the tissue to her face, but all I could see was her bun like a hare's tail, but rained on. I tried to think when she might have last unclipped and uncoiled it at the Chief's side. His weight on the mattress would have tumbled her into him, or maybe she would cling to the outer rim. It was true she used to be very physical with him. Not in the way of patting affection. It was something thirstier. A bygone behaviour anyway. Had it been years or months since he'd last mounted the stairs? Decades or years since she'd rested her head on his pilaster shoulder without fear of collapse? Would she pine after him when he'd gone, kneeling for the Angelus twice daily? A new phase might be in store. The Sisters of Mercy might have her back. She was only sixty-one. Her estranged parents were alive somewhere in County Wicklow. Granny Nugent, who we never saw nor spoke of. If genes were anything to go by, Nóra had epochs in her yet.

'What made you think of that story?' Cormac asked the Chief.

'What put it in my mind?' he asked himself, but turned to his son who had all the answers. 'Was it the hay shed in flames, no? Those were only field mice came scuttling out alight, Mum and Dad and Kitty inside. No. No, not that. Was it Mike and Bridie's, maybe? Oh yis, there's leverets beyond in the yard. That's what it was. 'Tmust be the time of year for them. A little family of them. Tell me: what month are we in, Hart?' The Chief consulted Cormac, opening his eyes for the response.

I could see Cormac's brow bent in the mirror. 'It's Cormac, Dad.'

'August?'

'No, it's … it's the first of October, Dad. But I'm Cormac.'

'Autumn?' the Chief asked, incredulous. He struggled to turn back to us for confirmation, but he couldn't manage it. He focused on Cormac's suited shoulder. Then he fell back into his doped position and looked ahead. 'But that can't be right. Would you look at the glorious daffodils lining the roads?'

Nóra rubbed her nose with the tissue. Cormac said nothing. I unclipped my seat belt and sat forward to put my hand on the Chief's shoulder. 'What daffodils, Dad?'

'Daffodils, all along. The length of my arm. If it's autumn, you say, I'll believe it. They're God's gifts.'

When I sat back, finally, Dolly took my cold hand between hers to stop it trembling.

24.

The lottery tickets won her ten quid and a jealous little sip of air from the man behind the counter, who registered that this woman was spending her winnings in the newsagents and not taking it to Lidl to make it stretch in the way it should rightly be stretched, in light of the economic conditions. She bought a pack of playing cards (as if props would keep me and Cormac from tearing one another apart), a family pack of Skips crisps (they 'melt on the tongue' so she hoped the Chief could manage them), breath mints and six cans of Guinness.

After dropping Dolly off at her call centre job, we had lunch in the hotel on Eyre Square. A sandwich was no good for Cormac, the working man. Cream of potato and leek soup with two white rolls, Lucozade, the pulled pork—and what vegetables had they? Garden peas, mash and pureed carrots and parsnips. 'You can leave the peas, so you can. And no parsley on any of it.' Cormac tilted his head until it cracked. After all that, Cormac wasn't done: 'I'm tempted to indulge the child in me and have the jelly and ice cream.' He must have been constructing that barriered sentence for a good minute.

The waiter half-smiled. 'Will I get you that, so?'

'Go on.'

'No bother.' The waiter took the menu with a nod. Cormac was wild annoyed when it came in a Knickerbocker Glory glass with pink wafers for sails. 'Now! Was that the ticket?' the waiter asked. 'Did it take you back to your childhood?' When no laugh was forthcoming, he advanced the ceremony: 'Tea or coffee, folks?'

'Neither one,' Cormac decided for us all and sniffed. I couldn't figure out what frame of mind he was in, or what he was like altogether, other than a cunt.

25.

Lakes were common as potholes on the N59, small fishing boats roped up in each one. Limestone shouldered out of the fields like half-excavated famine villages. The rugged remote majesty of the far west put me in mind of another country.

Nóra had been intoning names of plants as if recalling them from her days of tending the priest's garden—there being no better way to get on side with a clergyman than to ream off Latin vocabulary. There was something calming if not sensual in the whispered exotic names: *Crocosmia*, that's montbretia, yellow wort,

Blackstonia perfoliata, honeysuckle, *Lonicera periclymenum*, purple *Gentianella campes*—

'Arragh raven crock of genital warts on Edgar Allan's fucken toe!' Cormac snapped, wanting done with wistful impractical poetics for the day. He tailgated every car he came upon until he pulled into the long grassy campsite drive his GPS device had located.

The mobile home sat above sand dunes clotted with marram grass. In front, the leaden Atlantic Ocean was unembellished but for a tidal island crowning out. Behind, the weather-smoothed Twelve Bens mountains humped from the horizon like whales. There were only three other caravans, and one large tent with little transparent windows so the owners had at least a plastic veil between themselves and the neighbours. We were as good as alone. When the Chief was settled—wrapped in a rug on a collapsible chair that creaked with his weight, facing seaward—Cormac drove off to pick up a fresh fish supper from the chippie. Once he was gone and Nóra had busied herself sufficiently, I went out to the Chief and put a can of Guinness in the armrest cup holder. I handed him my copybook. As soon as I'd done it, I worried it was the wrong thing to do and would only upset him. But I couldn't take it back. I'd go walking on the beach and be back shortly. Had he his whistle? He took the copybook without a question and said he'd keep an eye on me. If I came across a dog, it would be chasing the waves and not the visitors. They do like the lapping waves. Not to worry.

Sliding down the marram grass, the tears slid likewise. Who'd tell me what I needed to hear tomorrow? Who'd keep an eye on me, or spare me a thought? The softer upper beach was pitted with ownerless footprints. The hard, damp sand by the water was unmarked but for two sets of prints and their return journey. Life itself was caught up in that venture, advance, abort, spin around, retreat, all trace dissolved. I took off my shoes and socks and carried them. It's good to be reminded of gravity

and that the state of falling is plain as day. Ironclad. I felt that
and the shiver of an early autumn on my skin, the damp earth
coming up to meet me. Sand hoppers leapt for a taste from
their seaweed tangles. The waves pushed in a lip of scum for
a reminder of the great chilling world that's in it, full of razor
clams and spiral conches people take home and hold up to their
ears to remember their holidays, but all they hear are the hollow
qualities of their domestic, logistical lives. I climbed onto an
outcrop of volcanic rock and clambered so far I couldn't see any
land or fences or houses before me. Nothing but the sea and the
rock drawing blood from my unhardened soles. It was a good,
focused pain. Dolly would have put it to work. How different
my perspective would've been had she her long fingers wrapped
in mine, then. She said she'd write letters until I was ready to
leave home. She said there was something old-fashioned about
me, and postal correspondence felt right. If she'd bother, I didn't
know. Listening to the water wrestling granite, I thought of all
the ocean stories she'd told me. She was a woman of the coast
and was formed by it. I had no ocean stories. Only river ones.
The ocean was another thing entirely and I didn't know why the
Chief had chosen to go to it.

'Do you know why I gave you that to read, Dad?'

The Chief's hazel eyes were pink-rimmed when I came back.
He had the copybook rolled up in the cup holder and the Guinness
can clutched in his fist. 'You say here you've never seen your
mother crying and you don't want to.' He looked up at me. 'Would
you rather it bottled up inside her, forming a cancer of its own?' He
waited for me to shake my head. 'You'd best get used to the sight
of it, I tell you that.'

Was that a threat? Was it the drugs? 'I only meant—'

'You meant well, Hart. But you'll have to do better than meaning
well, d'you hear? We all meant well, and look where it got us.'

I took a few deep breaths and felt an ant climb my bare foot on the grass.

'I've left the instructions for you, and you've a few choices to make.' Then he looked very worried, his thoughts pivoted. 'You'd never know the difference between a brown-tissued spud, plighted in the pith, and one that's perfect but has been stored too cold and the starch turned to simple sugar and browned.'

'What?'

'Have you a pen?' He opened the copybook and scanned it again. After a moment, he slowed down and breathed in short sniffs. His expression softened and he pressed the paper down with his left hand, the crimped fingernail of his ring finger infinitely consoling. He began to laugh. 'I'd forgotten about that mischief with the biscuits.' He looked up, pained. 'And devouring them with my two fit boys, happy as you like.'

I fell to my knees on the grass, and my father took my head onto his rug-covered lap and rested his hand on it with a comforting weight, but hard to bear. 'Thank you for giving me this,' he said. 'I worry you'll remember me too kindly. Doharty. You're a son to be proud of.'

No. No. No. I can't miss you this much. I choked on my own breath. 'I'll miss you so much.'

'I miss you something terrible, but there you go.'

26.

I hadn't heard Cormac pull up, with the Chief's hand on my ear, but I did hear the door shut loudly.

27.

There were wheels on the mobile home for tax purposes. The benefit of Mitch and Bridie having a trained barrister daughter driving a taxi was that she knew about property and vehicle tax both: that denying the thing was on a permanent site (a brown envelope agreement with the landowner), leaving it on its wheels (so it's 'mobilised') and forgoing an electricity supply would keep it economical. It wasn't technically a holiday home. So they felt well and truly gypped when a two-hundred-euro mobile home tax was introduced, regardless of whether or not the contraption was kept in one place or attached to land.

It had a 'master bedroom' and a second room with two single beds for me and Cormac, so no one had to hug their knees on the sofa-bed. The lounge and kitchen had nineties furniture—pine kitchen with ivy trellis wallpaper, a beige velour falcate sofa around a glass-topped coffee table—so you felt as if you were moving around the set of a sitcom, only no canned laughter came from the fancy Bose digital radio, just Connemara Community Radio, '*possibly the most interesting radio station you will ever tune into*', doing a feature on the Clifden writers' group:

'*And now we have Mairéad, who'll read her poem about the grey squirrels she used to see in Hyde Park in London, England, where she did her master's degree in Ecology, qualifying with Distinction. With her meditation on modern overpopulation through the metaphor of the English squirrel now, here goes Mairéad.*'

'I'll turn on the heater,' Nóra said, finding things to be busy with. The Chief was watching me and Cormac play Texas Hold 'Em poker in the lounge, cradling his Guinness can.

'How's there a heater if there's no electricity?'

'Solar panels on the roof,' Cormac said. 'Come on, stop foostherin'. You're small blind.' He pushed forward two crisps for big blind. Our Skips crisps were stacked up in two little mounds on the coffee table. We'd been playing for the best part of an hour and Cormac was so far ahead he occasionally ate one of his crisps. Our private bet was that the loser would organise the funeral. Cormac had sent me a link the week before to an article from the *Irish Times*: 'Funeral Costs Survive Recession's Deflationary Grip'. The cost of funerals had gone up over three hundred percent in a decade. It might as well have read: 'Despair! But Don't Do Away With Yerselves. 'Tis Dear!'

I looked out the window at the darkening beach. The days were shortening, but just then the sun broke through the cloud, glowing yellow as the tell-tale buttercup held to a schoolgirl's chin. I was glad not to have sisters for what flowers they might pick and hold up to me, what truth might be revealed. Though I suppose brothers have their ways of doing the same.

'Come on ta fuck,' Cormac said.

'Don't annoy me.' I had a jack and a king, off suit. I pushed a Skip forward. 'Call.'

'Check.' Cormac slapped out the flop. A pair of kings and a three, off suit. No flush or straight potential. I looked at Cormac. He gave a little smirk and pushed out four Skips, trying to let on he had a king. But even if he did have one—highly unlikely—I had a high kicker. And he didn't have the king. He was a bluffering, bragging gurrier. So I met his four Skips and raised him another four, leaving me skimpy. Cormac lifted a brow, gauging the cards. He pretended not to be giving the game his full attention, saying: 'Clifden town's become the right job, Dad. Gentrified to the hilt.' The Chief made a noise to say he'd heard. '*Fashionable* town now … so it is. Baler twine used to hold up their trousers, with all the belts in their wardrobes growing mould. Wellington boots turned down at the top. Art galleries.' He pushed forward the extra four Skips to call and burnt a card. He had an intent look on his face I knew too well. I checked the glass tabletop to see he hadn't angled a mirror under the couch. He set down the fourth card, the turn: a ten of spades. His small hazel eyes probed. I noticed a ring of yellow in them, by the pupils. You can pass your whole boyhood without learning the colour of your brother's eyes, it turned out. His lashes were practically transparent, unlike mine and Nóra's, which made his crow's feet all the more pronounced. I could feel my frown line rototilling between my brows. When had we gotten old?

'They're no better off than the rest of us,' Nóra called from the kitchen, where she was taking down the bluebottle-heavy fly-catching strips from the ceiling and replacing them with fresh ones found in a drawer. 'Four hundred empty rooms in the new hotel and a half-built multistorey car park beside it, they were saying on the radio.'

'That's it,' Cormac said. 'They roll up the sleeves of their alpaca cardigans before dipping their sheep.'

'The Bull McCabe is long gone,' I said, half to myself.

Cormac sat up. I pushed in two Skips of my remaining six. I needed him to bite. I gave an explanation of the reference that wasn't asked for: 'That's from John B. Keane's play, the farmer Bull McCabe. Maybe you know the film version, *The Field*, was filmed out this way, with Richard Harris.'

'He died,' Nóra stated. 'Would you close the curtains, Doharty?' She didn't seem to want to leave the kitchen. Or was it the door to the bedroom she was lurking nervously by? She'd be sharing a bed with him for the first time in months.

I frowned at her. 'The day's not done yet.'

'What do you know about plays?' Cormac's chin stiffened.

'Arragh, I know a few.' I stood and closed the curtains anyway. '*The Doll's House*, that's Ibsen. Nordic fella. What else? *Guys and Dolls*. A musical, that. I mostly know the Irish ones. *Philadelphia, Here I Come!* We know that from school. Same Friel fella wrote a thing called *Lovers* ... And *Portia Coughlan* is another ... Can't tell you how I know that one.' I sat back down and tapped my two Skips. 'Are you in?'

Cormac tilted his head. 'All in.' He unnecessarily pushed his pile of prawn-cocktail-flavoured crisps forward, only needing to move four.

I had three kings. The only hands that could beat me were three kings again, with a higher kicker, a full house (fat chance), or if he had pocket aces and he caught another ace on the river. More likely, he was chasing a straight—with a jack and a queen in his hand, say, so he'd need an ace or a nine for the last card. Maybe the all-in indicated that that's what he had. Good. Or maybe he had a ten and a three—two pair—in which case I had him. I decided he was either bluffing or he had pocket aces, and the odds were low he'd get the third. Pocket aces would be the kind of thing Cormac would lose on. But there were no re-buys.

'I'm thinking,' I said. I pictured myself phoning up Auntie Bridie and Uncle Padraig and Gerry Lardner and justifying the cremation. Writing an obituary for the *Roscommon Herald*. Would they want one for the *Connaught Tribune*, or were regional mortalities not high enough on the social ladder to note them falling off it? How long before I should move the bed out of the living room and throw the whistle in the bin? How would I transport the heft of him to the crematorium? There were only the two—one in Cork and one in Dublin—and his personal if not his political affiliations would've been with Cork. Cremation was half the price of a burial, and that's what he'd asked for besides, so it would be done. I looked at Cormac and didn't see those thoughts in him at all. He didn't like me observing him. He turned to the Chief and said:

'While she's thinking, Shane's collecting the cull on Tuesday. I know you won't be … just so you know, it's all arranged for after the grading. We're all set up.'

The Chief nodded slowly. 'Grand.'

'What's that?' I asked.

'Nothing,' Cormac said. 'Are you folding or what? Or will you try to scoop your way out of the grave with your four melting Skips?'

The cull. A new buyer. Right. From the scraps I'd heard in the house and on the phone, I should've pieced it together. The Chief was supplying Cormac's horse-trading business with feed—the reason most of the horse-owners had been forced to sell. The key component of Shane and Cormac's business model: keeping the horses fed while hay was unavailable or unaffordable. The culled tubers that normally go to livestock farmers or manufacturers of processed potato products were going to my brother for a song. For nothing. Because the Chief was trusting Cormac to save us financially. Because Cormac had the brains and ability to make a few cute moves, when all I could do was scrub the shite off the mattress my mother couldn't bring herself to touch. 'You're bluffing. Out with it, Ned, you liar. Call.'

The Chief straightened up a bit to watch and Nóra turned down the dire squirrel poetry on the radio. Cormac's disposition changed so quickly, I couldn't read it at the time, but now I know what had been the machinations of his mind. He burnt a card and lingered before turning the last card: the river. A three of diamonds. He didn't get his ace. His shoulders dropped.

I turned my cards over. 'Three kings, with the pair of threes on the table. Full house!'

'He has you bet,' the Chief announced, looking over Cormac's shoulder at his hand. His breathing loudened as he tongued the tooth that was bothering him, and the sound was like a gale trying to get through a millimetre gap in a window. I didn't even let slip a smile. Deep down, I felt improved, bolstered, but I didn't think it right to gloat the rare triumph over my brother, for what I would have been hailing along with it.

Cormac turned his cards face down on the table, placed his hands on his knees—fingers turned inwards so he made a kind of box of himself—and shook his head. 'You were *that* sure I was bluffing, you wouldn't even bother milking me on the last bet?'

'Not necessarily,' I said. 'You were chancing your arm on the river to make your straight … or you were bluffing all along … or you'd pocket aces and couldn't see past them to accept they were the lesser hand.'

'A chancer, a con artist or a cunt, is it? That's how you see your big brother?'

Nóra intoned 'God forgive us' from the kitchen, staring up at the framed Sacred Heart on the cabinet. She wore yellow rubber gloves.

'Sorry,' Cormac said.

'Don't be sorry,' I said. 'It's normal to get caught up in your own hand and not be mindful of other people's circumstances. That happens in cards as in life.'

'Right you are, Spuds. But sure, no one'd *blame* you for it, living with the auls till you're twenty-five.' He spoke with luxurious compassion, turning the sterling silver Ts of his cufflinks to pull them out. 'Sure, how could you be expected to know how other people play, when your life's been so blinkered the only thing you know—and know too well—is your own hand.'

Beneath the surface of my brother's glassy expression was a smirk like a large trout that might surface fleetingly for a hatch of mayflies. Even if it didn't, you could tell it was there all along: a dark, slithering scorn, full of small bones that somebody, someday, would swallow.

'Amn't I after saying he has you bet, Hart,' the Chief said, putting his Guinness can down on the couch, where it toppled and spilled. I watched it slopping out thickly. The laboured breathing was the only sound for a long moment. Blasé, Cormac set his cufflinks on the tabletop, then turned his cards. A three of clubs. A three of hearts.

He leaned into me. 'Four of a kind, would you call us? Until tomorrow anyways. Then we'll only be three, and the lesser for it.'

I could feel the pH level of my blood rise like soil with too much lime or wood ash or poultry manure that can afflict the whole season's yield with common scab. His hazel-yellow eyes necrotic in the half-light, Cormac added: 'Here, I'll send you a link to a grant you can apply for. They're giving out eight hundred and fifty euro towards funeral costs. There's a truckload of form-filling, but it might be the ticket back into Mam's good books.'

I did not lay into my brother's peninsular jaw. Instead, I lifted the table with a kind of horsepower that can't be earned through chin-ups or bicycle crunches or burpies in front of a mirror, but by succouring the fifteen stone of a dying parent and steering rust-heavy machinery in lines-without-end-amen. I let the table drop to the ground, so the glass top shattered. Nóra let out a banshee's scream at the bust table and her lock-horned sons, which set in gushing motion the Chief's bowels like the spilled Guinness by his lap. She exited the mobile home for the first time since we'd arrived, clad in rubber gloves. God knows what the fresh air might disturb in her, I thought: a gale sent into a catacomb. The Chief's guts went off again. A glugging sound. A film of sweat had formed on his paled skin, so he might have been a glass of milk taken out of a fridge. But it was hot in the caravan. It was stifling. Cormac stood up—shoes crunching on the glass. 'I'll go after her,' he said, hesitating for approval.

'Do that.' The Chief nodded. 'But can someone help me to the toilet first.'

Cormac was in such a rush, he left the door swinging. The cold draught signalled night-time. Relief.

'I might shower, too, if you don't mind,' the Chief said, dragging on my elbow. 'Save us doing it in the morning.'

'Are you sure, Dad?' I said, uncertain I could manage it. 'Isn't it a bit late?'

'Do you think?' He gave me the most fretful look.

I might have managed it with less trouble had Cormac resigned to witnessing it, just once—this one small sacrament of my adult life; if he'd stayed in the adjacent room, even, to hear a brief section of the coda—the primal, clattering finale—rather than stepping in when it was all over for the weepy ovation. But, of course … 'No. No, you're right. We should get you scrubbed up, so you're not mistaken for a pagan tomorrow. Wherever it is you're going.'

28.

The only holidays we'd gone on as a family were Christmases at relatives' homes or bank holidays exploring the surrounding parishes' callows and eskers and boglands. We revelled in the region's quantity of kills: Kilbride, Kilbryan, Kilcolagh, Kilcolman, Kilcooley, Kilcorkey, Kilgefin, Kilglass, Kilkeevin, Killinvoy, Killukin, Killummod, Kilmascumsy, Kilmeane, Kilmore, Kilnamanagh, Kilronan, Kilteevan, Kiltoom, Kiltrustan, Kiltullagh. There was the rare time the three of us would go fishing in the Suck—a tributary of the Shannon. It seemed the Chief was trying to find me a healthy pastime. Maybe he thought the river's unstoppable movement would inspire calmness, in the way you had to be resigned to it. He would sit patient as the moon in his collapsible chair, rising only to pull Cormac's fish hook out of my cheek or to rub night crawlers out of Cormac's hair or to knock our heads together, which was always a kind of relief. It gave us licence to leave one another alone for five minutes.

One Easter, we climbed the 850 feet (Cormac counted) of Slieve Bawn to the tune of the Chief's sermon on the Composition of Connaught, Oliver Cromwell, the penal laws, the land acts and all that developmental malarkey. 'Point out to me MacDermott county,

Cormac.' Shane tagged along with us on that one, so Cormac had carefully calculated the hero-worshipping a clip on the ear would earn him. 'Did they have penal laws in MacDermott county too, Dad, or were the MacDermotts allowed to grow their penises however long they'd go? Ow!' But a bit of elevation from the water meadows' slop was all the Chief needed to feel the buoyancy of our self-governance, seven hundred years in the making. That day was the closest he ever came to the surface of himself. Nóra was with us for that one—climbed the whole thing keenly in her Mary Hick dress and wellies. Us boys were goggle-eyed at her exultant perspiration. We didn't know our mother could climb a hill. We'd rarely seen her beyond the periphery of the farm, never mind the county.

She did come with us to Strokestown regular, where all the shops would be closed for lunch, so we'd visit the Famine Museum again and be made to think about the farmer feeding his entire family for a year on a quarter hectare of potatoes. 'He'd *have* to,' the Chief pulled Cormac up on his scepticism, 'because half the tenant farms in the 1840s were between two and six hectares in size. Minuscule ... No, Cormac. Potatoes were the highest calories per acre could be harvested ... No. The acreage was too small for diversity. Stock farming wasn't viable. The monoculture was a trap, leaving us exposed to the brown leaf spot, late blight fungus, mosaic, southern wilt, common scab, halo blight, the black dot ... Not pirates, Cormac. I think we've had our fill of your cuteness. The pictures aren't altered and the Holocaust isn't a hoax ... The *murdered millions* are the evidence ... My own grandfather ... "Oh" is right.'

You'd never see Nóra glowing like she did then: her sharp son endeavouring to outsmart her experienced husband. She scanned the museum to see who might have heard. 'You might look into lawyering, Cormac, with the cross-examining you're practising on your father. And *you* could give up the farm and go school-mastering, certainly,' she told the Chief.

'Ah, it's only local history I've a grasp of. And maybe a bit of bookkeeping. But I've no head for triggernomethry or geography, or crowd management, as it often comes down to in schools.'

'*Tá an Ghaeilge agat freisin.*'

'Not the way my parents had it. Much good it did them. I wouldn't do the language justice.'

'Stoppit.'

'Doharty hasn't said a word of conspiracy about the famine. Are you examining them well-fed crows?' the Chief asked me.

'They only had ta follow a starved kid along the road till he tripped.' Cormac clicked his fingers. 'Supper!'

'*Don't,*' Nóra said.

'Why have worms when you can have intestines!' Cormac said and gut-punched me.

'I said *don't* make him *cry.*' Nóra pulled Cormac back from me, but I wonder was it only to protect herself from my waterworks. I wonder was she afraid of water altogether.

It was the oil-black plumage of the taxidermied crow that had caught my eye. Like the pelt of the Labrador that was always tied up outside Paddy Power bookies on the weekend, made shiny by the cosseting of passers-by. Like Shane's hair coagulated with Brylcreem. Something in the guise of the crow captured my imagination.

'Do! Do make him cry!' Cormac said.

'He'll not cry,' the Chief said. 'He'll go home with a new appreciation of his health and fortune. Won't you, Hart?' The way the Chief said it made me think that I would.

So we never went far afield in the early years, when we could afford decent holidays. Then we went a very long way downhill. The Chief sickened, the weather burst open its bubbles, the purse strings had to make do as shoelaces, the hysterectomy tied its knot in Nóra's psyche—not that we knew—and Cormac and I became dangerous magnets that needed to be kept at a certain distance. Until the weekend of the mobile home and the signs nailed onto fences that read 'Beaware off Bull' and the tarpaulin of hardy sea that unrolled all the way to America. Cormac photographed that sign with the Hereford bull behind it and the drooping power lines thick with swallows. He photographed it on his phone for evidence of his diametrical opposition to it all. The sea wasn't calculable enough. The infrastructure wasn't wireless. The oxen were ungrammatically signposted. He could manage patricide after breakfast. Crispy sage potatoes with fried eggs, he cooked.

Nóra had been sitting in the car beside the mobile home, all packed up since dawn. I suppose I should've known she wouldn't take the ocean casually. All that about holidays was to say I don't know if she'd ever seen the ocean until that day in Connemara before the Chief died.

I got up in the middle of the night to piss—the poker hangover had me acid-tummied—but I didn't want to use the small plastic toilet the Chief had polluted. I pinned my ears for any animal sounds before braving the beach. My skin froze to my bones for the sky had come cloudless and my sight sharpened to take in as wide an arena of stars as I'd ever seen. Zillions of stars and satellites and asteroids like a load of pebbles cast into a lake to skim. For certain there weren't daffodils along the road, but there was that vast province of stars the Chief could've described intimately as the trees around our house. Maybe I should have swaddled him and let him sleep out under them.

Because the sky was flaunting magnificent as that, it took a minute for my eyes to come down to the level of the beach, to make her out. Nóra. There she was by the tideline, stooped over. The marram grass would have to do for a urinal. I didn't have room for another bitter word or thought or confrontation. But then I saw the bin liner and the yellow rubber of her gloves: she was bent forward, inching along the shore like a beachcomber. Except she wasn't searching for shells or by-the-wind sailors or sheep's wool sponges or driftwood. She was gathering seaweed, wrack by wrack, and throwing the brown, soggy mops into a bin bag. She recoiled from the sand hoppers that plumed from each fresh hulk, but she didn't stop to catch her breath. Up and down she went along the drift line like the Stations of the Cross, genuflecting diligently, tidying up.

Later, though the curtains were drawn, I could see the night was nearly lifted. I wanted sleep so rapaciously, I must have put her off. Hot-eyed, I went out to the grass again to let the cold dew pluck at my calves. The cows must've been sleeping still, all faced in the same direction, as they do, for no lowing countered the sighing, capitulating tide. I pissed under a sign for sea borne activities: *Safe swimming, sea angling, scuba diving, windsurfing, boating, and the famous 'drift dive'*. The latter involved volunteering your snorkel-fitted body to the sea and letting it pull you along an estuary. Those weren't activities for Irish tourists. They were for Greeks and Germans and Norwegians who could look at the sea and see something other than a baptism or a urinal. But maybe I could surprise myself. A dunk in the sea would give me the anaesthesia needed for the day, maybe. So I waded through the marram and climbed over the fence, and there they were: the conspicuous half-dozen bin liners stuffed to their brims, lined up by the rocks. The tide was very far out. Stood at its rim, Nóra clutched her arms across her chest, facing the beach, towards me. I don't think she was looking at me, haunted as she was by the mess of fresh brown gulfweed the night sea had coughed up.

Did she think there was no more where that came from? Did she think she'd got all of it?

29.

'Does it not take a long time ... for it to burn?'

'Ah no, we're well used to it. And there's not so much wood

used these days. We've all types. Bamboo, wicker, papier mâché, cardboard—'

'A cardboard coffin?'

"'Tis cheap and effective in the crematorium.'

'Well, even if it is, I don't think we could go with cardboard. It wouldn't sit well ... My mother, she's—'

'Ah no, she mightn't like that in the slightest. That'd only shift the connishurers' jaws. Tell me this: are ye primarily motivated by cost, would ye say? Or was your father, rest his soul, heedful of environmental factors?'

The mouthpiece crackled. 'The environment, yeah. He care—'

'Good on him. Good man. No doubt, he was.'

'If we went with wicker ...'

'Wicker's the stuff! Same as Saint Bridget's crosses. 'Twill cost you in the region of fourteen hundred bob or thereabouts. Cheaper than the traditional oak coffins, like, by a long shot.'

'Is it?'

'Chalk it down, boy.' He had a see-sawing Cork accent. 'Who am I speaking with, at the minute?' A pen clicked.

'I'm still unclear on how this works. Who else do I call? Or do you do it all? Do I pay you for everything? How do we get ... the body down to you?'

'Could I ask you at all: is he dead yet?'

'Excuse me?'

'You'll save on transport costs if he dies nearby. If not, we'll organise a hearse and movers.' I couldn't get a sound past the blockage in my throat, but the man kept talking. 'The costs are split 'twixt director's charges—the coffin, embalming, removal, hearse and other transport—and disbursements that cover the grave purchase, its opening, cremation fees, newspaper announcements and flowers. Though there's savings to be had there, if you're doing your own announcements, like, and pulling flowers from the garden. Or the neighbour's garden! If there's ever a time they'll forgive ye ... So, besides the plot itself, the coffin and headstone would be the biggest costs, but if you can call into us this week, or you could browse our website online—'

'We have the plot bought.'

'Have ye the stone?'

'No. Just something plain will do.'

'Why wouldn't it. His name's his name, whatever it's writ on. I'll tell you, we've a headstone supplier doing terrific trade at the minute. Lovely plain granite slabs going half price, if you're happy to have the stonecutter's contact details engraved in the corner.'

The sentence went up at the end. All of the sentences went up.

30.

The Chief had wanted to put a few things in writing. It'd been two hours since we'd returned from Connemara. Cormac was doing Sudoku puzzles at the kitchen table. He'd crushed the biro's plastic casing and was chewing on the end of the ink barrel. I didn't mention the blue stain on his lips, half wondering if it'd turn up on Nóra's tight mouth later, the way they coddled each other. I'd spent an hour cramming morphine overdose scenarios and tablet info stickers into my brain, and another hour pretending to read a page of the newspaper the Chief had set aside for me, about the IFA National Potato Committee chairman saying that potato growers are facing wipeout if a viable price isn't achieved. 'Prices to producers are at historical lows, running well below the cost of production on all potatoes sold.' Historical lows for the crop and the cattle. Historical low-low-lowing.

The doorbell rang. Cormac and I stood and eyeballed each other. The only visitor we'd get on a Monday would be Gerry, but he'd be managing contractors for the oats and oilseed rape tillage

and busy with cows raring for calving. Or it could be Pat and Frank
Lally from down the road, who had a load of tradition about them
except the Monday to Friday one. Knowing it wasn't snobbery
kept the Chief from the local, they'd want his ear on Dysart parish
matters now and then. From Nóra's discomfiture when their grimy
faces showed, I wouldn't put it past him to top up their dole if they
were in a bad way.

'Mrs Black, how are you?'

Father Shaughnessy! I recognised his voice.

'If it's the man of the house you're after, I'm afraid he's resting.'
Nóra was smooth as a Hunky Dory crisp in her small talk.

'Of course he is. Abiding the Sabbath all the way to Monday.'

'Was there something I could do for you, Father?'

'It's what I can do for you that I'm here for.'

Seeing that a cup of tea wasn't forthcoming, he pressed: 'I
wanted to offer home visits to Mr Black, so he might make his
confession from the comfort of his home. I noticed him struggling
in the pew yesterday, and I thought he'd want to know home visits
are an option. There's what we call "just cause" in his case. I'd be
happy to come on Saturday mornings, after the first service.'

Nóra had stiffened as if all of the potatoes consumed over the
years had suddenly exuded their starch. The 'aren't you very good'
was markedly absent. Cormac knew it and bounded out before I
could wrestle him back. He shut the living room door firmly as he
passed in the hallway, cutting off a feeble whistle blow from the
study.

'Father Shocks! Well?' He'd've shook hands across the threshold.

'The fighting full back, Cormac Black. I saw you propel the
sliotar a hundred miles per hour the length of the pitch against
Gort not long ago.'

'You didn't see me hit it the hundred and forty metres to make
the goal against Galway?'

'Against Galway, no less! I did not. I missed that. You'll be in the Provincial Championships next month?'

'Eh ... the verdict is a one-man army can't defeat a county.'

'Well, don't be discouraged. Are you keeping busy besides?'

Nóra couldn't help herself: 'Didn't you hear him on Shannonside last week, Father? Talking on the radio.'

'If I'd known, Nóra, not only would I have tuned in, I'd have strapped the radio to the pulpit microphone. Tell me, what procla-mation were you making?'

'I was being interviewed, so I was.'

'Fair dues. About the hurling or the engineering?'

'Would you take a cup of tea, Father?' Nóra blurted out finally. The thought of Cormac's interview being broadcast to the congre-gation had overwhelmed any fear that our plans to assist a suicide before lunchtime would be made known to a representative of God. I scooped the medication off the table and dumped it in the cutlery drawer. There was no legging it. The kitchen door was open, so he'd have seen me escape.

'To hear tell of this interview, I might take the cup of tea, Nóra, thank you.'

'Let me have your coat, so.'

'It was about one of the start-ups I founded,' Cormac said. 'They wanted to hear tell of innovation coming out of the downturn. Creative thinking and all that, making something out of nothing. Sure, you'd know that, with Jesus ... and his loaves and fishes.'

I imagined the owl face the priest sometimes pulled, with the black close-set eyes and the forehead lines making Vs like migrating geese. Nóra spoke quickly so that what Cormac had said wouldn't be dwelt on. 'You must be sick and tired of the recession, Father.' She was putting the coat in the closet under the stairs.

'I am and I amn't! The rainy days are great days for masses.'

'They would be.'

'Sure, once a country's gone belly-up, the next thing is to kneel down,' Cormac said. 'That's how we do church, isn't it?'

'Cormac Ionatán Black!' The Irish version of 'Jonathan' was for the priest's benefit. Meaning 'God's gift'. She sham-admonished her way to the kitchen.

'No, no, he's right. When the petrol runs out on the leased Mercedes-Benz, it's the church pews that get filled up. When half-built shells of holiday homes threaten to fossilise ...' Father Shaughnessy paused in his speech to give me a nod as he followed her into the kitchen, then carried on, '... it's the homily that's sweet music to the ears. When the pyjama suit is turned away at the disco door, the wearer knows that the Lord doesn't distinguish Prada from Penneys from Salvation Army handouts, and they appreciate being welcomed and warmed by the Catholic community.'

'They would,' Nóra said—the *they* resounding.

I kept my hands on the keyboard of the laptop. Father Shaughnessy brushed his gaze over his audience members equally. '"Donor fatigue" is what the charities call it. We've to be very mindful of that. To treat each confession with gravity and to deliver and beseech support with a fervency worthy of the plight, no matter how often that means repeating ourselves.'

'Oh,' Nóra inhaled, humbly absorbing the word 'fervency' and letting it do its work on her, like white vinegar on the unseen grime of a range hood. He accommodated modernity better than most. Her long lashes pressed against her eyebrows, her eyes were that wide.

'Doharty, isn't it?' Father Shaughnessy addressed me, pulling out a chair at the far end of the table. Nóra busied herself with the tea and Cormac reclined against the kitchen sink behind me, arms berthed. I glanced at him to go in and silence the Chief, whose whistling was starting up.

'You've a good memory, Father,' I said.

'Oh, I remember you well. I remember you especially, because of one time in the confessional.'

I could sense Nóra pin her ears back, squeezing the life out of the single teabag firstly in the priest's cup, secondly in Cormac's, thirdly in her own.

'Would you take a bit of sugar, Father?'

'A spoonful only. Is there something whistling, or is it a ringing in my ears from too much proselytisation?'

That was the first time a six-syllabled word had been uttered in the house. I quickly typed it into the keyboard for making sense of later. 'Bedad!' he said. 'There it is again!'

'It'll be the TV inside,' Cormac said. 'I'll get it. But tell me first, what did Doharty say that time in the confessional that was so unforgettable?' He sauntered hallward.

'You'd be looking for one up on your brother to this day, would you, Cormac?' Father Shaughnessy cocked his chin to loosen his collar.

''Twas probably the time Hart threw our cousin out the window and broke his arm just for calling him a girleen? But he did his penance there, a summer spent sorting through vines and clods and waste on the back of the harvester, and was forgiven.' He grinned and left.

I straightened my arm so that it clacked at the elbow, where it had fractured. Cormac had recast the story.

The priest leaned into me: 'You won't mind me saying ...'

'Will I not?'

Nóra gasped.

'No, I don't think you will—'

'I might, Father. I might mind.' I gave him a sharp look and did him the favour of leading the conversation elsewhere. 'I can tell you now, on his behalf, that our father won't need weekly confessions. Not that he's ever committed anything you could call a sin, but he certainly isn't committing them from his bedstead.'

Father Shaughnessy blew his tea at length, watching the ripples he set off in the cup. After quite a silence (the whistling from the study had stopped too), he said: 'We all have our bindle sticks of wrongdoing we carry around with us, Doharty.'

I looked up at the clock above the radio: 11.55 a.m. My computer screen said twelve. Once the clock caught up, Nóra would turn on the radio for the Angelus and we'd have to sit through it with Father Shaughnessy's muttered oaths adding credence to our light-weight souls. Nóra's mouth was twitching with unformed wisdoms. Father Shaughnessy looked out the kitchen window at the gruel-dreary day. Then he turned back to me and stared. Nóra hadn't taken a sup of her tea but wrung her hands around the cup so that the sores cracked and bled. Cormac was back at the door, to her rescue: 'Well, I'm glad to see the clergy out and about, offering the old-style "knock on the door" for the locals. For some of them, it's the only knock they'd get, so it is.'

'I'm afraid to say you're right there, Cormac.' Father Shaughnessy dropped his gaze from me.

'Oh yes! Certainly,' Nóra said, with new zeal. 'We need to see more priests, nuns and monks walking among us and bringing Christ to the godless masses again.' She caught her breath and waited for a hum of approval. 'A few habits in sight keeps a community civilised.'

'Right you are, Mrs Black. There's something to be said for the rectoral garb. Collar, cassock and fascia,' Father Shaughnessy said, getting up.

'An S&M kit, if there ever was one.' Cormac slid into his seat.

'What's that?' Father Shaughnessy asked.

'If the costume fits …' Cormac said loudly. He took a slurp of tea.

Father Shaughnessy nodded slowly. 'There was a day you might've wanted it to fit, Cormac. There was a day in Scoil Náisiúnta Naomh Seosamh, after a practice run for the First Confession, you approached me about your brother's arm—not your cousin's—and the accident. He'd be missing from class and would I say a prayer for him. And you had a question for me too: could you be an altar boy.'

I looked at Cormac, who'd gone a bit lobster. Father Shaughnessy continued: 'But I wasn't sure if you were asking for the right reasons. Some boys want to do it for the bit of an audience. The showmanship. Or even to carry out some wily prank on the congregation, innocuous really. I wasn't sure of your reasons, so I left you to follow it up. You never did.'

Cormac took a loud sup of tea and gave the priest a baffled look, with his blue-stained lip. 'You've me mixed up with some culchie.'

'No—'

'Ah yeah, you have. Sure, young boys all look the same to priests.'

Nóra cleared her throat. 'I'm sorry, Father, but I've *just* had a delivery of a dozen day-old chicks and I should have them out of the box after their journey. I've been waylaid with this, that and the other ...' She attempted to usher him out timidly, but any words she uttered—no matter how mundane she laboured to make them—he saw as offerings it was his duty to celebrate and multiply.

'Waylaid! Very good. You're a hoot. It's where the boys get their humour. One final thing now, between ourselves, Nóra, before I go ...' He popped his head back into the kitchen. '*Beannacht libh*, Cormac and Doharty. I hope to see you soon.'

'Goodbye, Father,' I said.

Cormac said, 'Cheers.'

Father Shaughnessy continued talking to Nóra in the hallway as he put on his coat. 'I wanted to mention that the generous donation Mr Black left yesterday didn't go unnoticed or unappreciated.'

'Just a *token*,' Nóra said. I heard a splash of water from Mary and Joseph's interlocked porcelain arms by the door.

'Tokens like that could buy entrance to Heaven!'

Nóra made a sound like a cat birthing.

'I'm joking, of course. Give my blessings to Mr Black, and to all. Next time it could be I'll catch him awake?'

'Well. He could phone you if he needs you.'

'Next Saturday would be no trouble. Run it past him, will you?'

'*Slán leat.*'

When the door had shut and Father Shaughnessy's Ford Fiesta had eased down the drive, Cormac went to the cutlery drawer where he'd spotted the medicine bag sticking out and brought it to the table. He upended it so the brown plastic pill bottles rolled out. He cracked each one in his palm like the biro casing so the tablets spilled all over the tabletop. Next, he rummaged in the cupboard for a mortar and pestle. I separated the tablets from the plastic shards. The grinding began. Cormac's chin-ups made light work of milling the pills to unadulterated powder, giving off a pall like incense smoke from the spectral thurible the priest had left in his wake.

31.

The Chief soon took up his exasperating whistling again. *Whewwww.* Cormac and Nóra exchanged looks over their mugs of tea.

'You'd make a shite altar boy,' I told him, going to the medicine cabinet. 'You're supposed to *do something* when the bell is ringing.'

'Kneel down, is it? Or turn around?' Cormac said. 'You'd know, sure.' Nóra pretended not to understand.

When I got to the study, the Chief was red in the face. We were cruel not to have bought him a bell. 'Isn't that what the mobile phone is for, if he can't manage the whistle?' Nóra had said in defence. The Chief was holding his cheek where his tooth had been aching. I was bringing him the Aprepitant anti-nausea pill, a 125-milligram capsule Cormac had procured from some poor sod undergoing chemotherapy. The Chief took his hand away from his cheek to take the pill, revealing a shiny pink swelling along the jaw, halfway between his chin and ear.

'Ah, Dad, have you … a … what's it? Abyss?'

'Abscess? I think I might. But what harm can it do me now?' He threw the pill in his mouth and swallowed it with a slug of Guinness, baring his yellow teeth. He panted from the effort. 'Sit yourself down.' One of the kitchen chairs had been brought into the study so that Nóra could sit during the administering. Cormac and I would stand. The Chief had a folder in front of him that suggested closure.

'I've appointed you executor of the will,' he said, looking up. There was a vigilance to his eyes I hadn't seen for months and months, not since he slept in his marriage bed. 'Your mother will be in no state for arranging anything and your brother has work, so I'm asking you.' He handed me a printout from the internet with the receipt for the purchase of an online legal will for €34.95. The sheet was a checklist of the executor's tasks, which I scanned:

- *Notify family, friends, colleagues and associates of death and funeral schedules*
- *Obtain a medical certificate indicating cause of death*
- *Register the death at the local Registry of Births, Deaths and Marriages*
- *Get disposal certificate from the Registrar*
- *Make copies of last original will for banks, Inland Revenue, beneficiaries, etc.*
- *Pay inheritance tax, if applicable*
- *Contact local Probate Registry to obtain your grant of probate*
- *Draw up accounts providing details of estate division. Gather documents relevant to the will and compile a list of assets, debts and liabilities. Debts and liabilities should be paid off, and funeral expenses should be subtracted. The remainder can be distributed accordingly. An income tax form must be completed for the deceased.*

(Beside this point, the Chief had scribbled: *Cormac to arrange. Call Donal for help.*)

- *Make funeral arrangements*
- *Notify all businesses (utilities, banks, building societies, brokerage and mutual fund accounts, social security and tax office)*
- *Distribute the contents of the will, including pecuniary, specific gifts and legacies and the distribution of the residue*

'I thought you'd all this organised already, with Mam.'

'We've the estate and finances largely tied up. We had advice on that long ago. And the paperwork, deeds, title to the house and car is all arranged. I won't go into it now. The facts won't improve for tidying them. 'Tis a far cry from the will I spent my life bedding, but.'

'Don't start that, Dad.'

'Inheritance tax won't be a burden for my children, is all I'll say. That's the small favour I done ye.'

I couldn't sigh away the tightness in my chest. 'Was Cormac involved in this?'

The swivel chair complained less than it once would have under the Chief's weight. Although he was a shadow of his healthy self, sitting opposite him, I felt I was looking up. The stack of papers and folders between us were like a cinema ticket counter—me trying to stand casual at the Cineplex kiosk of a Friday night, playing tired from scholarship and sportsmanship like my brother. I remember jutting out my chin, but the demand was inevitable: 'ID.'

'Doharty, you'll be your own man from this day on. Not your father's helper or your brother's lesser. We've put together a small sum for your college education so you might have a shot at—'

'What? I'm twenty-five, Dad. I'll not go to college. I didn't even—'

'You might.'

'I won't. I want to *do* something with my life.'

'You'll have the choice either way. I'm your father and I'm saying you'll have the choice if it's the last thing I see to.'

The tightness worsened. 'Is that everything, then? I'm executor because Cormac's busy, and you've deprived yourself of proper healthcare and retirement so I can go to college?'

The Chief tongued his sore tooth and his wheezing loudened through the gap in his dry lips. 'That's the talk gives Doharty reason to call you simple.'

'I'm Doharty, Dad!' My throat might have discovered some sudden allergy. I was so angry I could barely breathe.

The Chief shook his large head—the only part of him the recession couldn't shrink. Maybe the skin was finer—more like a crumpled tissue than a cardboard box left out in the rain, as it once was—but the skull was formidable. 'One day you'll realise,' he said, breathing invisible grains, 'that your brother wants the best for you. To see you out and about. Tourism might suit you, he says, with your desire to travel. It's not just women do tourism these days, he says. You'd be your own man.'

A rush of movement drew my attention to the two black rock roosters waging war out the window. One bullied the other across the back garden, the victim cock turning to flap his useless wings in defence. Their green-black feathers blended into golden necks, as if in imitation of the coniferous trees behind them, drying out for the autumn. Their fleshy red combs and wattles like Mohawks and sideburns wobbled as they circled one another, occasionally bumping chests. Nóra must've had that pair four or five years, and they fighting still. Hens clucked noisily from the run, maybe enjoying the show.

'Settling flock dominance,' the Chief commented. I hadn't realised he was watching.

'Settling the pecking order,' I improved his comment. If it was

Cormac that said it, the Chief would've had to acknowledge the joke.

'One of these days, they'll fight to the death,' the Chief said.

'D'you think? After all this time?'

We were watching them pecking and flapping and kicking for a while before Nóra arrived on the scene. 'Oh. Here she comes,' the Chief said. 'They're in for it now.'

Heedless of her audience, she marched to the coop and run, where she put down a metal bucket and took a length of twine from it. Then she fished out a hammer and a large nail, which she drove into the side of the coop, about head height. The sight of her eczema'd hands working the rough twine around the nail and fashioning a clove hitch knot was at once impressive and repulsive. The hands needed cream and care, but they'd get neither. She wore a plastic apron over the funeral frock she had on still from the drive (with all the buttons up the front and wrists and the accordion skirt), and the yellowish skin of her face and neck ruddied in the fresh air. When the twine was knotted to the nail and draped down a foot on either side, Nóra set the bucket directly beneath it, then she looked at the fighting cockerels who had danced to the left, not quite beyond our view.

'That's how they're alive up till now,' the Chief said, 'thanks to herself prying them apart.'

The chest tightened further in anticipation. Somehow I knew that this mindless aggression would not be allowed to play out any longer. With certitude, Nóra seized the bigger of the two cocks, carried him to the coop, hunkered down and wedged his beetle-green body between her skirted knees, straightened his golden neck like a ribbon with one hand and, with the other, drew the kitchen knife from the bucket. She piloted the blade through the bird's neck and out the other side—as if the spine was a flower stem. She strung its twiggy talons together and hung the headless carcass upside down to bleed out before the plucking. She threw the knife into the bucket and pulled up a clump of grass to wipe the gore from her hands. After undoing the tie at her lower back, she lifted the apron over her head—careful not to pull on her tightly-pinned bun—and folded it into a neat square.

The Chief seemed to struggle for air through all the gristle of his lungs and trachea—as though it too had been cut into, if not clean through. 'Hart ... Do me a favour, please, and change the bulb in that light once and for all.' He shielded his eyes from the ceiling light. 'It's been flickering like that all morning. 'Twould drive a body up the wall. I don't know how I'll manage to go out to that blinking.' The Chief looked at his knees: not wanting to see any more of the ceiling light, which was off, or the window out to his future, or the stacks of folders on the table, which were as final as they come. Dandruff fell from his ruddy-grey hair. I got up before he could ask was it snowing.

'I'm glad we talked, son. It's a grand auld time we've had, would you say? Like Séamus and the leveret. It's as good a time as any, now, to ...' He made a gentle jabbing motion with his finger, as if to press the Enter key, or Return.

I looked out the window again at the strung cock. Nóra was nowhere to be seen. I drew the curtains shut. The tension in my chest reached a point where it could be squeezed no further without snapping. 'Is that what you want, Dad?'

He looked up at me and held out his hands until I gave him one of mine, which he clutched. He shook it and kissed it with his thick, dry lips. 'You'll be your own man before long. Bring them in now and let's get it past us.'

The tightness did snap then, and I fell apart. 'So I can go to college and become a tour guide for the Potato Museum?'

The Chief smiled widely and shook my hand even more surely with both of his fists. 'Precisely that.'

32.

It went as I'd imagined it would go in the dreams and night-mares I'd had in the weeks leading up to it. Strange and clinical, sickening and snagging. Even though he wasn't lying down, it felt like a hospice—like we were standing awkward around his deathbed, talking grapes and air-conditioning. There was the same manoeuvring of conversation to keep the patient distanced enough from the fact of his being the only one in the room to wear a nappy; that if he doesn't eat his supper gladly, it'll be spoon-fed to him.

Nóra was seated at the desk, clinging to her moulting tissue and some script, but she wasn't really present. She'd left her valour beyond at the coast in the bin liners of seaweed. All she had left for that day was the cold ink countersignature. And I suppose I accepted that. It was a horrible thing, the lot of it. I forgave her absence as self-preservation. I even forgave her the savagery with the cock. She wasn't to know of her audience.

Cormac, who had mercifully changed out of his suit into jeans and a casual shirt, stood behind her with his hand on her shoulder. I could tell she didn't want to be touched, not even by him, and that she was battling an urge to shake him off. I remember his frown: the little omega sign at the bridge of his nose, there to stay. But he wasn't red-eyed. He supervised me from a safe distance, demanding I verbalise my actions at every stage.

Several quiet minutes passed after the Chief had swallowed the cup of ground morphine powder mixed into soluble Oramorph. He chose to wash down the chalky paste with a pot of lukewarm tea. I could tell from his screwed lips that it tasted bitter as sloe. He suddenly sat upright and asked with hopeless urgency: 'What did the priest have to say about this?'

'Don't worry about that now,' I said. 'The priest can well under-stand unreasonable suffering.'

'It's not the priest I mean,' the Chief insisted. 'Cormac said he called this morning with the scriptures. Cormac told me. I forgot to ask ... what he'd found.' Tears welled in his eyes, from the lie. I gave him a look as sympathetic as I could manage, until he resigned with a small nod. He seemed childish almost with the lines of his face tented upwards, struggling to keep his eyes open. The bristled skin at his jowls dropped as though he was visibly disassembling before us. He'd shaved his own face to the end. It was a matter of dignity. But, taking in the patchwork of his cheeks, I regretted not offering to do it. His eyes closed, finally, and he seemed to have calmed.

I don't know why Cormac couldn't see that the job was done: that he would go quietly now, if he was let. But Cormac took a slip of paper from the table and began reciting biblical passages that sounded forgiving and loosely to do with illness and the taking of life. The words didn't sound made-up but they weren't on that piece of paper. I knew that sheet to be a farm lease form, signed sorely by the Chief in red biro. The land had been remortgaged, and when the payments weren't met the bank foreclosed on it and auctioned it off, so we had to lease it from its new owner. I hadn't known, until those last weeks. The sheet of paper was a prop. Cormac had learned the few lines for the occasion. He was rewarded by the Chief nodding gently, not opening his eyes.

'Thank you, Cormac.' Nóra glanced back to where he stood, plaque-chested.

'*Mo mhac cliste*,' the Chief croaked. My clever son.

Then his maracas quieted entirely. The ceiling light blinked and I cursed myself for not changing it, but the Chief's eyes stayed closed, thankfully. A few minutes came and went and it seemed that the Chief might have faded out as simply as that, like a song that has no great climax or clean cadence ending. Which suited him, I suppose, the lack of fuss. No sound of a gunshot. Aside from the unspeakable disgust I felt at the Chief's last words, it was undoubtedly the dream ending and not the collective nightmare. That was until a sweat broke out on his forehead and on the tight skin of his cheeks around his nose. Only I saw it at first. Nóra was keening within the bottle of herself and Cormac was, I think, flummoxed. The sweat was followed by a gurgling sound from the Chief's throat, then a small convulsion. I knew what was going to happen. My own stomach threatened to give out, but I turned to see if Nóra had noticed.

It might have been the flickering light, but she looked as pale yellow as buttermilk. 'Is it the tremors?' she asked. 'He gets those from the morphine.'

'No, Mam,' I said.

Her long eyelashes batted against her eyebrows in disbelief and a wail emerged from her chest, so that it was all Cormac could do to get her out of there before she would shatter. With one hand already on her shoulder, he put the other beneath her elbow and hurriedly pulled her up.

'Come on now, Mam. It's done.'

'Cormac!' I cried. *It's not!* I wanted to shout. The Chief's convulsing redoubled and I could feel the grave commotion of his lungs where my hand lay on his back. 'Cormac! Get me—'

As he led Nóra out of the room, fast as he could compel her to move, Cormac turned back and gave me the most warnsome look I'd ever seen, laying plain what it was I had to do, with my own bare hands. He pulled the door after them. I wept uncontrollably, standing behind my father.

'This is the worst bit,' I promised myself.

Later, when I was going upstairs to shower, Nóra passed me in the hallway. Cormac had driven off to buy her a mobile phone of her own. She'd changed from her funeral frock into trousers, a blouse and a buttoned cardigan. Colourful, almost. I watched her. She went to the study for the first time since, and I waited to see if she'd need collecting from the floor. She stood at the study doorway for a long moment, looking in—the way she had stood at the top of the beach the morning before, and it freshly littered with seaweed. She could tend to it, but the shame was all-pervading and unabsolvable. She pulled the study door firmly shut.

The next day, the funeral frock and the sheets from the downstairs bed were hanging on the line. Alongside them were half the contents of the Chief's wardrobe: trousers long gone at the knees, piled jumpers, the elbow-reinforced corduroy jacket Bridie'd bought him for his fiftieth.

Kitted out in gardening gloves, trousers and kneepads, Nóra spent the morning spreading chicken droppings onto the vegetable garden and pulling out rhubarb shoots she didn't like the look of, as if the time had come for small jobs that needed doing. Cormac had taken off after breakfast with an icebox, a *Cooking for Chickens* recipe book and our father's last words. He'd be back to visit at the weekend, if he could manage it at all, so he would.

It's Tuesday morning, I thought. I opened a bottle of spirits with my teeth. Where's that knife and bucket, till I cut off my … foul … these foul, disgusting … hands. That was the last coherent thought I had until the doorbell rang four days later.

33.

It rang three times at one-minute intervals. Nóra answered, rambling about manners. It was the first sound of the outside world I'd heard since Cormac's car had careered out the drive on Tuesday. I hadn't gone downstairs. I'd brought provisions to the bedroom with me the night of, though nothing had any taste or smell or feel, but the hard liquor and harder bread kept my head and stomach from hurting. They did fuck all for the heart. That incessant doorbell stirred some sensation in me though, so I staggered to the window and swung it wide open. My bedroom was almost directly above the front door, and it was a rainless, windless day, so I could hear their exchange clearly.

'We agreed I'd come for the house visit on Saturday,' Father Shaughnessy announced without a hello, 'and today's Saturday, if the reluctant faces of the morning congregation were anything to go by.' He was forcing friendliness.

'There was no agreement, Father,' Nóra said, soberly.

'Oh? Forgive me, I thought we'd it settled.'

A moment passed where a swallow making a nest in the eave drew attention to itself. I remembered the Chief asking me to string up some catgut to stop them making a mess of the front wall. If it was the rear wall, he might have left them at it, for the sake of their music. Remembering that made my eyes hot, and they had only cooled off hours before. This was why leaving the closed room was a problem: there were wells all over the place you could trip into. Bucketing up to consciousness was dangerous.

'Nóra, I don't like to be an imposition, but I owe Manus a Christian look-in.'

'I'm sorry, Father, but you must let him come to you in his own time. It's not good to be stirring him from his sleep, and it hard-won.'

'Tell me, is he very poorly?'

'He's all right.'

'Is he?'

'He'll manage.'

A silence.

'With the help of God,' Nóra added, to balance the atmosphere.

'Oh yes. Is it ...' Father Shaughnessy's voice diminished as he poked his head inside, sniffing. 'Have you something cooking? Or, is it ...'

'I'm cleaning,' Nóra said abruptly. 'I'm sorry, Father, to turn you away, but—'

'And how are the lads? Doharty and—?'

'You couldn't keep up with Cormac.'

'Very smart lad. And Doharty?'

'He does his bit.'

'Has he no woman to keep him honest?'

Nóra let out a whinge and I realised that it was because Father Shaughnessy had stepped inside. 'I'll just take a splash to keep myself honest, in lieu of the women!' I guessed he'd gone for a dip in Mary and Joseph's porcelain arms. It made me giddy, knowing how close that step inside for the holy water came to keeping us all honest.

'The lads might come along to the town hall tonight?' He was on the safe side of the threshold again. He seemed to be trying to pass off the sniffing as a cold.

'Why's that?' Nóra asked tightly.

'I'll have my silver jubilee this week, and they're throwing a little shindig.'

'Congratulations.'

'They want to present me with a trophy! D'you know the way they'd be going over the top?'

'It's deserv-ed. All the best for it now.' The door creaked.

'Right so. I'll leave you to it. You'll tell Mr Black I was after him, and to phone me as soon as it suits?'

34.

That Saturday night, Bridie rang relentlessly until Nóra picked up. (I was half drowned.) Bridie wanted to check was everything fine. They hadn't had any thanks for the loan of the mobile home. They were hoping to hear how it went: had the Chief managed to enjoy himself despite the pain and the loo you couldn't swing a cat in? Could she speak with Manus? Surely he could manage the phone. He seemed very morose the other day. Was it the terrors? The passive figures he mentioned? The passive figures who do lurk along with the morphine and who sometimes become hostile. Herself and Mitch had been very disturbed by that. Could she not speak with her brother?

Nóra disconnected the phone line.

35.

She was still wearing her knee pads and gardening gloves when we were arrested. 'Green-handed,' Cormac would've quipped if he was there, but he wasn't. I heard the patrol car sneaking up the drive, its siren off. It was a Sunday morning so it couldn't be the postman and it surely wasn't Cormac living up to his promise, coming to see how we'd coped with the week. Would he be in for a shock or did he know deep down what we'd done? That we *hadn't* coped. My scarce conscious moments I'd spent googling methods to off yourself. Samurai sword to the gut; lepping out of a hedge onto a motorway; asking Shane for a go of his motorbike. One night, I'd nearly died laughing from the thought of dressing up in a chicken suit and sitting in the coop and awaiting Nóra with her breadknife, bucket and twine.

I'd woken up in a cesspool of my own sick, so I'd showered for the first time since the trip to Connemara with Dolly. How all the fat crows in the sky hadn't descended around our roof was beyond me, we reeked that profoundly. Showering was a mistake. Half-clean, I was out of true with my environment.

It was ten or thereabouts when they arrived: a Lego-headed fella with hooded eyes, enjoying the baton swinging by his hip, and a disconsolate-looking middle-aged ban-garda with a few red highlights poking out under her cap and a large continuous bosom and stomach that was kept at bay by her anti-stab vest. Though it was autumn, clawing ten degrees outside, they were in their short-sleeved pale-blue shirts. Navy neckties. Little caps kept their heads toasty.

Looking out the window, I mistook Nóra for a scarecrow away off to the left: a particularly interesting scarecrow that some romantic agrarian had taken time over, to keep the scavengers away from our blighted potato farm. I watched her with drunken sympathy, half-remembering the story of a Japanese scarecrow deity. He couldn't walk, but he knew everything about the world. I couldn't recall much about him but that his name meant 'the disabled prince'. It was the Samurai sword I'd got for my fourteenth birthday that prompted me to read about things Japanese. When I was that age, I wanted nothing more than to travel to a country that had scarecrow gods. I wanted to live there. How could there be dogs or Tony Morrigans in such a country? It was sobering to see the scarecrow frantically pulling off her garden gloves to draw the new mobile phone from her pocket and dial for help. Her lips weren't made of straw. She didn't march on a peg but on two legs, all the way to the house to barricade our front door—her behaviour already incriminating. The ban-garda's hand hovered over her utility-belt radio as Nóra strode towards them, clutching her phone.

'Mrs Nóra Black?' The guard's voice was high-pitched for the breadth of his chest. 'I'm Inspector Adrian Mooney, this is my colleague Detective Sergeant Cliona McCarthy. We'd like to have a word with Mr Manus Black and yourself. Might we step in out of the cold?'

'That's already several words.'

'I suppose it is.'

'There's no supposing about a fact.'

The guard glanced at his colleague and said: 'Is Mr Black home at all?'

Detective McCarthy stepped forward and pressed the doorbell for several seconds, sending a current between my scalp and skull.

'What is it regarding?' Nóra asked.

'We'd prefer to speak with Mr Black,' Inspector Mooney said, somewhat softly.

'Wouldn't we all?' Nóra said.

Waves of nausea arrived along with each exchange, watching Nóra cling to the filament of hope that the problem of the Chief and her problems with the Lord might gently dissolve like quail's eggs in vinegar.

'What do you mean by that, Mrs Black? Nóra, if I might?'

'You mightn't.'

'Do you mean to say you haven't spoken to Mr Black recently?'

'I've work to be doing.'

'I understand. But if your husband's inside, we'll need to speak with him.' Inspector Mooney moved towards the front door.

'You'll need a warrant to step inside my house!' Nóra enunciated sharply, putting a halt to his movements. I was sweating and shivering. How long would this go on for? How long could we put up with it?

'We've received a call, Mrs Black,' Detective McCarthy took over, 'urging us to check on your husband.'

'You might check on your own husband,' Nóra said, eyeing the glinting gold band on Detective McCarthy's finger and following her gaze through to Inspector Mooney insinuatingly. She was using insolence for adrenaline.

'We're going to ask you one last time if Mr Manus Black is inside this house. If you don't answer, Inspector Mooney will wait here while I obtain a warrant to inspect the property.'

Nóra's hand was blue-white from holding the phone like an oar. If it was possible for a human being to implode, she would be the one to try it.

'He's in the study!' I called out.

The dark moons of the two gardaí caps became crescents suddenly, as they looked up. I knew they couldn't see me. I could barely make out Inspector Mooney's eyes for the brim of bone cloaking them. I could see McCarthy's, though. They were like my mother's eyes in her younger, questioning days.

'Please. Take him,' were the words that came from my mouth.

Nóra gasped when the garda lurched for the door handle. 'Don't open that door!' she shrieked, but it was no use. I learned later that as soon as they crossed the threshold and encountered the smell, instantly identifiable, they radioed for backup, forensics and a paddy wagon.

Lying on the carpet, the wide window finally giving me air, I held my wrists up to Detective McCarthy as she moved into my room, hand on baton. I was like my dribbling father the night I caught him in his dressing gown and boxers in the field, shooting down the scarecrow. I suppose I was crying. If I was, it was those silent outbursts babies have when something is uncommunicably wrong and can't be fixed by sleep or bottle. I'd tried both. She drew out the handcuffs.

'Doharty Aengus Black.'

I nodded.

'I'm arresting you under section four of the Criminal Justice Act of 1984——'

'What time is it?'

'Mr Black, you'll have to come with us now to the station. Do you want to put on trousers and a jumper or will the mat on your chest keep you snug?'

I hadn't put on any clothes after showering. No wonder I hadn't been able to stop shivering. She helped me to my feet. She didn't have much on five foot. I've always been afraid of small dogs, I said, unaware if I was speaking aloud. 'They've more to prove. I don't know enough people ... to know ... if they're the same.'

'I'll leave the handcuffs for a minute so you can dress yourself. Then we'll take you to the station and get you sobered up.'

'Have I a right to an attorney?'

'No,' she said. 'That's only in America.' I dropped the jumper because there wasn't any feeling in my hands. She picked it up and handed it to me, so a few strands of the red bob stuck to her cheek. 'In Ireland, we only have solicitors. Will that do you?'

'Will everything I say be used against me?'

'Come on now before you waste your story on an audience of one.' The tone of her voice was dismissive, but it was an act. Dolly would've known. Dolly would've stuck her belly out, tucked her chin in and mimicked it perfectly. I stepped onto a pair of old running shoes, flattening the heels.

'I don't want an audience.' I recall being very concerned about my lack of socks.

'By the looks of things downstairs, I'd say you'll get one.'

'It's Cormac likes an audience.'

'Is that so? And who's Cormac, when he's at home?'

'He's not … at home.'

'And who's he to you?'

'My brother.'

She took me by the elbow. 'We'll have a talk to him as well, so. See what we can muster up in the station for an audience. Superintendent Goulding has a soft spot for theatrics, Cormac may be glad to know.'

36.

Most likely they thought I was stunted: living at home at twenty-five, uneducated, feral. I'd been polluted drunk or hung-over to the point of a swollen tongue since I'd been arrested, so that didn't help my making of impressions.

Superintendent Goulding placed on the table a pen alongside two photographs: one of my bathtub still; the other of the bruising on the Chief's neck, zoomed-in enough to look like an abstract colour study. I knew it was the Chief's neck from the twine necklace for his whistle. Goulding's hooded blue eyes were sharp and solemn. He had side-swept silver hair and a thick moustache. Inspector Mooney sat on the seat to the side, his legs door frame-wide to compensate for his voice.

'Doharty Aengus Black. Dunmorris Road, Dysart, County Roscommon. Twenty-seventh of January, 1989.'

'Mr Black—'

'I'm Doharty. The Chief was Mr Black, and it feels … Can you say Hart? Please?'

Goulding broke his gaze for the first time to put pen to paper. 'Doharty Black. Can you confirm that our member in charge has explained to you what section of the Criminal Justice Act you're being detained under, and the reason for your arrest?' We went through the whole rigmarole—everything I told them was a correction.

'So you were planning on taking over the farm while your father was first sick. But plans changed when the bank foreclosed on the mortgage?'

'No, I never said I was *planning* on taking it over. I had the option, was the point.'

'How our young people hold dear their options! And tell me, would you have taken it?'

'No.'

'Why not?'

'Because I don't like physical labour. Because it'd remind me of my father. Because I'd be trying to fill his shoes and my feet'd only blister. Because one day I might want an education like my brother.

I'm scared of dogs. I can't abide my mother. I hate the smell of shite. I'm sick and tired of root vegetables. I'm too good-looking to be a farmer. I don't want to belong to a parish. The fields are full of crows and magpies and I have a thing about them birds. There's better-looking birds fly in from Mayo and Galway. I'd—'

'Take a good long sup of your tea, Doharty. Calm yourself. These are the easy questions. Relish them while the tea lasts.' The tea was Lyon's and not Barry's, which put me in mind of Dolly and her red silk mouth. 'When did you start to work on the farm?'

'I worked on it full-time since I left school.'

'What age were you?'

'Eighteen, nineteen.'

'When's the last time you worked on the farm?'

'Last Saturday. Before we went to Connemara.'

'From the age of eighteen to last Saturday, you've worked full-time on the farm?'

I shrugged.

'Seven years?'

'Not full-time, but yeah.'

'What do you do for money?'

'I'm on the scratch, since I left school.'

Whenever Goulding wrote something down, the dimple in his chin deepened. I could see he'd written down 'NO WAGE'. He rubbed his moustache upwards, seemingly for the feel of it.

'We'll get back to "last Saturday" and "Connemara" later.' He looked to Mooney, who nodded and scribbled. 'First, answer me this: did your father ever broach the subject of his death with you?'

'I already told you.'

'I'm referring to his declining health over the past two years. Did he mention anything about death, dying, or any action or treatment he might take, beyond his usual health difficulties?'

'Yes. He asked me and Cormac to research what the Church had to say about suicide.'

Rapid scribbling ensued. Detective Sergeant McCarthy entered, bosom-belly first. Now that she'd taken the garda cap off, her red hairdo was in its proper tea-cosy shape. She stood by the wall.

'Have you anything in writing to confirm your father's request?'

'He didn't *really* want the research done. He knew there was no way of doing right by God. 'Twas just his way of acknowledging his religion—especially for our mam, who's an ex-nun. It was his way of telling us he wanted to end it. So it wouldn't be a shock for us, I suppose. But we weren't about to let him do it on his own and botch it. I don't know if he was expecting our help or not.'

'Did he or did he not put the request in writing?'

I felt my face flush. 'I don't know.'

'Did Nóra know about the request?'

'I don't know.'

'When did you next speak with your father about the suicide—assisted or otherwise?'

'I … I didn't really.' It was very uncomfortable with the wool jumper on and no T-shirt under it. It was hot and itchy and I knew that my shoes would pong without socks. 'We talked … in metaphors. Around-about. The Chief and I were always that way. Like Gar Public and Screwballs in *Philadelphia! Here I Come …* except the Chief was—'

'Do you read a lot of books? Tall tales?'

'I read the odd book.'

'Is that why Manus asked you to read the Bible on his behalf?'

'Maybe. No. It was a way of letting us know his mind. He wasn't really asking us to research it …'

Goulding sucked air in through his teeth. 'Did your father often say things he didn't mean?'

I boiled up. 'No.'

'Did you often know he meant something other than what he said?'

'No.'

'Did you talk to your father about the method of suicide he planned to employ?'

'No.'

'There was no agreement made or discussion about his suicidal thoughts? Did he speak to a doctor about it?'

'No.'

'But you agree, Doharty Black, that on Monday the second of October, you were present while your father took an overdose of morphine sulphate?'

'Yes.'

'A toxicology report will confirm the quantity. But who procured the morphine for him?'

'He got it himself. He had a prescription from his GP.'

'Whose name is?'

'Dr Kelleher. I took him to the clinic to pick up a new prescription. I think he asked the doctor to switch to liquid morphine and Kelleher prescribed it and didn't request the leftover tablets back, so. That's how we had enough.'

'We?'

'The Chief.'

'Who?'

'Dad.'

'Who told him how much was enough?'

'No one.'

'How did he know how much to take?'

'We researched it but we didn't *tell* him … He didn't ask—'

'Who prepared the morphine dosage for him on the morning of the second of October?'

'Me and Cormac.'

'Who gave the drugs to him to swallow?'

'He took them himself.'

'Who handed them to him?'

Sweat tickled my upper lip and I wiped it, making a crackling sound. 'I did. But he took them himself. He wanted to take them. He called me into the study an hour before and asked for the anti-nausea pill and he told me he'd bought an online will and he made me executor and he said to me, "We've had a grand old time".' Tears arrived in my eyes. 'He said, "It's as good a time as any to ..."' I made the jabbing gesture the Chief had made with his finger. The camera blinked. 'I asked was he sure that's what he wanted and he said it was. To ... call the others in.'

Of all the people, I think I saw a sheen on Mooney's recessed eyes. McCarthy was unchanged. Goulding was unreadable beneath the frowning brow and the moustache. He asked what happened when everyone convened in the study. I explained it, step by step. About the Chief remembering, finally, to ask what the Bible had said about it. How Cormac's reamed-off lines seemed to appease his conscience as much as we could hope. How he thanked Cormac. How him praising Cormac was his last words. How softly he had retreated into himself, like the moon into the background of the morning, where it couldn't be seen to linger. Where it couldn't ...

'Please answer this directly. Did Manus Black die by strangulation?'

'It wasn't strangulation.'

'How did he die?'

'Morphine overdose, cancer, the recession, mortgage arrears, obsolescence, an abscess in his molar tooth.'

'Was he dead when you put your hands around his throat?'

'Nearly.' My head ached from suppressed crying.

'"Nearly" dead means alive. It means Manus Black was alive when you put your hands around his throat. Is this correct?'

'He was *very* nearly dead. He was gone. He wasn't there.'

'Was he dead after you put your hands around his throat?'

'No, it was the morphine. Holding him was only to help him keep it down. The anti-nausea medication he'd took wasn't enough. It would have been horrific … He would've choked on it. My mother would have died on her knees from the horror.'

Inspector Mooney put his head down so I couldn't see his eyes at all. McCarthy's brows were still raised, but she seemed to be biting on the inside of her cheeks.

'Was he breathing after you took your hands from his throat?'

My shoulders danced. I shook my head.

'What did you do then?'

I kept shaking my head, sobbing. 'None of us did anything wrong. We never meant to.'

They'd stopped note-taking. McCarthy stepped forward: 'That you're innocent until proven guilty is the Golden Thread of the Criminal Justice System, Mr Black. It's not the silver lining.'

Goulding let out a groan. Then, after a moment, he placed the fingers of his left hand on the table, the Claddagh ring upside down—heart outwards, crown inwards—and began to chuckle. 'Did you ever hear Niall Tóibín tell the one about the American tourist who bought oranges off a street stand in Dublin?' I glanced at Mooney's rapt expression. Goulding continued, putting on a Morgan Freeman American accent for the tourist and Dublin North-sider for the vendor: '"May I please have a dozen oranges?" the tourist asks the vendor lady, sat at her Moore Street stall. "Dare luvli jewci Spanick aranges!" says she, putting them in the plastic bag for him. "How much is that going to cost me?" the American asks. "Owny fawr euros." The Yank thanks her and walks away, glad of his interaction with a real local. But when he checks the bag down the street, he sees there are only eleven oranges. So he walks back to the stall. "Excuse me, ma'am? I guess that even in Dublin a dozen means twelve?" "It does indee-yad," your wan says, pleased with herself. "But, ma'am," says he, "you only gave me eleven oranges?" And she says, "Yessir. One o' dem was bad. I thrun it away".'

Mooney slapped the table. McCarthy pushed her lips out, as if she was holding on to a mouthful of wine for the tannins. Goulding gave me a thick, moustachioed smile.

'All right, Inspector Mooney, we'll leave Detective McCarthy here to complete the formalities. And we'll try the other two once more. See if we can make the District Court before five.'

'Yes, boss.'

'Tomorrow's set to be a fine day for Cloverhill,' Goulding said, getting up.

'Cloverhill?' Mooney asked.

'For the bail hearing. The District Court has no jurisdiction to set bail for murder charges. We'll have to see if Dubliners still have the same philosophy when it comes to bad oranges.'

37.

Next time I saw Goulding, he came with a mug of coffee, a freshly combed moustache and a charge under the Offence Against the Person Act of 1997. The three of us were driven in separate patrol cars to the District Court to reply to our separate charges. There, we met Cormac's solicitor: our cousin Cáit.

I hadn't seen her since she was in her school uniform with half the length of the skirt rolled up at the waist and her knickers admittedly wet from laughing clannish malice. But she'd mellowed since, Bridie insisted. Oh yes, over the years, Cáit had 'come into herself'. What she'd found inside was sharp, we'd find out, as well as shiny. She had the same pink Connemara marble complexion, grey eyes, the upturned face and whiffy blonde hair high up in a ponytail that swung side to side even when sat still. Her ticklish-girleen clothing—a pastel-blue blazer and fishtail skirt with a silk top and pearl earrings—was by design. Female lawyers often dress in macho charcoal suits with licked-back hair to be taken seriously in a sexist system, she explained later, but she didn't want any 'cold and calculating' associations.

First thing she said to me was: 'Why is it that birds save up all their crap and offload it on your car as soon as you get it washed?' Then she said, 'Don't reply.'

'What?'

'Give no reply. To the charge. I'll sort out legal aid for you and Auntie Nóra. We can share a legal team. But there'll be separate representation. I'll be Cormac's barrister. He won't qualify for aid. He earns too much. And there's only so many days I can wear my pyjamas in a row without them embedding in my skin. This is a career case.'

'He won't pay you?' The acid pooled in my stomach.

'We've an arrangement,' Cáit said. 'If I get you off the charge.'

'Me?'

'All of you. Athos, Porthos, Aramis. We'll need to get you psyche evaluations. Sooner the better. And don't lock eyes with anyone at Cloverhill. Make sure your mam keeps her opinions to herself.'

'Cormac'll look after his mammy.' But Cáit didn't seem to hear. She passed her steel eyes over me, seeking out the offending article.

'Fuck, Hart. It is a crime. You've lost your looks.'

38.

Dear Hart,

I had an audition on the back of a good review I got in the Tribune for Bailegangaire: 'An unflinching performance. Aleanbh Cullinane is a rough diamond.' Diamond's good, but I'm not gone on the rough part. I was in Galway Youth Theatre three quarters of my life, can't they tell? 'Youth' should be taken liberally or not at all. The audition was to play Pegeen Mike in a musical version of Synge's The Playboy of the Western World *and it got me thinking of you. I've been thinking of you non-stop. The audition was diabolical. I felt so sick from the chanting and breathing and yelling our deepest angers at the wall that I just left. I didn't even excuse myself. I can't sing anyway. I threw up my breakfast in someone's flowerpot in the Claddagh. For all that, I had to cancel a shift at the call centre, phoning up the overnight middle class to ask if they think their combined household income is significantly below average, slightly below, about average, slightly above, or 'I can't answer that. I'm just the sous-chef. Mr Ahern is meditating in the panic room.'*

Some good news I definitely shouldn't tell anyone yet. My sister Emer is pregnant. She's only a few weeks in, so it's just a missed period and a lot of googling. She won't go in for ultrasounds or screenings for a month but she's peed on enough sticks to build a boat with. Our brother Kenneth has three kids but they live in Sri Lanka, so it's good for me to be here. Stay close.

You'll come west when whatever's going on in your peculiar life is done with and put in the drawer. I don't mean to say you could put your gracious living statue of a father behind you. But it's not an unreasonable distance for weekend visits, Galway to Roscommon. For when he moves to the hospice, as he must. Just because you don't know what you want to do with your life doesn't mean you should default to unpaid caregiver-potato-farmer. There's less sense in paternal reverence than the culture lets on. Sorry if that's cold. The lament is rarely the last act.

I thought I had you puzzled out, but that car journey taught me otherwise. Maybe we don't know each other at all. Shall we start now?

I'm a compulsive liar.

I'm forty-one, not thirty-three.

I, too, lived on the dole for years, without the excuse of an ailing parent. My folks look after themselves well enough, not that I'd step in. They wouldn't support me after I'd given up the baby, which was a vile thing to do. Sixteen, loose-bellied, empty-armed and kicked out to fend for myself. Told I might earn back their respect after a decade of Responsible Living. Apparently two decades never quite saw me Respectable. Nothing responsible about playing patient at the teaching hospital, they said. They were probably right there. On a good day, I'd be given a script to follow, regale all the medical students with my complaints. On a bad day, I'd take some untested pill or go in for an invasive procedure that was better paid and sorted me for a week, but it could knock me out for a week equally. That was just term time. Summers, I'd take the bus out to Spiddal to be an extra on soap opera extraordinaire, Ros na Rún. *You'd get an endless supply of Nescafé and Kimberley's biscuits and you could look at all the paid actors walking up and down their polystyrene street with their faces excessively Irish and you could hold out hope for getting the Special Extra bit once a season that might give you the big break if the director of* Fair City *accidentally flicked channels just in time for your one line, milked to high heaven.*

So that's what the stretch marks are from. Catriona, I'd called her, though she'd go by some other name now—Apple, maybe, or River. It wasn't a fat phase during college. I never went to college. Lie

number … Is that enough for today? Three feels somehow absolute.
But that could be the convent schooling.

Now your turn. Tell me what your brother ever did to you. Tell me
it's not just the national penchant for victimisation.

Yours,

Dolly

P.S. I've enclosed a play.

39.

Grief dried me out something violent. I'd've drunk the ragwort
spray if that wouldn't have left us stuck the following season and
if I hadn't finally got the distillery dripping out pestilential liquid
in the bathtub. Nóra let me have it—the bathroom—so long as I
kept the door shut. Well, she hadn't uttered a syllable. I took the
go-ahead from her non-complaint. That was something Shane and
I had, to keep a friendship going without Cormac. We cobbled
together a still from hardware shop bric-a-brac. It wasn't anything
posh. Potatoes, sugar, water, yeast. I took some of the cull before
Cormac got at it with his trailer. The fussiest step was making
the wash: fermenting spuds. Shane got me a steel-top 2,100-watt
plug-in hotplate with a heat transfer of up to 360°C and dual heat
shields to keep the case cool to the touch. That set me back a few
favours, but it was what you'd call critical. Next, a big old pressure
cooker with a hole in it and a lid. The modern ones have fancy
valves to release the pressure, but with the old-fashioned cooker,
all Shane had to do was remove the weight and weld a fixture so

the tube would fit the valve. The lid kept it covered enough to stop wild yeasts and mould spores from getting in, but loose enough to let the rank air out. When the wash came to the boil, the alcohol evaporated and sent the lovely inebriating mist through the long copper tube (refrigeration tubing—€2.10 a foot) that twisted down from the pot into the bathwater, which I changed frequently during the two-week refinement, to keep it cool, all the while condensing the vapour into liquid and it dripping into my kitchen crock. Nóra wasn't using the oven any longer. She ate things raw from the garden or dipped eggs briefly in hot water to make sure a downy chick wouldn't emerge. No more ice baths would be needed, so what better use was there for the bath but a wash? Flush out the mind. Relief tap-tap-tapped into the drum like the Raven, as if he'd forgot the Chief had opened the door to him already.

We were due in court on Wednesday, which gave me two days to see if I couldn't blind myself. There'd be disability allowances, surely. And I had my looks to fall back on. Dolly'd probably take me sightless and legless, now that I knew she was forty-one.

40.

Dear Hart,

Not that you wrote to ask me, but the Synge casting man phoned and said I couldn't sing for loose change, so 'regrettably' they couldn't use me for the musical. Here's me about to tell them where to shove their loose change when your man goes: However ... we liked that you walked out. It was the most authentic reaction of the afternoon and we're willing to forgive a bit of amour-propre for the sake of authenticity. We think the fire in you would be well suited to the part of Juno in Sean O'Casey's Juno and the Paycock, *he said—a play they're producing for the Arts Festival. The first run's in January, then there's a rerun for the tourist throng in July. I had to catch a hold of my jaw. Am I not a bit young to play Juno? I said. He said no. But isn't there … what's her name, the young socialist love interest, that'd be closer to me? I asked. Juno is the bigger part, he said. But if you're not interested? So. The transition has been made, clearly, and denial's not my style. The wizened mother character it is. See how one day to the next our roles change. I can't tell you how fluky this is, two paid acting jobs as good as in a row. By paid I mean they've strung the figurative Halloween apple from the ceiling with the euro coins wedged in and I have to bite the euros free without using my hands. Little do they know I'd do it for nothing. I'd pay to be overpowered by another life, as long as it's convincing. I like to think that what they 'saw in me' was the fire you put inside me. With the Deep Heat, I mean. You quare hawk. Wouldn't it be great if, in my pained auditioning, they'd mistaken a fetishist ache for uncontainable talent?*

In other news, Emer has awful morning sickness. I'm lying. It's worse. I neglected to say before that she's thinking of terminating it. It wasn't planned. She's a bit older than me and has always been a career person in the way I'm a roaming person. We're no altruists. Choice is everything. But the haranguing Emer's getting already … People get very involved and concerned once you're pregnant. They like to put collars on your choices in case they stray too far from the sanctioned area. And there's the risks, she keeps being told, of age-related complications. She's not the type to give up her life for a child. And fair enough. I mean, if it's a sickly thing, she'd be shaping her life around it. Part of me thinks, well, that could be an enlightened way of living. But then I think: fuck enlightenment. That type of forced change could kill somebody's spirit if they're not able for it. If they don't really want it or accept it. It's no criticism not to be able for it. It's human. Some people can. Some can't. She's got a very full life. I just think ... no. I think life is complicated enough. I think ... it's hard to be rational. Cormac would have a way of reasoning it, don't you think? With his self-certainty, the originality that makes room for. What do you think? You'd have feelings on it, having given up your twenties. Maybe I'm more selfish, but I'd have made your folks liquidate the house and the farm and use that for retiring to a small town house with a nurse. Or to a home. But I suppose it's not as simple as that. Is it not??

All this makes me think of Catriona. Makes me hanker for the teenage daughter I could have now, who might come and see me in my plays. Even the ones where I play the granny. A daughter who'd roll her eyes at my exaggerations. Who'd have pulled me up on my lies long ago. But there you have it. Proof I shouldn't be a parent. The first thing I think about is how my child could coach me.

Before the tests, Emer asked me if I wanted to be an 8–4 nanny. I'd be able to give up the teaching hospital gig and the inquisition centre. I'd be able to do plays in the evenings and weekends. I'd have 150 euro cash in hand every week on top of the dole. We drank two bottles of Claret to seal the deal. She vowed it'd be the last drink she'd have, that she'd do pregnancy by the book or not at all. Well, by the pamphlet, anyway. So, I agreed, didn't I? We drank to it. Can either of us go back on it now?

Dolly

41.

Dear Hart,

I never watch the news. That usually keeps me safe from the false child harassment memories taking root in my brain. I'd go around suddenly recalling how I'd been leap-frogged by Mr Púca, the Irish Dancing teacher. Never underestimate a story's scarring potential—a story can be just as wounding as an experience. So, no news. Sometimes I mourn the characters I played long ago and forget it wasn't my own twin that drowned or my own senile mother eating Complan, unable to finish her war story. I delude myself into thinking something might come of my taking on other people's tragedies. As if I can fulfil them. Act the tragedy out of their system.

So I forgo it, for my own health and sanity. Characteristically selfish. But I lapsed. I turned on the news. Only the radio—you'd think I'd be safe. There were no names named. Two brothers, 25 and 27, and their mother. Arrested on suspicion of murder in Roscommon.

Hart. I can see the stone there now, and I don't want to jump to it, but the more I think about it and the more I'm left alone with my thoughts, it's the only stone I can make out. Tell me if I jumped to it, it'd sink and I'd drown for my baseless assumptions. Tell me I'm a fanciful citybitch, sensationalising other people's lives. Give me a piece of your mind. I've enclosed a stamped envelope to make it easier.

But if you don't tell me that, Hart, I still want to hear from you.

Tell me something. Anything you need to say. I know you better than the leeching Dublin journalists. Give me that.

Love,

Dolly

P.S. Emer's keeping the child, she thinks. She made the mistake of letting slip to our parents. So now it's a case of cutting the baby or the mother out. And Emer's softer than I am. Feels our mother has a right to our children somehow. Entitled to our fertility like you farmers to the output of your fields, no matter the incentives to let one go the fuck fallow. So it looks like it's coming into the world, the dote, harmed from the outset. I wish you'd tell me what you think. I wouldn't normally need to know. You have me ruined.

42.

I had *her* ruined? She didn't know the meaning of ruin. A hundred and fifty euros cash in hand weekly over and above the dole for child-minding and play-acting and living sovereign in a dockside flat. She wasn't landlocked. She wasn't usurped or injuncted or out on bail. It wasn't even her babby or her decision to brave. She lived in a fashionable coastal town where a phone call to the estate agent was the answer to all manner of watersheds, and if that didn't do it, there was always the sea and someone would have a dingy or a tyre or an ox-leather Gladstone bag she could drift away in. If I phoned her up and told her the truth, she wouldn't care to know my thoughts any longer. One word of the truth is all it would take to minify her caring.

Just one night remained of free life, before the trial. I twisted the radio dial, giving life to the adenoidal telecaster:

'*Local TD Denis Naughten has condemned the Government for further cuts to the farming sector announced last month: the latest in a series of austerity measures. In oh-eight and oh-nine, an average of seven farmers a month walked out on their farms in County Roscommon. Since then, the cuts have been compounded by lower prices and rising costs, putting a squeeze on the pay packages of farmers who have weathered the worst years of the recession. Naughten said: "Now the minister for agriculture has turned sneak thief and is set to pick their pockets too. Despite all the spin and spoof about fighting for farmers' interests in Europe, the reality is that the minister has sold them out. Instead of cutting jobs in agriculture," Naughten alleged, "the minister should be focused on driving this key export sector."*

'*A four-year-old girl from Boyle is in a critical condition after being savagely mauled by her cousin's dog, a Boxer named Brutus. The girl, who has not yet been named, was playing Cowboys and Indians with a toy gun with her cousin when the dog sensed a threat and attacked, inflicting severe wounds to the girl's face and arms. The dog's owner claims that Brutus was reacting in an instinctive, defensive manner and should not be euthanised as a result of its protective nature. The owner told reporters: "It was a mistake. There isn't a mean bone in that dog's body." The girl's parents have not pressed charges.*

'*In local news, the Glinsk Ladies' Club's twenty-second annual waltzing competition for the Eilish Tiernan Memorial Trophy took place in Glencastle Lounge on—*'

Just one night and one morning remained—the dregs of my freedom and youth. One night and one morning to take a walk along the road and breathe the countryside air, a free man. *Your own man. If you cannot walk this road, you'll find your own road to walk along. Take a stick*, the Chief counselled, among all the echoing horrors in my mind. *No, Dad. I'll not take a stick or a stone or a slingshot. Haven't they already proved my weapon of choice is poison?*

I went out to the garage deep freeze and rifled through the

snowy sacs of vol-au-vents and plastic bags of five-year-old salmon and sliced pan and tinfoiled ham and mushroom quiches and wholesale ALDI prawns like frostbit infant fingers until I found it. At the freezer's deepest remit—where a new-age couple might keep their placentas—there they were still, after all these years: the lambs' livers. I disinterred the plastic container from the ice and brought it into the kitchen. I put the pot in the microwave to defrost and went to the garage for the rat poison, Rodend. I cut the five slick brown livers in half so I'd have enough pieces, made a neat incision into each and spooned in the blue pellets. The livers were piping hot. I counted in swigs of *poitín* how many houses there were between ours and the cemetery. The Lallys. The Mullans. McDermotts. O'Rourkes. Joe Heffernan has only a cat. The Qualters, ohgodtheQualters. Five miles return. That'd do.

It was a bleary-eyed drive to the graveyard and back, but night air slicing through the open window kept me vertical. I drove on the wrong side of the road so I could fling the livers out the driver's window with a fistful of ham. I could hear the scrambling of paws, furious sniffing, the odd yippish bark. I told myself: the morning was forecast to be a fine one for walking.

The long night came, but a curtain never closed on the day's journey into it. I slept barely an hour before a tossed-gut feeling yanked me back to my undreamly surroundings. The drink, no doubt, filling my head with muffled sounds. What noise could the house give out when the doors were locked, his lungs were long set to rest, the dogs had been doped, the combative rooster had no rival or sunrise to augur? Why couldn't I sleep just this once? That *sound* … a kind of mewling … Acid burnt in my stomach when I sat up and groped through the ditch-black for the wall. The wall was an ice block against my cheek. It was feverish. Fraught … the sound was. A kind of smothered howl … Was she crying? Was this her calling out, for help, to me … the lonesomeness too desperate to suffer silently, needing … company … and only me here to hear? But there was no snivelling or staggered inhalations, the gulpy hiccupy breaths of lamentation … No hollow moan, but a *tense* one … the sexed, muscular violence … and then a thin note sung high and quavering.

Tripping away from the wall I bashed my hip into the corner of the dresser and the pain burst through me as a billiards break. *What* in all *hell* … the *fuck could* she? *Where* in the *fuck* was her *head?* Neon lights streaked across my vision. I closed my eyes, pressed my fingers into my sockets until everything went squiggly brown. It didn't bear thinking. The *filth. Rancid rag* for a heart. My own liver needed throwing out the window then. I was too drunk to drive away from this hell and I couldn't walk the road until dawn. Where was she—the moonshine to snuff out?

43.

It could've been a heart attack: the thump on my back that made me tumble forward, sending daggers through my knees. It could have been a stone thrown at me by a bereaved dog-owner or a tazer-happy guard. But it was the thwack of Shane's leather-clad hand as he passed. He swung a U-turn on his racer until he was facing me in the swath of exhausts, and lifted his helmet visor. I was out for my walk. To establish my territory, out of the house, unattended. I was deaf with adrenaline. Dizzy with homebrew.

'Spuds!' He cut off the engine. 'Is it the night before or the morning after?'

Which is it? I doubled over and tried leaning on my aching knees but they wouldn't stay still. I'd dropped the stick I'd been carrying, to save being seen with it. I must've been going at some clip, for my skin was scalding. I felt the heat of my knees through my jeans. The air wasn't cooling me fast enough. The ground floated like a bog mat till I upchucked half a pint of *poitín*, a fistful of sliced pan and a can of baked beans, now refried. I shut my eyes to the mess and I felt instant sweat-drenched relief. Holy fuck.

'No harm done,' Shane said, amused. 'There's more in the bathtub!'

I held the two sides of my head together and opened my eyes to search the fields again and make sure no half-poisoned dog was chasing down from Qualter's yard.

Shane eyed my stick thrown into the roadside. 'If yer runnin' from the dogs, yer goin' the wrong way.' I couldn't speak yet. 'I'll look the other way while you pull up yer knickers.' Shane proceeded to whistle a shrill old Irish tune, 'Geese in the Bog', which was amplified by his helmet so I was sure whatever dogs had a modicum of life left in them would come chasing. 'You're lookin' majestic as al'as, Spuds. Come here to me and have a lean on Pamela.' He slapped the flank of his motorbike. 'Rearin', she is, for two at a time! Front-the-ways, back-the-ways.'

Queasy again at that, I staggered over to him. 'What the hell has you up this hour?' I asked.

'I've to meet some fella in Strokestown afore work. He commutes to Sligo, the gack.' Shane took off his helmet and ran his gloves back through his sleek black hair. He'd grown a kind of Tetris goatee.

'You've a centipede on your face,' I said.

He stroked the facial hedging. 'Fu-Manchu-Soul-Patch combo, thanking you. I was thinking to look shlick like, for the big bijness.'

I grunted.

'Did I tell ya Cormac sent a partnership contract for me to sign for Colt Horse Cash? After twenty-seven months in the bag. Sent it in the post.'

'Hey?' I said, coming back to myself.

'On legal-headed paper. Says I've to contribute an agreed amounta hours on a weekly basis to match his inveshtment of the cull and storage and I can't go selling my own half or "buy out" for the first four years.'

I shook my head and instantly regretted it. 'The Chief said if you need a contract with someone, don't deal with them at all.'

Shane narrowed his eyes. Threw a pack of chewing gum at me. 'It's yer own blood you're warning me against?'

'Watch yourself with him, Shane.'

'I dunno which is the shly dog of the two of ye. But I hear what you're telling me. When are ye headed to the big shmoke? Today at some stage?'

'Cormac's picking us up soon.'

'I'll come up fer it … jusht in case.'

I swallowed the gum. 'Why would you?'

'For the *rí-rá* and *ruaille buaille*!' Shane winked.

'You realise it'll be long and boring as Cormac's ranger. Court'd depress a pothole.'

'Listen to ye! If there's cameras rolling and you take the shtand—the ride that ya are, even not at yer besht at the minute, with the feckin' charm on ya, the tongue—ye'll get a sentence on the *Bowld and the Beautiful*, minimum. Only a head-the-ball would shkip that soap opera.'

'I'm serious, Shane.'

'So am I.' He looked down the road before explaining. 'Cormac told me I shouldn't bother coming. He said ye wanted to keep it private as ye could. Good luck with that! But, yeah. Your dry job of a brother gave me a rake of shite to do, almost as if to keep me too busy to go, if I was wanting to. D'ya get me? I think if I'm right by you, Spuds, I besht come. I can give a character reference, if they need it.'

'The solicitor has all the witnesses settled long ago. We're over a *year* in and out of the District Court, writing the bloody Book of Evidence.'

'Here was I thinkin' you'd spent the year polluten yerself and reading stage plays from yer wan what's been postin' letters. Yer educated Rita. Prima donna, what's-her-tits?'

'Dolly. It wouldn't be any use, Shane, only waste your time.'

'Let me be the judge of that.' Shane pulled a wicked smile. 'See that now! It's catchen on, I'm telling ye. All this wheelen-dealen has me half turned into a slogan.'

'It takes weeks to get going. It'll probably get pushed back, too, you know. We went up to Dublin last week for interviews with our barristers and were told trials collapse every day. They said even the jury selection can take a few days. Be wasted petrol for the lot of us.'

Shane held his gloved hand in front of him to say: *I believe you.* 'We'll mitch the first few days, so.'

That was enough to send my defences to the ditch and my strength along with them. I'd to put all my weight on his bike. Thinking of the days of mitching school, scurrying along fields with plastic bags, hunting magic mushrooms; then, tired of our posturing as older boys, building maze forts from bales of hay ... back when we were dopes enough to want rid of our innocence. But that thought was tainted too by my sobering up. I was never really in it—the minute, the friendship—for I had to sentry the landscape always.

'What're ye at out here, anyways?'

The dire hangover loomed. I thought about telling the truth. 'I came out to be sick,' I said instead. 'Nóra doesn't like a mess in the house. She has a thing about smells.' I gave him the stormy eyes. He took one look at me and laughed wide and soundless as a sinkhole opening up in the Burren. He smacked Pamela. He liked me. He did like me. But liking's no good for evidence. *Hart's a sound job, Yer Honour.* I took the chance of a lift home, though. It would've been tempting fate to carry on down the road to the cemetery, where the stonecutter's phone number is writ larger than an Irishman's lifespan.

44.

Humans eat three times their body weight in dirt during their lifetimes, but us Blacks ate twice that with all the muddy spuds and maggot cabbage pigswill. Walking into the enormous glass-fronted new courthouse in Dublin—the 300-million-euro pantheon constructed in heyday-oh-seven—I had the feeling we'd be eating a whole new lifetime's worth of dirt.

Eleven storeys. Four hundred and fifty rooms. Twenty-two court-rooms. Two hundred thousand cases a year. One hundred convicts kept in the basement: held, heard, herded, heralded. Cormac tried holding his chin aloft like the Liam McCarthy Cup, but none of us could've been tall enough, well-dressed enough, tight-buttocked enough, lactose-intolerant, suburb-settled, electric-car-keyed, possum-haired, air-mile-loaded or Latin-tongued enough for the place. Standing in the atrium entrance with its see-through lift shafts and Sistine ceiling, we could only stare at Cáit to keep our heads above the trough, to get past the caped and wig-wearing overachievers trotting along the marble floors, comparing barge lease rates on the Shannon. Cáit saw our dread.

Leading us to our pre-court holding room, the rhythmical swishing of her ponytail and her high-heels clacking were like Morse code. At least *someone* was sending out signals. She wore a cropped lilac blazer and a silk scarf over a black dress that hugged her lithe, sinewy body. Prissy shoes made her calves tense and release like the two halves of a heart. She smelt of cough syrup. Though me and Nóra had our own barristers, the public would see Cáit as our representative: she'd make the family tie known to the jury, and that would make a unified symbol of her. The damaged chain-links of us clicked behind her along the corridor.

'Make sure you hammer home the fucked insurance costs,' Cormac started.

'Judge Gilroy might be a bit of a Leninist,' Cáit said, 'but she's—'

'Commie, is she?' Cormac cut in. His swagger would knock you sideways. His silver suit, red tie and breast pocket hankie were designer buys from TK Maxx. I went without a necktie because there's no beautifying a muck-brown suit, and hair dried to yellow, and a once-chiselled face scoured-like, a too-young-tragic job. Cormac had more pointers for Cáit: 'If you make the insurance the root of the problem—'

'We're at least a fortnight from closing speeches,' Cáit broke in. 'For the love of God, Cormac, spare me the advice till then.'

Nóra wouldn't have that. She cleared her throat shrilly by my shoulder. 'We've had fifteen months to think long and hard about our case, Cáit. Would it occur to you that Cormac's advice might be worth the time of day?'

Cáit kept walking, glancing at the yellow Post-it Note she'd stuck to the front of her zipped leather folio. 'The insurance cost's a sob story,' she said. 'So's the property fiasco. So's Manus's bona fide attempts to dig himself out of a ditch.' Nóra piped up but Cáit carried on talking over the breathy outrage, piloting us along the corridor. 'In eight years of litigation, I've only seen room made for sob stories in losing cases, to soften the sentence. If Cormac has evidence for me—or you, Nóra—I'm all ears. Anything left out. Videotapes? Depositions? The presence of a certified physician? The pretence of lawfulness?' She stopped and twirled back to us, her ponytail and lilac scarf floating in the air for motion lines.

'Well. We'll pray that's not your closing speech,' Nóra said, 'or you'll surely fall into the ditch after us.'

Cáit raised her bleached eyebrows at Nóra, then looked between me and Cormac. 'Isn't she a scream?' She reached out and knocked on the holding room door we were stopped at. We'd passed no one since the great hall, so successful was the circulation system that ensured separation, privacy, security and protection for all manner of court users. When the door was opened by a cow-eyed, fair-haired junior counsel, I looked past him to see my barrister, Alastair Waters—bald and relic-like at the huge varnished table with his legal team fascinated around him. It was a windowless room. Nóra's barrister was there too, Paul Sheehan: an enormous, middle-aged walrus of a man. Imperialist gentry type with a comb-over. I'd seen him before, but he lorded over this environment all the more. He was drinking from a Starbucks paper bucket, guffawing with his senior counsel.

'I have to gown up,' Cáit announced. 'Charlie'll look after you.'

The cow-eyed lad nodded and stepped aside to let us in. Cormac bullied in first, but I stayed at the threshold. My legs wouldn't stop trembling.

'You alright, Hart?' Cáit said.

'What? Yeah.'

'Fuck, it's muggy. Or the perimenopause is staking its claim.' She handed me her briefcase and leather folio so that she could remove her blazer. Then she draped the blazer on her arm and took her things back.

'Giving up?' I eyed the nicotine patch on her bicep.

'Do I seem like a quitter?' She gave me a sarcastic look. 'I patch up for court appearances.'

I hooked my shivering hands beneath my armpits. Then she tilted her head to the side so the ponytail became a pendulum.

'Alright, then?' she asked.

I shrugged.

'You're all ashes no fire, Hart. Stoke yourself. Your fire's your advantage. You care too much. You always have. High EQ. The schoolgirls loved it.'

'You're after saying sob stories don't make the Book of Evidence.'

She nodded, changing her tone. 'Getting a murder conviction's extremely difficult without non-circumstantial evidence. They need a confession.'

'Which I gave them.'

'Which you gave them along with a lot of poetry the jury'll go in for. And the others didn't confess. That makes you look soft, which is good. Then the autopsy, thank fuck, is indeterminate. It's not good, but it could be worse. They need witnesses to the "murder". Cormac and Nóra weren't in the room for the act of interception. For all they knew, the overdose did the job. The cancer did it. A coughing fit did it. The crushed pride. You said yourself. They'll not testify against you. They witnessed suicide. That's what their statements say. That's what the Book says. They're guilty of not taking appropriate action to prevent it, and not reporting it.'

'And what am I guilty of?'

She clicked her tongue. 'Doing what your daddy told you.'

I turned away. Through the gap in the door, I saw Nóra sitting, wringing her hands. She had on the olive trousers, the posh ivory chiffon tunic and the fawn, pearl-buttoned cardigan regalia Cormac bought her when we were arrested: an immaculate costume. I couldn't catch her eye and I didn't know if I wanted to. Cormac stood behind her now, sipping coffee, cufflinks glinting. That was how the pair of them had been positioned in the study on that day that wrapped its hours around my life and tied a knot.

'I forget what you call the judge.'

'Your Worshipful Holiness,' Cáit deadpanned. 'You won't be addressing the judge, Hart. Alastair will. He's world-class. Actually, I'm nervous he'll upstage me. I need referrals from this case. From now on, ixnay on the pro bono.' She sighed. 'Da's always talking about this place being full of criminals. Quangocrats, he calls us. Thinks it's great craic to write us all off as auctioneers. Criminals tried, cash-criminals doing the trying. But I'll tell you one thing, Hart. However Da wants to simplify all this, he couldn't reduce Alastair to anything but salt of the earth. He's honest and loyal. And that's how you should be represented.' She paused. 'Isn't it?'

'Isn't it?' Was she asking me?

'Isn't it just!' She jigged her shoulders. 'Fuck. It's freezing.' She glanced at her watch. 'I'll see you in there. Go to the toilet first. Adjourning for a shite's rude.'

45.

'Ireland is where strange tales begin and happy endings are possible.' Charlie Haughey said that, and mind what a hammer of an end he got. That's the difference 'twixt possible and probable. Whichever way it would go, I hadn't a bad seat for the finale. At the end of the defendant's bench, I was closest the gallery. Nóra was in the middle, gaze glued to the smooth, varnished furniture penning us in. Cormac was closest the judge. We all faced the empty jury box.

Red carpets. Lights like out-of-reach halos. Panelled wood for walls. Three huge TV screens. Carafes of water. A gold harp ornament above the judge's cathedra. Above that again, a big tract of window showing a puny treetop lurching in the south-westerly gusts. A sky unforgivingly white.

Red figures of the digital clock threatened to mete out all time eternal. 09:46:17; 10:52:35; 99:99:99. The gallery was full of note-taking trainee lawyers who came and went, half the Gardaí payroll lined up along the back wall, more than a few complete stranger pikeys mighta been media men, an aul biddy twosome sporting clip-on earrings and cartoon frowns, some other bored retirees, a pair of tourists (judging by the Alcatraz anoraks), an exhibit officer minding the white cardboard boxes of 'evidence', and too many groin-forward court officials. I expected Father Shaughnessy to bend around the door in his garb, shamefaced as if he'd been at the altar wine. Uncle Mitch showed up and, separately, respectfully, Gerry.

Underneath her bobbed forensic wig, the judge wore hooped

metal earrings that carried another hoop inside the hoop, and a third hanging from the second. Whatever Olympic sport she practised, I hoped it wasn't one of the endurance ones. Her face was set with fault lines whose activity you might spend your whole life failing to predict. She looked over half-moon glasses at Alastair, my barrister, Cáit for Cormac and the enormous, puce Paul Sheehan for Nóra. Judge Gilroy addressed them: 'Let's see if we can't do right by the taxpayer and settle on a jury in one day.'

Sheehan, who jerked his head before each statement to reposition his comb-over, replied: 'Quite.'

'I'm calling up thirty jurors instead of twenty since we have three defendants,' the judge explained. 'With seven peremptory challenges each, that's twenty-eight potential challenges without cause shown alone. Let's hope we can find more than two out of thirty representative citizens to empanel before lunch.'

Sheehan nodded, jerked. 'Let's.'

A garda marshalled thirty members of the public into the courtroom from a side door, all clocking us clan of culprits. Why was it that the jury would be selected so carefully to weed out bias when the counsel was picked quick as dock leaves for the nettle sting? I kept looking at Alastair for reassurance, but he was lost to his wig, a black poplin gown with flaps and long sleeves and the coat on under it. A stiff white collar and bands sheathed his neck, which had a raggedy scar by his Adam's apple. Given how much time he'd spent poring over my life—even Dolly, our letters, the still, how well each of my neighbours knew me ... he'd inspected every detail—I knew nothing of his.

Beneath the judge, the stenographer sat in front of a computer monitor and beside him the registrar pulled names from a drum. The first twelve were called and their excuses were humoured before being qualified for the jury. The clerk brought the names of the first eligible twelve to each counsel so that they could strike people off the list. During a toilet break, Cáit told us she'd phoned euthanasia advocacy groups and, despite what you'd think, there wasn't any 'type' of person who tended to be pro or anti, so there was neither a typical supporter that the prosecution could challenge nor a demographic typically opposed to euthanasia that we could veto.

Cáit adjusted the white bands she wore over her blouse—the bands the men wore, in contrast to the starched bibs that covered the necklines of the female prosecution counsel. Uncle Mitch was ogling her, desperate for his progeny's stardom.

Cormac watched her too. 'Are the horsehair wigs on the out,' he asked, 'or is there any trade left in them?'

'Try not to look so cocky, Cormac. The jury's sussing you out.'

'Should I look like Hart, so? Half-cut and brickin' it?'

'Hardchaw cunt,' I said, as an involuntary reflex.

'Don't you *dare* make a holy show of us,' Nóra whispered, without shifting her gaze from two feet in front of her, yet infinitely aware of the goings-on of the courtroom.

Despite no recommendation to do so, it seemed our side was vetoing any sketchy-looking gippos, new parent types and any brew of skin other than milky. Top of that, an auld wan was challenged owing to the cross strung round her neck, the principles she was showily upholding. Off away home with your glinty principles. Contrariwise, the prosecution was culling the too well-educated. College types. Laudy-daws. On and on it went. Purgatorial ceremonies. Two hundred members of the public duty-bound to their inglorious democracy waited backstage in the theatre of law for the day and a half it took for the casting. Finally, when the troupe of twelve were settled, the judge loomed over her glasses: 'Do refrain from reading articles or viewing any of the media coverage this case will attract. Do not do independent research by way of the internet or otherwise. You are required to make your decisions on the evidence only. Article 30 of the

Constitution of Ireland provides that all indictable crimes shall be prosecuted in the name of the People.'

But how heavy are the bindle sticks the People carry, Your Honour?

'The first, the second and the third named accused should now be rearraigned, Mr Registrar.'

Mr Registrar stood up and turned to me: 'Are you Mr Doharty Black?'

Not Mister, no.

'I am.'

'You are charged on the indictment as follows: that you, Doharty Black, of Dysart, County Roscommon, did on the second day of October 2014, with intent, unlawfully kill Mr Manus Black—the deceased person, who is your father—by way of asphyxiation, at his home, situated at Dysart, County Roscommon. How do you plead: guilty or not guilty?'

Kill?

There were no magnets force-fed in the name of the Holy Ghost. Only tablets swallowed in the name of the Human Spirit.

No.

'Not guilty.'

46.

Stopping drinking over the weeks following returned my vision to me. I could see myself in the mirror—the eroded statue of myself. One too many bits had been chipped away over the months: whole muscles from my shoulders and thighs, the meat from my cheeks, the grain from my chest. I could rest Dolly's stack of letters on my collarbone. No amount of her theatre would move me either. I was soft as September weather below. That's what I saw in the mirror. My impotent, hairless, slackened, orphan self. The mirror was the way of my recalibration. It was wojous as an AA shindig or an AA bra tag on the unpinging. Society was soberer than when I'd left it.

Since the easy bits were over, a pair of weeks into the trial—it would've been December 2015—Cáit gave us a talking-to before Judge Gilroy arrived and the prosecution began calling its witnesses:

'When Hurricane Katrina flooded New Orleans hospital, the staff had to carry the patients downstairs. Just being moved was the death of some of them, poor bastards. Doctor Anna Pou was working on the seventh floor with the sickest of the sick. A lot of them on ventilators went out with the electric.' Nóra gasped by my ear. Cormac sniffed and clicked his pen. He was eyeballing a bearded man in one of the front benches who was observing our exchanges, maybe reading lips. Cáit ignored the rest of the room. 'One of the patients wasn't terminal, though. He was young, just getting his bowel scooped out. But he weighed *twenty-seven* stone. The weight of a piano. So—'

'Nowhere close,' Cormac rubbished. 'Twenty-seven stone? Definitely not a grand piano.'

Cáit lifted her robes to put her phone inside her jacket pocket and addressed Nóra: 'He couldn't be carried. Dr Pou gave piano man a lethal dose of morphine. Eleven days later, mortuary workers recovered two dozen bodies with lethal morphine levels in them. Some called it euthanasia. Others called it homicide. The nurses called it harsh conditions. Treatment with the lights out. Nine of the bodies were on the seventh floor. Pou was arrested, charged with multiple counts of second-degree murder. A few months down the line, the grand jury decided *not* to indict Pou or the others. The charges were expunged. The state of Louisiana forked out half a million in Pou's legal fees.'

We all sat there, staring at the metronome of Cáit's ponytail leading us in. Cormac was still fuming at the prosecution's opening the day before—how we'd had to sit back and listen and none of our counsel did a thing. He didn't want to hear Cáit talking hurricane poppycock. He wanted legal citations only.

Cáit turned to me. 'What do you make of that?'

'How is a gang of nurses making a hames of a hurricane equal to this?'

Cáit thrummed her tidy nails on the dock bannister. 'Ha! Hames of a hurricane. Doharty quits *poitín* and takes up poetry. Well, Hart, for your troubles, I'll tell you what makes them equal. The coroner's report. He knew the report would change the case, so he called in a second opinion. Doctor Steven Karch, a specialist in post-mortem toxicology tests. Karch flew to New Orleans, took one look at the evidence and said it was absurd to try to determine cause of death in bodies that sat in hundred-degree heat for ten days. He said the medical cause of death should remain—'

'Missus Roe,' Mr Sheehan interjected, placing his hand on Cáit's lower back and moving her against our bench to let the tipstaff pass behind with the judge's water.

'—undetermined,' Cáit finished.

Everything about Sheehan put him at home on the red carpet, even if his skin tone clashed. He thrust his comb-over leftwise. 'I'd ask that you refrain from addressing my client. While I doubt this eleventh-hour counsel is ill-intended, it's causing Mrs Black undue stress.'

We all looked from Sheehan to Nóra, whose skin had aged like foxed paper. Her long eyelashes were clogged with tears and tissue fibres and her lips were pursed white. She concentrated on clasping her hands.

Cáit shook her silver bangle watch to the end of her wrist and checked it against the red digital clock. 'You're ahead of yourself, Mr Sheehan. It's the tenth hour. Not the eleventh.'

He smiled. 'That remains to be seen.'

'All rise,' the tipstaff called out, leading the judge in with a stick. Gilroy took her tractor seat above us and let her glasses drop from the chain to heed the jury's foreman, who said that one juror had a training course and the court would have to adjourn next Wednesday. Mr Jonathan Enright, the DPP barrister—a fella with the small eyes, flat nose and whiskery lip of an otter—said that the defence might still be working through the witness list on Wednesday and there were *many* witnesses and *eleven* other jurors taking time off work in the interest of civic duty, so *one* person's training—

'The current unemployment rate in Ireland is 11%,' Judge Gilroy cut in. 'If a member of the jury has a training course, the justice system won't jeopardise that juror's professional development or employment status. The court will adjourn for one day on Wednesday, December sixteenth.'

'Yes, Your Honour,' Mr Enright said. 'I move to have all witnesses excluded from the courtroom.'

'Your motion is granted with the exception of members of the Garda Síochána and clergymen. All other persons who expect to be witnesses in the trial must leave the courtroom.'

Whingeing followed at the prosecution's bench. The rest of us turned to the congregation to see if anyone would leave. Even Nóra looked. I took from their pseudo-sympathy that the two linked-armed biddies were Nóra's friends. I vaguely recognised them from mass. But Nóra wasn't looking at them. Uncle Mitch was there again, and Gerry. Beside Gerry—inexplicably—were Pat and Frank Lally, almost grotesque with clean faces and grins ear to ear. And, I only saw him then, Father Shaughnessy, whose close eyes flickered when they met mine. That exception to the witness segregation rule had been made for him—on whose request, I didn't know—and the prosecution couldn't decide if they were one bit happy about it. Just then, Shane tried to slink in rat-like at the back, but all the faces staring doorward made a hedgehog of him. He sat down on the back bench, beside the police witnesses. He smirked, unpeeling the Velcro of his biking gear.

Mr Enright cleared his throat. 'Your Honour, the prosecution calls Detective Inspector Adrian Mooney as a witness.'

And so it began. The long game I'd told my small cousins about. The shots of laxative the prosecution gave us all to swallow, one after another: interview, memo, statement, deposition, exhibit, all read out excruciatingly by a barrister and backed up by the guard in the witness jacks; you swallow each mouthful and sense no movement at all, even though your motion is granted; swig, swill, slug; something should be happening by now; morning, mid-morning, early afternoon, mid-afternoon; sergeant, inspector, detective.

'Detective McCarthy, please interrupt me if your own notes diverge from what I'm reading aloud for the jury.' Mr Enright shifted his weight from one bony hip to the other while he recited:

(Q) State your full name.

(A) Cormac Jonathan Black.

(Q) Do you realise you aren't obliged to say anything unless you wish to but anything you do say will be taken down in writing and may be given in evidence?

(A) We'll try to make it entertaining, so.

(Q) Is patricide a joke to you, Mr Black?

(A) I'm Irish, sure. Everything's a joke.

(Q) Is a life sentence a joke?

(A) The way I heard it, the minister for justice can grant temporary release to someone doing life. A murder convict on a life sentence, off you trot! What's it one of them academics called it? The temporary release dodge: 'A Damocles sword hanging over the head of the licensee'.

(Q) Do you know a lot about the loopholes in criminal sentencing?

(A) I know a bit about a lot of things. But this case has nothing to do with my mental faculties. It has to do with our father's bodily health, so it does, and his wish to die in a modicum of comfort.

(Q) Do your family members come to you for advice on various matters?

(A) They'd run a thing past me.

(Q) Is that why your mother phoned you when we arrived at the house?

(*No response.*)

Do you generally supervise your family members' actions?

(A) That's going a bit far. Mam has a strong will of her own, needs no advising. Dad would've seen it as pure cheek if you tried directing him. And Hart can take charge of his rare aul mind, so he can. I wouldn't go near it.

(Q) What do you mean by that? 'His rare aul mind'?

(*No response.*)

Are you saying that Doharty has angry, dangerous or aggressive impulses?

(A) All dark thought, no dark action. Hart wouldn't swat a fly. Couldn't if he wanted to. He'd be afraid its tiny ghost would haunt him.

(Q) Is Doharty afraid of a lot of things? Is he afraid of you?

(A) God, you're an awful literal crowd. Do ye find me very scary, is it?

(Q) Was Doharty afraid of Manus?

(A) Our father wasn't threatening. Awesome, maybe. Fearsome in that way. But not someone to be afraid of. Hart was always hankering after his approval, but he wasn't *afraid* if he didn't get it. He just wanted it. Anyway, Hart's afraid of some things and not others and half the time he has it arseways.

(Q) What do you mean by that?

(A) Ah, sure. He's not afraid of women, but he's petrified of dogs! I mean, where in the bog do you find that logic?

(Q) Where do you think he got that logic?

(A) (*Accused laughs.*) Oh, did he tell tales, did he? Did ye have a bit of psychotherapy in here, did ye? Go on so.

Accused holds his hands above his head. Superintendent Fintan Goulding enters the room. Accused nods to the superintendent, lets down his hands. Accused continues his response:

Guilty as ye'll have me, but not guilty as charged. Sorry to let ye down. The charge isn't for having undue influence over my little brother, is it? I'm … what's her name … culpable on the dog front. But sure, I'd no clue Doharty heeded every word I said. I'd'a gone soft on him if I knew his mind was easier broke than an egg.

(Q) What did you do to him to make him afraid of dogs?

(A) I didn't do a thing. It takes words only to break his bones.

(Q) What did you say?

(A) I told him if a dog gets a hold of your leg, he'll bite down till he hears the bone snap. And that's why you're always to carry a stick when you go outside. So that when the dog has you, you can snap the stick. The dog will hear that and will let go, so he will. You've only to hope he doesn't nick the popliteal artery. (*Accused laughs.*) Hart loves a bit of vocabulary. Words, sure, they're safe. Easier to look up than a skirt. No word of a lie, it was the 'popliteal' sent him over the edge. And the way it went: the more scared he got, the more Dad would tell him to take a stick with him. The mantra for cycling to school, going out to the storage shed, the shop, going out the front fecken door. 'Take a stick, Hart. Take a stick.'

Cáit objected for the fourth time during this recital. An expert witness would be called to speak to the psychological profiling of all three defendants regarding the defence of trauma as a reason for not reporting the death. This memorandum was irrelevant, leading and opinion-based. She wanted it redacted.

I wasn't sober yet, it turned out. Judge Gilroy's hoop earrings were the only things I could focus on to keep from reaching out and pounding a hoop of my brother's skull. Right from the outset, from his first interview he'd been building his case ... and it wasn't against the People. Maybe he took it for granted I'd do the same: set myself against him. How far back had he contrived my incrimination? He slid his notebook across the bench to me then with a page open where he'd written: *Jury needs a stooge to pity and jeer at. The fool is always guiltless. You're welcome.*

The journey home might have been our last if I'd got in the car, within a body's length of him. The instant the judge and jury had been led out, Shane came to me with the offer of a ride home on Pamela. 'She has a long back on her! And I brung ye a helmet—protection and all!' he said, hoping to take the lid off the boiling rage in me one way or another. Queerly, it helped. 'I'll wait outside for ye, Spuds. You've yer fans to attend to.'

Father Shaughnessy was first, looking more burdened than ever, with all the weight of the souls he conceived to be on his shoulders. He was buckled halfway to the floor, apologising his way up the aisle. He'd brought us leaflets from the Sunday mass. 'The sermon is abridged in it, but it might be of some use. We're sending the prayers up in their droves, I can tell you ... God bless you all.' Cormac wouldn't take the leaflet, so Father Shaughnessy had to place it on the table in front of him. I took one and saw what was highlighted: *'I speak to your shame. Is it so, that there is not a wise man among you? No, not one that shall be able to judge between his brethren? But brother goeth to law with brother, and that before the unbelievers. Now therefore there is utterly a fault among you, because ye go to law one with another. Why do ye not rather take wrong? Why do ye not rather suffer yourselves to be defrauded?' (1 Corinthians 6:5–7)*

Then my barrister finally had something to say, to my shoulder: 'Mr Gerry Lardner would like to have a word with you, Doharty. Would you prefer me present?' Cormac overheard that and frowned. Then he left. Most of the courtroom emptied out. I wasn't sure what Gerry had to say or what Alastair was withholding, but

Alastair's eyes were shut while he collected himself to say, faintly: 'It's a particularly sensitive matter ... given that eight of the twelve jurors own pet dogs.' He opened his eyes and allowed a flicker of contact before focusing again on my shoulder. He wore his wig still. It was hard not to stare at his neck scar sagging over the stiff white collar like the leg crease of an uncooked chicken. Then Gerry approached, cap in hand. 'I'll be gathering my papers,' Alastair said.

The exhibit officer was busy loading the boxes of evidence onto a cart.

It had been too many weeks since Gerry's hair was hennaed, so the roots were a ruddy-grey contrast to the mahogany waves behind his ears. He was a strapping man, like the Chief before the illness, and he made me feel small, though he went out of his way to do the opposite.

'How's the farm?' I asked. 'Weathering a skyload?'

'No more than yourselves.'

'Yeah.'

'Bad aul dose of it, to be sure.' Gerry clocked my brown suit through his permanently smiling eyes, though his words weren't smiling. He gauged the shoulder span wider than my own, the safety-pinned ankle hems. 'Them's your dad's clothes?'

I hesitated. Gerry straightened the peak of his own cap. 'She dumped all his clothes in a charity shop,' I said. '*Concern*, my arse. She'd've sold them if she thought they'd've bought a pack of biscuits, or feed for the hens.'

'Be wide, Hart.'

The floor between us was what I saw then, so my eyes must have gone to it. 'I bought his suit back from them for eight euro. Half in flitters. His only suit from his lean youth and he never bought himself another. Maybe if one of us had got married ... Given him a day out.'

Gerry took a deep breath. 'I keep saying Manus was the man for forgiving. And for understanding.' His thick cheeks reddened.

'He was the Chief! Kind a man as you are.'

'No!' Gerry shook his head so his cheeks waggled. His voice resounded in the chamber, despite his efforts to be discreet. 'I'm not.'

One of the guards lengthened the route of his back-and-forth pacing and Alastair gestured to him to give us space.

'I'd a thing taken long ago, Hart. A thing I loved. Gone in a blink. And I can't abide seeing others done the same, for no good reason.' Gerry shook his head again. 'You mean well, Hart. But you done a bad thing with them dogs. I know it was you, and I wish I didn't.'

I felt very hot suddenly, the suit hanging on me as if the seams were weighted down with rat poison. 'I only wanted … I wanted to walk the length of my own road before being locked in … for good.'

'I'd have walked the road with you and minded you from the dogs, if it was fresh air you wanted. You know that. That's no job at all.'

'I didn't *want* help. I didn't *have* help. Not for years now. Not from then on. I don't have the Chief. All I have besides a summons is what he left me and that's the road and the stick and the way he'd be proud of me.'

'Manus wouldn't be proud of what you done.'

I swallowed hard. I wished the salt that reached my lips tasted stronger. I wished it strong enough to blind me.

'I'm sorry, Hart, to say that.' Gerry sighed and made himself smaller. 'I didn't come here to sadden you. I came to tell you I called into each house on the road. I'd words with the Qualters. I'd talks with the lot of them and I told them, I said I'm convinced Manus was long planning to end it, and he did that. 'Twas only an err in the end what put ye here. You especially, Hart. You were as dedicated to your father as a son ever was, and I said that. You were shook to the bone, with the trial about to start, out of your wits. I said that. If it's the truth or it isn't, there's truth in it. They understood, in honour of Manus. They respect him more than their dogs they'd some of them ten years trained. They listened when I told them, I said if you phone the guards or report deaths to the vet, I said it'd turn the case on its head. You'd be done for. Your lawyer said the same. He said if it came out you as good as kilt nine dogs the day before ...'

I'd never in my life heard Gerry say so many words in a row. I remembered Nóra mouthing 'he hasn't a *whole lot* going on upstairs' all those years back. But there was a power of thought going on, as he stood exposed as an uncastled king in front of the red digital clock on the courtroom wall. _ _: _ _: _ _.

'You might think you done me a favour, leaving my Collies,' he said. 'But you put me in a tight corner in the community. And not everyone took it the same.'

I tensed up. 'Morrigan?'

Gerry shook his head and looked to the door.

He hardly meant ... 'The *Lallys?*'

'The Lallys. They're waiting. A lift back and forth was part and parcel.'

'Part and parcel of *what?*' Gerry didn't like my riz temper. 'My father was *good* to them,' I said. '"They've an older manner of opportunism we'll never see the like of again", the Chief said once. I never understood it.'

Gerry almost smiled at that. The mole on his cheek angled up. 'Manus had it right. 'Twould'a been opportunism put them in mind to tell me that one-eyed Max was worth a few bob. That it'd be hard to tolerate the loss of him.'

'*What?*'

'Max was a great guard dog, they said to me. Had I a spare Collie to replace him? If I hadn't they'd take the remains of Doharty's bathtub still and a trip to Dublin.'

'For quittance? They can have it!'

Gerry punched shape into his cap and put it on. He looked up at the gold harp above where the judge had sat, then back at me. 'You might be wearing his suit,' he said, 'but it isn't Manus's footsteps you're following.'

The treetop in the window yawed out of sight.

I'm sorry, Gerry. You were right. I *was* out of my mind. I'm still out of my mind. I'm destroyed and I've no one to … not even my barrister. Not even my mother. I don't know how much of that I said aloud. The noises were layered and electric: words seemed indistinct above them. I wanted someone to bind my head with bandages until the soberness settled. Everyone was declaring me out of my mind, so why not own my alleged condition?

'I'm not doing this by the way to protect you,' Gerry said. 'You've the makings of a good man and I hope the law comes out favourable. But if there's one last thing I do for Manus, it's to make sure he isn't likened to a poisoned dog.'

Out he went.

Next thing I knew, Shane had shoved a weighty full-face helmet on my head and the world outside it was the slippery, garbled, uncontained thing that couldn't get at my immunity. I touched the helmet and felt something hard-wearing. It would do for bandages.

47.

It costs an arm and a leg to break a neck in Ireland. In the roughest weather, when people couldn't feed their horses, they sure as debt couldn't fork out three hundred euro for the tidy injection. So they'd take them to the nearest forest and set them loose, let them roam free, *Tír na nÓg* style. But waterlogged woodland's no place for horses. They need constant grazing. That's how the forests came to be littered with dead steeds. Shane thought that a story fit for telling when he dropped me home. That I'm not the only animal killer in the country was the moral. That he's the one to tell scary stories was the secondary moral.

It wasn't Cormac who told me about the dog biting down till the bone breaks and to take a stick. It was Shane. 'And it was a shtory about badgers I told ye one summer fishin' on the Suck river.'

I knew it wasn't Cormac's story. I remembered the glee in young Shane's face as he said: 'Shnap!'

Why Cormac lied about it, I couldn't figure. If he really had known it would be read out in court a year and a half later, what convoluted itinerary had he planned to coxswain in the minds of the jurors? Or was it just that he wanted ownership of my crippled mind—to have been the dominant influence?

'Came close to a forest visit oursels lasht week,' Shane said. 'Overstuffed the horses on the cull spuds. One o' them near Nagasakied, I swear ta feck. Ballooned up so we'd to pierce her under the rib with a knittin' needle to let the gas out. It's not like cows that regurgitate, chomp away on the cud. We've a Bloat Kit bought for it now in case it happens agin. Like Jesus said: "Once punctured, the foal's the fool. Twice punctured … it's twits all round".' Shane smoothed down his Tetris goatee and thumped his helmet back on.

'Well, that's me told,' I said.

The tail end of a laugh escaped as he lifted his visor. 'I can give ya a lift agin in the morning, but I've ta head back twelvish, so you're on yer lonesome then. It might shtave off the murderen, though. Will it do?'

'Thanks, Shane. I don't know what I'd've done—'

'Here. No poisoning yerself tonight, right? Ya need yer head about ya.'

I unstiffened my shoulders and gave it a thought. Could I manage another long night in the emptied house, with its deadlocks and antiseptic smells, abstemious?

My sober thoughts were half-made bridges, arcing out

every-which-way for safe mooring. My drunken thoughts had leapt blindly, had been better at landing on water. A new letter lay on the kitchen table. I would read a few of the old ones first, build myself up to it. I needed to build up to it. I'd dismantle the bathtub still and drop it off to the Lallys. I'd bring them the last of the poison and swap it for a few cans of beer. I'd wash my only good white shirt and sew the hems up on my brother's cast-off suit instead for Gerry's sake and, I suppose, Nóra's … who I could ease up on. I'd put four dinners' worth of food in the oven and roast it in oil. I'd do a hundred push-ups and run up the stairs twenty times. I'd take a blistering shower. I'd shave. Then I'd write back.

48.

Dear Hart,

This letter may be recorded for quality, training and satisfaction measurement purposes. Time to quit the call centre. Someone's complaining about the pyjama index in their neighbourhood. Probably the very same person spent the college fund on a mature olive tree for their garden in 2006. I'm acting appalled-but-unsurprised. My default mode at this stage. Shoot me now. Do I've to tell you not to take me literally?

Sorry.

I'm sorry you've to go through this when you're heartbroken to the nines. I would've come to the funeral if I could've got off work. I read Cormac's firm are keeping him on the whole time! Holiday leave for high court dates and GAA gallivanting! Nuts. It's busy here. On top of work, Emer needs loads of help getting ready. Due date's in four weeks. We're painting her room tonight. It's a girl. I think I'll paint a giant floral vagina in the vein of Georgia O'Keeffe so the little petal gets positive reinforcement.

In other vulva news, I got to stand in for a statue in Antony and Cleopatra. My parents came to see it and I can safely say they'll never enter a theatre again. I did warn them the part was a gilded statue but they must've thought I was being facetious. Their faces at the sight of my gold spray-painted pubes! Are you smiling?

You must be drained. I can't even imagine … though not for want of trying. Do write back, Hart. Tell me everything. How on earth are you surviving in that house all alone with your mother? Does she ever take off that costume she goes around in? The emblematic Shan-Van-Vocht outfit. Self-sacrificing, loyal, ascetic, moralistic with shoulder pads of indignation. Sorry to say she has nobody convinced. Except maybe you. She wears it so tight, it's as if she wants to cut off the blood supply to her whole lower body, lest it betray her. What service was it she provided the priest again, before she married? Housekeeping? Anyway, sorry, it's just hard to watch women like that vacate themselves.

Easier to watch is your hot blonde cousin, though. The media loves her. Prim as a cucumber sandwich. Is it unusual she was allowed to represent her own clan? Someone her age wouldn't normally get to cover such a high-profile case in the high court. Anyhow, she flatters you both, so that's a good thing. There was a picture of the four of you in the Independent. At least, I think it was you. You minus your father. What's left of you. You've shrunk. I don't like that it's happened. Can't you look after yourself, Hart? And where in Botswana did that brown suit come from? Come on. You're in the limelight. Some people would kill to be in your position.

Sorry. I'll stop that now. I feel giddy for some reason. In that odd way of a kid at a birthday party who's been sniffing sherbet for hours, on the brink of getting a nosebleed and vomiting all over the Tibetan rug. I wonder should I just stick my fingers down my throat to get it over with?

Dolly

P.S. That story about the hares your father told in the car, that was the story of a man readying himself for death. A man who knew the departure timetable off by heart and was standing early on the platform without a suitcase. I've never known real death, only stage death. And Catriona. But she was unformed, so it wasn't a whole death. Only Rhionna or Rían ... ~~The whole girl was never~~ I only meant to say it was his own choice and there was no pressure on him from any of you. You were the ones that seemed pressured.

49.

I wrote back.

50.

Nóra was nowhere to be found in the morning. Shane arrived at eight and I locked the house. I wondered was Nóra hiding inside it. I suppose I didn't look very hard, afraid of what I'd find. Despite the ways I felt about her, the image of her in jail—really in jail— was suddenly harrowing. Out of all of us, she was the only one better off in the house, and it folding in all around her.

There she was when we got to the courthouse, bound in her green-black frock buttoned from elbow to wrist, midriff to throat. I asked was she okay as we strode in a nervous clique along the corridor, and she gave a stiff nod but her eyes caught mine for a moment and gainsaid.

'This is part of an interview conducted by Superintendent Fintan Goulding with Nóra Black at Roscommon Garda Station on 21 October 2014 at 4:45 p.m. Detective Inspector Mooney was present. Mrs Black was tearful.' Enright proceeded with his next recitation:

(Q) You and Cormac witnessed Manus swallow the morphine sulphate, fall asleep and appear to pass away. Is that correct?
Defendant nods.
(Q) And what did you do then?
(A) Mourned.
(Q) Is that so? If weeds are anything to go by, it would seem you did the gardening.
Defendant doesn't respond.
(Q) What sort of a woman are you, Mrs Black? Are you a good woman?
(A) Excuse me?
(Q) Are you religious?
(A) I am Roman Catholic.
(Q) Do you attend mass?
(A) Yes.
(Q) How often?
(A) Less often than I would like.
(Q) Why did you leave the Sisters of Mercy Convent in 1975?
Defendant doesn't respond.
(Q) Is it true that you were asked to leave the convent?
(A) I left. That's all.
(Q) What did you do after?

(A) I was housekeeper to Father Jarleth Scanlon.

(Q) How long did you do that for?

(A) Seven years.

(Q) Do you know that the typical reasons for leaving a convent are falling in love with a priest, developing a special relationship with a fellow nun, sustaining an injury or losing your faith?

Defendant shakes her head.

(A) Faith isn't a handkerchief. Either you choose to relinquish it or you discover you never had it in the first place.

(Q) Are you speaking from experience?

(A) Do you mind the boldness of it!

Superintendent Goulding interrupts.

(Q) Did you read the Bible while you were at the convent?

(A) Was I born naked? Do I breathe oxygen? Did I read my Bible at the convent? Have you neither common sense nor decency?

(Q) Have you read the Bible since?

(A) Yes.

(Q) Do you know that, according to your Christian Roman Catholicism, the suicide you say you witnessed and permitted to happen sent Manus Black to Hell?

Defendant doesn't respond.

(Q) Was it your intention to assist in your husband's eternal damnation, Mrs Black?

Defendant doesn't respond.

Defendant makes a request to speak to her son Cormac, which is refused.

Defendant makes a request to speak to her solicitor, which is arranged.

Defendant refuses to sign interview notes.

On the witness stand, Goulding enjoyed the re-enactment of his bull session, even if Mr Enright's delivery hadn't much of the matador about it. He upset the defence counsel by voicing observations that were hearsay only. Though the objections were sustained, the jury heard it as Goulding put it. Mr Sheehan was the only defence counsel to cross-examine Goulding that first time he was called. It was to highlight Nóra's emotional fragility during questioning, to show she'd been suffering. Goulding pronounced it muddy suffering—part way over loss of face, part way over loss of spouse, half over holy injury.

Nóra's back was ironed so flat against the bench that a few in the gallery had to crane their necks to see her. Specially the Amish-looking couple—formal as two pints of tap water without a slice of lemon between them. I supposed they were 'pro life' scouts, but equally they could've been old friends of the Chief's. Could nothing be done to defend a man's magnanimity or his wife's? Was there no resting place for the old Irish in the new Ireland—a patch of land resistant to liquefaction?

On the next bench, Nóra's friends sported life-sized crucifix necklaces and figurine-sized faith. Father Shaughnessy's lips were aflutter. Gerry wasn't in the crowd. He'd have work to do. My shite to clean up. Uncle Mitch, contrarily, took his self-employment lightly and—I could barely believe my sobriety—he'd brought small Thomas and Neil, who I hadn't seen in over two years, since they'd come round for tea that time. Twelve and fourteen, they'd have been, or thereabouts. Neil wore an expression like a whoopee cushion. The innocence was there still in the upturned nose and giraffe freckles. Thomas rested his head on his knuckles and eyeballed the buxomest member of the jury, which could've been the middle-aged man in the V-neck or the curly-haired forewoman. Bridie wasn't there to give Thomas a slap because the defence counsel intended to call her as a witness. The State wasted a technology specialist's day to go through our phone records for circumstantial evidence: that me and Cormac were texting leading up to the Chief's death, which we were:

Cormac gives one to the opposition:

Make sure he won't lump us w 2 year leases 4 them threshers

Hart scores for the home team:
Chief can't drive any more. I've to take them to mass

Hart scores own goal:
Chief near caught pneumonia last night shooting scarecrows.
Not good sign sanity-wise. Got the thing yet?

Ya got anti puke pill. The tumour chick's pure sound.

Chief wants to go away weekend 23/24 You free?
I sent you a link check your email

You there?

Cormac! You getting my messages?
You free or not?

Busy that weekend.

Unbelievable.

Fuck off.

30/1 then?

Ya.

You'd have to stay at home with us Sunday 1st,
then we do it Monday morning

Fine. Make sure Mams changed the sheets

Matchpoint:
*Why bother? If you've to stay in a house with a
dead man you'll wake up itching.*

How farcical the depth and breadth of the pit we'd dug ourselves. The blatant intent. Cormac's calls with cancer patient Anne Daly, whose deposition was admitted on account of her incapacitation. My laptop search history (*Can you dissolve a morphine tablet in water? Taste of morphine sulphate. Cost of lethal injection for horses. Do suicide victims get a funeral? Suicide liturgies. Dignitas. Proselytisation meaning. Bible word search suicide. Old Testament book of Samuel, Saul sends David on suicide mission. Cheap flights Zurich. Benefit of the doubt meaning*). The PC's history too (*Buy online will. Agricultural relief to avoid inheritance tax. Dá fhada an lá, tagann an tráthnóna* ('However long the day is, the evening comes'))—my activity or the Chief's, it couldn't be said. Nóra's phone call to Cormac at the precise moment the patrol car entered our drive. Cormac's arrival thirty minutes later at Roscommon Garda Station to give himself in for 'failing to report the death of a person'. He thought that his mother and brother had reported the death. He'd only discovered that they hadn't. He thought it his duty to inform the Garda Síochána as soon as possible and to officially apologise for not ensuring it had been dealt with. The busy working week that was in it. Would they mark it down now as 'self-administered overdose'?

'May we take another look at exhibit forty-seven, Detective McCarthy?' Alastair cross-examined the gazillionth witness. 'The receipt for the online will.'

'Yes, My Lord.'

'How did you find this particular document, Detective McCarthy?'

'How?'

'Yes, how.'

'By looking, My Lord,' Detective McCarthy said, to laughter from the back bench and Thomas. Neil snickered loudly for fear of having missed something.

'Objection, Your Honour. The question was ambiguous,' Mr Enright said.

'I mean under what circumstances did you find it?' Alastair added, before Judge Gilroy gave a ruling.

'I found it on the study desk, My Lord. On October the eighth when we recovered the body.'

Alastair breathed more loudly than he spoke. 'Was it in an envelope, in a pile of papers, on its own, or was it specifically affixed to any other document?'

Mr Enright piped up. 'Objection, Your Honour. Mr Waters is leading the witness.'

'Dismissed,' Judge Gilroy said. 'Mr Waters is getting to the point.'

The cross-examining barrister is only supposed to revisit topics raised during the direct examination. Cáit told us that to explain why we were going soft-Mick on the prosecution's witnesses. She promised that we'd pack our punches soon enough. But Alastair had decided to pack them now. He used the cross-examination to prove that the will had been paper-clipped to the list of executor's tasks on which the Chief's handwriting could be identified. Therefore they were the Chief's documents. Not mine. No coercion. He got Detective McCarthy to admit that the handwriting—which read 'Cormac to arrange. Call Donal for help'—was the Chief's by comparing it to other exhibits. Then Alastair turned to the jury and picked a shoulder to fix his gaze on. 'If you can identify the handwriting on the list of executor's tasks—to which the will was paper-clipped—as Manus Black's handwriting, then the implication—'

'Objection, Your Honour. Argumentative!'

'Mr Waters,' Judge Gilroy declared. 'If you were about to

propose that the jury take inference from a proved or assumed fact, you would be in contempt of court. This isn't your closing speech, I hope, so your questions should be intended to elicit information only.'

'—then the implication … is that Manus Black wrote on the document,' Alastair finished.

He sat down slowly as a feather, which doesn't fall as fast as the hammer, it turns out.

As long as that day was, the night came. We were wasted for the drive home.

The following day was off. I've work to do, Cormac muttered when I suggested we go for a pint. 'Ah, come on. Let's see who'll buy us a last round. We *actually* killed our father, unlike the Playboy. We might get a riot going yet. Give the pigs some real fucken muck to roll around in.' The giddiness of Dolly's letters must've caught on. I felt impulsive. But Cormac wasn't in any humour for toasts or talk. He must've been so cocksure of his acquittal that he hadn't planned for an outcome the like was upon us. Maybe he hadn't known that the legal system was a cyclone from which, if even a hair off your head got sucked in, no manner of intelligence or sly manoeuvre would extricate you.

The fridge was empty. The eggs were caked in shit out in the coop, halfway to armadillos. Devoid of herself, Nóra locked herself in one room, then another, sorting the last of the Chief's belongings into bin bags. The post box was empty. I got into the car to drive to Galway to see Dolly. I could stop off in the post office and take out money and my pockets wouldn't be empty and I could buy breakfast and maybe Dolly would be in a play and she would fill the hearts and minds of the west coast and the ripples of her influence would stretch to the West End and the world's idea of us would be substantiated. And maybe the play would be in Irish and I could fill the seat in my mind where the Chief's voice had upped and vanished. (*Mo athair caillte.*) I could listen and be the jury for Dolly's curvilinear story, to-be-continued. I could go easy on her.

The car had no registration or insurance but what fine could be greater than life? My heart didn't skip a beat when I pulled in to the Roscommon police station to sign in. After, I hung south-west on the N63. Though I'd never driven to Galway town and I had neither map nor phone, this was my day and I could take ownership of its direction. Her address was scrawled on my hand. I could hunt down the call centre or wait outside her house, which was a mouldy town house in the Claddagh with pulled velvet curtains and a stench of seaweed and fancy dress—not an apartment on the docks like she'd said. I could knock on the neighbours' doors. I could pass the cathedral for drive-by mercy, cross the merciless Corrib river over to the town hall and search for her in playbills and ask after her and find the pink slip of a parking ticket tucked under my windscreen wiper. I could sit in the pub where we'd had lunch on the way to Connemara and spend half my savings and the last hours of my last free day on three pints and try her house once more in the dark. I could fall asleep against the wheel, blocking her ramshackle gate, dreaming of the pink slip of her, hands on me making good and bearable the fluke of my existence. I could do all that.

51.

The fuss of media umbrellas on the courthouse steps was less intimidating than the anti-euthanasia activists harassing Parkgate Street when we arrived the following morning. There was only a score of them, but they knew how to yowl. 'Not Dead Yet!' 'What do we want? Natural Death! When do we want it? Whenever it happens!!' 'Right to Life.' 'Die the Death Jesus Designed.'

'Dignity is God's to Give!' Their banners took up half the street. The picket sign that was fixed to the back of a teenage girl's wheelchair read: '"The taking of a human life for any reason is wrong. You cannot nudge the moral compass from its true North without losing something vital"—Jessica Fletcher, *Murder She Wrote*.'

Cáit, Mr Sheehan and two police officers hurried out into the pelting rain to take us by the elbows. We'd been stunned by the noise of the hate. The rain stung, pelting down with toy syringes. Cormac stamped on one of the syringe-shaped highlighting pens so the plastic cracked and spattered luminous pink. Cameras flared. A newshound called: 'Mr Cormac Black, are you culpable for tormenting your psychosocially vulnerable brother into committing patricide?'

Cormac pulled away from Nóra and stood bear-like, staring down the crowd. 'Who the fuck is funding this?' he asked.

'Why did you leave your afflicted mother and brother in the house with the body for six days?' someone shouted.

'Mrs Black, why didn't you encourage your husband to seek treatment that would have extended his life and saved his soul?'

Cáit wrestled Cormac inside. Metal detectors looked how Hell's fire would look to a new arrival: better to walk through than to stand in front of, the skin slipping off you. I was waiting for Nóra to whimper that it was insufferable and when would it end. But she didn't. Her eyes were bloodshot, like waxy green leaves veined red by a fast change in season.

52.

Finally, the priest was called for confession.

There we were again: a queer congregation, berserk with piety but hesitant to fall to its knees just yet. Gilroy looked down at Father Shaughnessy with his blue cloth Bible and judged its fit. The People looked up to him—most zealously the Amish couple, his cronies maybe. The jury looked askance: a generation that needed proof. The legal counsels tried to look squarely at him, but there was that sense that his collar was thicker than theirs, that his robes had more function. We three persons acting in concert together tried not to look any-which-way or to hear or speak but Cormac was static electricity. He wasn't wearing his cufflinks to transmit the shock in a handshake or a puck. He took no more notes. He hadn't spoken to me in days. Mr Enright took the reins on our side and let the others examine only the driest of evidence.

'I led the funeral liturgy for Manus's parents and his small sister, Kitty,' Father Shaughnessy attested, 'when they died tragically in a fire. It was my first year out of the seminary. My first year in Dysart parish.'

'When was that?'

'Nineteen sixty-six. Manus was sixteen, I remember it clearly. He was old enough to take over the farm with some help. An aunt went to live with him and his sister Bridie until Manus learned to cook a bit. Then Bridie went to live with the auntie up in Boyle and Manus faced God's good earth alone. Lord have mercy on his soul.'

'Can you describe your contact with the Blacks beyond that—Manus in particular?'

'He was a humble, hard-working Samaritan who attended mass weekly through the years of his solitude, and later with Nóra to whom I married him. He made whatever contribution he could manage. He didn't receive the Eucharist, mind you, but I never pushed him on why. Attendance is what counts.'

'Did his sons attend also?'

'Cormac stopped coming at fourteen, with the excuse of hurling. I administered him the Sacraments of Baptism, Communion and Confirmation, so we'll consider him Christian, though I suspect he wouldn't identify as such. Doharty, conversely, attended most Sundays right up to his father's passing. He was devoted to his father, it should be said. Hart has the makings of a fine God-fearing man and he is one of the most spiritual youngsters I have come across.'

'Objection!'

'Stick to the facts, Mr Shaughnessy,' Judge Gilroy warned. 'You're not here to give character references.'

Mr Sheehan jerked in agreeance.

'Did you know about Manus's health?' Enright asked. 'And if so, how and when did you learn of it?'

'You'd be doing well to get Manus on the topic of himself. It was his sister Bridie who told me. She's in Skrine, so they'd go to the cathedral for mass. But she dropped in one time, in … when would it have been? Two thousand and nine, and asked would I do a mass for him. From what she said, she didn't know he'd decided against treatment altogether. She seemed to think he was on a waiting list.'

'How did you know that Manus had decided against treatment if you never spoke to Manus about his health?'

'I have the priest–penitent privilege to uphold.' The microphone amplified his nose whistle. 'Suffice it to say I knew he was beset. He was very troubled financially, so, that was going on. He kept his morality in check.'

'When did he stop confessing?'

'Objection, Your Honour.'

'Sustained.'

'When did you offer Manus Black home confessions?' Enright's altar boys shifted papers and glances in a flurry of purpose.

The priest could say when, yes. He could say why. Could he say if there had been any indication of suicidal tendencies? 'Among the religious community, there's a conviction that the drop-off in religious practice has played a major part in the increase in suicide rates in this country. However, as I've said, it was never my suspicion that Manus cut back on his practice for any ideological or cynical reason. Merely a biological one.'

'So, Manus was not suicidal?'

'Objection!' Both Cáit and Mr Sheehan stood up. 'Leading, Your Honour,' Sheehan protested.

'A priest is not an expert witness,' Cáit added. 'The jury should be advised. Mr Enright is soliciting opinion evidence.' The white rain lashing the rampart of window above mirrored her agitation.

'Sustained. The stenographer will strike that from the record and Mr Enright will refrain from leading the witness or soliciting opinions.'

'Yes, Your Honour.'

'You may continue your questioning.'

'When did you first visit Manus's household, regarding home visits?'

Father Shaughnessy looked troubled by the ructions. The state of someone's soul wasn't a topic for debate and, if it had to be, it could only be spoken of in analogies. A human being outweighed the sum of its parts, as did the Shepherd's flock. Why couldn't he be asked if he'd found the lost sheep? He could have answered that. But no, they insisted it was a day of the week and not a moment in the time after the death of Christ when Father Shaughnessy first called to the Black household: a particular minute of the hour of the day of the week. The morning we'd returned from Connemara. He didn't mention how long it took Nóra Black to invite him inside.

'What was Mrs Black's response to the offer?'

'She said that she'd pass it along to Manus when he was awake. I said I'd call in again next week.'

'And what was Mrs Black's response?'

'Well, she was gracious. She'd pass on the message, that Manus would phone if he wanted home visits.'

'Did she tell you not to call in again?'

'Well … she said no, Manus would phone me if he wanted me to.'

'Did she or did she not say that you may call in again?'

Father Shaughnessy looked down at us, in the negative. I was the only one to meet his eye: his was driver's eye with lowly human reflexes—unable to change course upon sight of the huge animal.

'You received no phone call from Manus, but you called back anyway?'

'Yes, I did. The following Saturday after morning mass.'

'Why did you flout Mrs Black's wishes?'

'I didn't mean to do that, but I didn't know what Manus himself wanted and I'm long enough in this occupation to know what one person wants isn't necessarily what another is capable of communicating.'

Mr Enright allowed that to sink in. It looked as if Father Shaughnessy's collar had tightened. 'Before we look at that second visit, do you recall what you talked to Cormac and Doharty about? Did you ask why they were both at their family home on a Monday morning?'

'No, only small talk, it would've been. Cormac had been interviewed on the radio, he was telling me.'

'And Doharty?'

'Hart was on his laptop computer at the kitchen table. He seemed very anxious … morose.'

'What did he say for you to infer that? Did he say anything about the whereabouts or well-being of his father?'

'He wanted to know why I was offering confession for a man who was lying sick in bed, unable to commit any sins. Hart would be very philosophical like that, you see. He thought Manus a saint, which is a rare attitude for a child who has been overly relied upon.'

Objections all round. If he voiced opinions again, Judge Gilroy warned him that a large part of his testimony would become inadmissible. Was that clear? The priest would be made to drive on—forbidden philosophy, prayer or the bemoaning of roadkill.

'Did you notice anything unusual on that first visit of October the second, 2014, the day of Manus Black's death?'

I looked for Father Shaughnessy's sympathy, but he didn't turn to me again. Instead, he turned to the Bible on the witness stand and his nose anticipated what he had to say. The whistling. Cormac dismissed it as the television, he explained. When it sounded the second time, Cormac left the room. When Cormac returned, the whistling had stopped. Father Shaughnessy presumed Cormac had turned off the television. No—no presumptions. Only the facts. The fact of the whistling sound. The fact of it being ignored. The fact that Manus Black was caught dead with a whistle around his neck and the seal of his son's hand.

'Were you aware that Manus wore a whistle for calling when he needed help?' Enright asked.

'I wasn't.'

'Was it Manus whistling for help that you heard?'

'I couldn't say.' Father Shaughnessy's long words were cut to stubs, but he tried to make them work. He parted his hands and laid them on the bench. 'That would be speculation, only. The *fact* was that Manus had sent in a large donation at Sunday mass the week prior and I came to express gratitude. It was the type of donation that comes from a person who knows it will be their last. And it was Manus put that envelope in the basket, not anyone else. I saw him do it. That was the fact of it.'

It wasn't enough. The jury could hear whistling still and knew where it came from. It was too shrill to ignore. The rain lashed so fiercely that the window might have broken open like a pen rupturing paper from the pelt of writing. But it was Nóra who broke open. She rose to her feet beside me and drew a slip of paper from her sleeve. She faced the jury, waving the white envelope like a handkerchief. 'I have evidence,' she croaked.

Cáit, Alastair and Paul Sheehan all rose suddenly. I tried to stand too—*what the?*—but Cormac reached across and pressed my shoulder hard. The yellow rings of his eyes mimicked the lights above. His jaw was gritted. Way too calm.

Mr Sheehan pitched his hair leftward so the others knew he would be the one to speak: 'If Your Honour pleases, the defence counsels require a brief adjournment to discuss this matter with our friends.'

Judge Gilroy let her glasses hang from their chain and excused the jury. Only when the clerk called 'All rise' did Cormac take his hand off me. He walked beside me like a bouncer as we were ushered out the side door. But we weren't led along the purgatorial corridor. We stopped right outside the courtroom. Nóra, Sheehan, Cáit, Cormac and Alastair formed a circle of which I was involuntarily part. I looked at Cáit, but she was busy scanning the long, hand-written document that Sheehan, with a plastic glove on, held out to each counsel to read—ladies last.

'Given the retrogression of the proceedings, my client has been prompted to submit a new piece of evidence, just come upon, which will have a significant impact on the case.'

'What?' I said.

'Your mother is submitting a document to the Book of Evidence,' Sheehan repeated. 'On one condition.'

'What document? What evidence?' I said. Why was everyone swaying?

Sheehan licked the corner of his bulbous mouth. 'The Statement of Wish to Die.'

I became very aware of my knees. *Why are we here? Standing still?*

Sheehan had more to say, directed at Alastair: 'Section two of the Suicide Act of 1993 says that a person who aids, abets, counsels or procures the suicide of another, or an attempt by another to commit suicide, shall be guilty of an offence and shall be liable on conviction of indictment to imprisonment for a term not exceeding fourteen years. Involuntary manslaughter would be closer to five years. A decade in the detail.' He held up his stubby fingers to me, to indicate the years. 'The condition upon which my client will submit this document is this: Doharty pleads guilty to all charges. We three can barter with the DPP: the statement submission and Doharty's guaranteed plea if they'll reduce the charge to manslaughter. My client and yours, Ms Roe, will be *nolle prosequi*. Doharty won't get life, thanks to this evidence, which acquits the intent element of the charge.'

Cáit looked at Cormac, who gave her a quick nod, arms crossed. Then she turned to me. 'Hart. This trumps what Alastair and I had up our sleeves. Alastair's aide took a deposition from Aleanbh Cullinane. To confirm the trip to Connemara and to describe Manus's health. But it might be considered hearsay because her excuse for not being here is that she can't leave her daughter. Not a great excuse. Besides, it might not have won over the jury. This is better. It's the best outcome. A much lighter sentence. If the DPP go in for it.'

'Which they will,' Mr Sheehan said.

'If they go in for it,' Cáit repeated. 'Which they might do. They're nervous about Bridie's testament—how it will reveal Manus's state of mind. And what the priest might reveal when we recall him. This document confirms an unlawful killing, but on the basis of a request. It's the difference between abetting suicide and involuntary manslaughter. It proves there wasn't a mental element.'

I felt Alastair at my elbow. Was he propping me up? Did he know what I'd just found out?

'Why ...' I tried to speak, to speak over the word that had stuck. *Her* daughter. But I had to fight for it too. 'Why are you all saying "Doharty"? Wouldn't we *all* get manslaughter?'

'Ah, yes,' Sheehan started. 'While Nóra and Cormac are complicit—'

'I asked *her*.' I tried to point at Cáit but my limbs wouldn't work.

Cáit leaned forward—the lovely androgynous smell of her the only consolation. 'It'd be difficult to get a charge on the others, Hart. Because the death was strangulation secondary to overdose. The DPP know that. I'll still have a battle getting Cormac off the aiding suicide charge, but they only have evidence of him procuring one pill, not even the morphine … which *you* got. They'll probably drop the charges on the others … in exchange for the statement and your guilty plea.' She gave me as sympathetic a look as her sharp face could muster.

'Guilty? Of slaughtering my father?' I looked to Nóra, who stood in Mr Sheehan's huge wake. 'Mam?' Her face looked stretched across her bones like cling film, but the air had got in; she had turned. Her eyes were gashes. 'You'd put me in jail?' I said. 'You'd have me take the blame? For what? What did I do?'

She sounded some word, but it was nothing recognisable. A blank bit of wall between Stations of the Cross. She wanted me to quickly pass by her. Sheehan advanced. 'Your mother cannot endure the stress of the trial's continuation. You might think of your widowed parent's well-being when you decide whether or not to wrap this up today.'

Cáit told everyone to give me space. She led them a few metres away, except for Alastair, who held my arm. A full minute of silence passed before I could hear beyond the tinnitus. Alastair's laboured breaths reminded me of the Chief. I couldn't face all the damage of him now, so we stayed side by side, not face to face.

'This is your decision,' he said finally. 'Your change of plea must be voluntary. So listen to your own instincts as well as my recommendation.' Another pulsing silence. 'Some manner of assault charge must be borne, by one if not by all. If you plead guilty, the jury becomes irrelevant. It reverts to Judge Gilroy.'

The ache of grief returned to my throat, a tocht the size of a fist, and my mouth opened for the poison it needed—the fire that would burn me as innocent as the Chief's parents, his small sister who never got to live this strange, fucked life. My knees buckled, but Alastair had me.

'Come, now,' he said. 'She's quite like you.' He spoke softly and breathed at my shoulder like crunching footfalls in hard snow. 'Green-eyed.'

I gasped and searched his face. Alastair's neck scar looked waxy and white as an envelope seal in the corridor light and, from so close, the stitch marks on either side were unmistakable. Ellipses along the jugular vein.

'She's very small, yet,' he added, 'but give her five years. You can look at her and, perhaps, see a fresh start. Aleanbh agrees you might just be ready for a child, then. A thing not to be afraid of.'

I asked, in so many vowels, if I could see her.

Alastair looked at my bowed shoulder. 'Only to say goodbye.'

53.

Our father was no God. He couldn't hold his fields in his hands and make them replete. He couldn't hold his sons in his hands and make them heroic.

That that didn't make his hands smaller took me years to understand. Five dark years cemented around me. Father Shaughnessy guided me through them. He knew a person needed help when left with nothing, no thing not a thing. He knew what a loving son does with the body of his father: how he lifts him over his head and tries to carry on living with that cargo and muscle burn and skeletal compression, all the while hoping his Chief will be raised up in tribal estimation.

On one of his many prison visits, Father Shaughnessy reminded me how sons are small gods too to their fathers, how what's good in them—what's unmarked save for the thumbprint of the Lord—is held up in awe. He told me a story the Chief had shared when he was young and fit and glad of fatherhood:

One hot Sunday, the Chief drove by Pat and Frank Lally traipsing through the fields, the sweat pouring off them. I was a small boy in the back seat. Gerry was in front. The Chief pulled over and called them out of the rude sun. Was it a lift to town they wanted? She'll go wherever there's a good feed, said Frank. He'll swally a bandage for the hunger pains, said Pat. They stuffed in on either side, and me stood up between them, testing out my new-found balance as we drove. Pat held onto one ankle and Frank to the other with the filthiest hands I'd ever seen, brown and hairy as tarantulas. Frank said I had the makings of a jockey if I'd go in for silks. And infertility! Pat added. The smell that came from their laughter overpowered the other smells. My four-year-old face was thistle-grimaced and I blurted out: 'Is tonight the night for the bath, Daddy? Is tonight the night for the washing?' I kept repeating it, plying subtlety for all it was worth. The Chief could have killed me, he told Father Shaughnessy, only for he'd never known a child more honest. He feared it. The standard it would hold him to. Father Shaughnessy agreed that honesty was my biggest strength and my weakness. Too much honesty is incompatible with this world. It is water poured onto droughted soil. It can only spill off. The earth is too rigid in its poverty to absorb what wealth is given.

It's true that the outside world is the wayward thing. The exposed, riotous, pitiless prison. What were the final images then, when I held the word in my mouth: the magnet that had been arranged on my tongue for swallowing? (Not arranged all along by my guileful brother, but by the undying Father who knew that I would come home to Him, given time.) I'll remember now, so that I know the route I took to where I've come, so that I never go back on myself or lose my way for lack of paternal direction.

This is what I saw when I pleaded Guilty to the People and bore the cold lash of their shackles:

Judge Gilroy—gauche in the horsehair wig and weary of her steel jewellery—didn't offer to fast for thirty days on my behalf.

My mother. Passing her keys to Cormac, who was to become her property manager, for she would go to live with her parents, the old couple for whom she'd had me convicted, the generation to whom her sins could never be exposed, to whom the Chief's disgrace could never be bared, who might forgive her one Cain son. We're *human*, she'd beg. 'Now the brother shall betray the brother to death, and the father the son; and children shall rise up against their parents, and shall cause them to be put to death.' She wouldn't do the same. She would be rescued from the cyclic flame. She would carry her parents to the City Gates, if only to see them off. What was it that happened so long ago between them? Her leaving the convent? She might tell me tomorrow, when they come for me, to take me home.

Finally, there was Dolly. Dolly, costumed in a blue dress with fine white stripes crossways, a white linen blazer and flat-soled shoes. A thin gold rope with a nautical anchor marked where her waist was, which had thickened. Her black eyebrows were as the crow flies: undeviating. Why had I waited so long to write back? Could I not read between her lines? The child was outside in Emer's arms, but it was her own child. It might be my child too. Depending. Did I know that Doharty means 'harmful'? Would I live up to my name? The mole on her chest had sprouted a hair. I nearly went to pluck it, but nothing was my own to move or do or say. I was between places that were nothing like a woman's pale, muscled thighs.

I turned to the door as someone exited the courtroom, in the dread hope of glimpsing my child in the gap. Seeking out that crescent of life, I remembered one of Dolly's letters had named her Rían. She'd been born with a congenital heart defect: a small hole in the upper septum. It had closed on its own. Was that irony? Cormac wouldn't care to put me right any longer. Perhaps

I'd been gazing there a long time, for when I turned back, Dolly was handing Cormac his cufflinks. He slipped them into his breast pocket furtively and angled his neck until it cracked. He patted my back and said something unintelligible. Then he went about his business.

'Don't get me wrong,' Dolly said.

Tears tumbled down her cheeks and chin and were captured by her blue naval dress and were captured by my gaze and the gulley of recollection. She was sorry as Faustus, she said, whatever that meant. Be good, Hart. Aren't there things to look forward to? She asked no end of questions, like one of her letters, only I wasn't there to receive them. Nothing needed saying. There were no plots to concoct or guises to perfect. I would have to hold my own, without stick or kin or book of evidence. That much would be asked of me, until I had nothing to answer for. Until I could be my Father's son, at last.

ACKNOWLEDGEMENTS

Thank you Bill Clegg, for all that you do, and for being my ideal reader. To the Clegg Agency's brilliant, thoughtful people: Marion Duvert, Simon Toop, David Kambhu and Lilly Sandberg. Anna Webber, Seren Adams and folks at United Agents, thank you. To my editor and publisher, Juliet Mabey: thank you for believing in this book, and for your extraordinary energy and dedication. Everyone who worked on this book and on *Orchid & the Wasp* at Oneworld: Margot Weale, Paul Nash, Alyson Coombes, Thanhmai Bui-Van, Caitriona Row, Polly Hatfield, Laura McFarlane, Helen Szirtes. Ben Summers: for this perfect cover. Publicity in the US: Richard Nash, Emily Cook, Caitlin O'Neill and Phoebe O'Brien. Publicity at Bloomsbury in Australia – Genevieve Nelsson in particular. In Ireland, Cormac Kinsella and Louise Dobbin: folks who make the book world feel entirely unlike an industry. Thanks too to the booksellers and librarians who do just that, whose generosity changes readers' and authors' lives.

Thanks to the Queen's University of Belfast, Victoria University of Wellington and Maastricht University for support over the years. Thanks to Culture Ireland and Literature Ireland for helping me get out and about, to find and meet readers. The knowledge of a Literature Bursary Award from the Arts Council of Ireland for my next novel helped keep me sane while I edited this one. Thanks to the Ireland Funds Monaco Award, I wrote at least four thousand words of *The Wild Laughter* in the extraordinary location of the Princess Grace Irish Library. Thanks too to the Faber Academy in Olot, where I spent a week working on edits.

Friends who read parts of the work along the way, or whose support I exploited: Judge Petria McDonnell, David Fleming,

Jessica Traynor, Jane Clarke, Ronan Ryan, Doireann Ní Ghríofa, Mary Cregan, James Shapiro, Maria Tivnan, Beverly Burch, Brian Lynch, Paul Lucas, Alicia Hayes, Elizabeth Behrens; the Dutch writer and ex-student Priscilla Kint, whose poem about the Irish phrase *tá brón orm* ('I'm sorry'/'sorrow is on me') inspired a moment in this book; my PhD supervisors Harry Ricketts and Geoff Miles; my siblings Donnla, Evin, Rían and Rowan; my parents. Paul Behrens, for loving this book more than anything else I've written and telling me that whenever I gave him any other work to read.

In 2013, Marie Fleming challenged the Supreme Court to establish a constitutional right to die, hastening a long-overdue conversation.

Caoilinn Hughes is the author of *Orchid & the Wasp* (Oneworld 2018), which won the Collyer Bristow Prize, was shortlisted for the Hearst Big Book Awards and the Butler Literary Award, and longlisted for the Authors' Club Best First Novel Award and the International DUBLIN Literary Award 2020. For her short fiction, she won *The Moth* International Short Story Prize 2018 and an O. Henry Prize in 2019. Her poetry collection, *Gathering Evidence* (Carcanet 2014), won the Shine/Strong Award and was shortlisted for four other prizes. Her work has appeared in *Granta*, *POETRY*, *Tin House*, *Best British Poetry*, BBC Radio 3 and elsewhere. She has a PhD from Victoria University of Wellington, New Zealand, and she was recently Visiting Writer at Maastricht University in the Netherlands.

Orchids are liars.

They use pheromones to lure wasps in to become unwitting pollinators. In nature, such exploitative systems are rare. In society, they are everywhere.

Gael Foess is a heroine of mythic proportions. Raised in Dublin by single-minded, careerist parents, she learns from an early age how ideals and ambitions can be compromised. When her father walks out during the 2008 crash, her family falls apart. Determined to build a life-raft for her loved ones, Gael sets off for London and New York, proving how little it takes to game the system. But is it really exploitation if the loser isn't aware of what he's losing?

Written in electric, heart-stopping prose, *Orchid & the Wasp* is a dazzlingly original novel about gigantic ambitions and social upheaval, chewing through sexuality, class and politics with joyful, anarchic fury, announcing Caoilinn Hughes as a rising star of literary fiction.

'Highly ambitious… Kick-ass, whip-smart.' *Sunday Times*
'A gem of a debut about the way we live now.' *Elle*